PK.

Faith started to laugh, because it was that or cry.

"What are you laughing at?" Dean asked as he fought a smile.

Faith got up on her knees and lifted a muddy hand, smacking it down on his shoulder. "We're hopeless."

Dean stared at the new mud print on his shirt. "That's going to cost you."

"I'm not scared of you," Faith said, making a second attempt at standing. "You look more afraid of getting dirty than I do."

The challenge had been presented, and Dean Presley didn't back down from a challenge. Faith wasn't sure how she could have forgotten. Dean used both hands to grab fistfuls of slop.

"Not scared, huh?"

Faith's heart beat a little faster. If she didn't move, she'd be washing mud out of her hair for sure.

The twinkle in his eyes reminded her of the boy she once loved.

Dear Reader,

There is nothing more important to me than family. I have two younger brothers whom I have always felt the need to look out for, even as they have grown into men with their own families. So I can relate to Faith Stratton in so many ways. Faith and her brother, Sawyer, have relied on each other since they were little. When their father died and left them in charge of running his horse farm and equine therapy center, their need to watch out for one another only grew stronger.

Dean Presley understands the importance of being there for a sibling, as well. Only, he's struggling with the guilt of not being there for his sister when she needed him. Twelve years ago, Dean left Grass Lake, Tennessee, with no desire to return. He'd rather stay away than face the reminders of what was lost there. His new responsibility is to his record company, Grace Note Records. And what Grace Note needs is some new talent. Talent that Sawyer Stratton has in spades.

The Girl He Used to Love is a story about knowing not only when to hold on and when to let go, but what to hold on to, as well. I love my brothers, but I know I have to let them make their own way in this world—even if I am the older and wiser big sister.

I hope you enjoy this first story in the Grace Note Records series. It's bound to be a bumpy ride, but the happy-ever-after is always worth it!

xoxo,

Amy Vastine

HEARTWARMING

The Girl He Used to Love

———

Amy Vastine

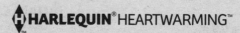

Recycling programs
for this product may
not exist in your area.

ISBN-13: 978-0-373-36796-2

The Girl He Used to Love

Printed in U.S.A.

Amy Vastine has been plotting stories in her head for as long as she can remember. An eternal optimist, she studied social work, hoping to teach others how to find their silver lining. Now she enjoys creating happily-ever-afters for all to read. Amy lives outside Chicago with her high school sweetheart turned husband, three fun-loving children and their sweet but mischievous puppy dog. Visit her at www.amyvastine.com.

Books by Amy Vastine

Harlequin Heartwarming

The Hardest Fight
The Best Laid Plans
The Better Man
The Weather Girl

To my brothers, Andrew and Adam. Always remember that I will be there to pick you up when you fall...but give me a minute to finish laughing!

CHAPTER ONE

LUCK WAS A funny thing. People could be blessed with the good kind and then cursed with a string of the bad. Good luck made people millionaires overnight. It caused paths to cross and lost valuables to be found. The not-so-good kind led to much less desirable endings…like standing umbrella-less on the side of the road with nothing but a cell phone for a flashlight in a torrential downpour that had begun at exactly the same time as the horrific thump-thump-thumping noise coming from the front passenger-side tire.

Dean Presley was fed up with the string of bad luck that had become his reality lately. Not only was he still over an hour away from Nashville but he most definitely had a flat tire.

"Seriously?" he shouted up at the heavens.

Climbing back into his car, Dean would have given just about anything for a towel. He held his phone out until it touched the windshield, desperate for a cell signal. When that didn't work, he reached back and pointed the phone in the other direction. Still nothing. He might as well have been in the middle of the Smoky Mountains given the complete lack of cell service around here.

He tossed the useless piece of technology in the backseat and turned up the heat, hoping to fight off the chill. He never should have gotten off the highway and taken these deserted back roads, even though he knew them well. He rested his head on the steering wheel. When it rained, it poured. Literally.

The unceasing rain might be the reason there was no one on the road. Dean had gotten off the interstate because of an accident that had shut down all lanes going north. The alternate route had been a blessing at first, but not so much now that he was in need of some help. Tonight was full of shouldn't-haves, starting with making this trip in the first place.

Driving down to Birmingham to scout a band he'd heard about from a friend had been a complete bust. Maybe the band was having a bad night, but the drummer couldn't keep the beat and the singer kept forgetting the words. Their lead guitarist was decent but, unfortunately for him, he was doomed to playing hole-in-the-wall bars in Alabama for the rest of his life unless he found new bandmates. Basically, Dean's time would have been better spent searching YouTube for some undiscovered talent.

Two brightly shining headlights appeared in the rearview mirror. He switched on his hazards, praying the driver would stop, but the sixteen-wheeler whizzed by, spraying the broken-down BMW with water from the flooded road. No one was going to save him.

There was only one thing to do and that was to make a run for it. The sinking feeling in his stomach kept him right where he was, though. It had been a dozen years since he had been back to the place he used to call home. Grass Lake, Tennessee, held too many painful memories. Dean had left the summer before his senior year of college and had never come back. Not even for holidays.

Holidays were the worst.

"In and out," he said to himself. "Find a phone, call Landon and leave. No one will know you were there."

A flash of lightning lit up the sky, making him question his sanity. He turned the car off and opened the door.

"ANY COOKIES LEFT?"

Faith gave Old Man Middleton an apologetic smile. Every Friday night the Sundown Bar and Grill featured one of her alcohol-inspired desserts. "Sorry, Hank. I made Rum and Coke Swirled Shortbread for tonight. Those went pretty fast."

Hank snapped his fingers as he sat on the stool beside her. "I knew I should have stopped by earlier. That's what I get for coming for a nightcap instead of an imperative."

"I think you mean an *aperitif*," Faith said, trying hard to hold back her laughter.

"That's what I said," Hank asserted. He leaned across the bar. "You sure your brother ain't got a couple hidden away? I came out in the pouring rain for your cookies."

Faith shook her head. She'd have to run a special batch of cookies over to his place in the morning to make up for it.

Hank sat back. "Guess I'll have to settle for the liquid version."

Faith's younger brother had already anticipated his order and set the drink down in front of him. Sawyer had a way of meeting people's needs before they even knew what they needed. It was a gift he had inherited from their father. Faith's heart ached a little at the thought.

"You got here in time to catch my second set. That's got to be worth something," Sawyer said.

For a couple months now Sawyer had spent his weekend evenings tending bar and entertaining the customers with a few songs. Faith had made him promise this little side job wouldn't interfere with his responsibilities at the farm, and so far, Sawyer had made it work.

"Well, your father used to brag about you playing a mean guitar."

The Sundown had been their daddy's favorite place to hang out after a long day on the horse farm. He loved chatting up the other regulars and telling stories that were oftentimes more fiction than fact. Nothing ever brought the guy down.

Nothing except one fatal heart attack that ended his life way too soon.

"If you ask real nice, I bet Sawyer will take a request," Faith said.

Sawyer shot his sister a look. Faith was sure her little brother didn't know many tunes from back in Hank's day, but ever the quick thinker, he offered up a suggestion instead. "Are you a Johnny Cash fan?"

"What does a young man like you know about Johnny Cash?"

"Oh, I'll show you what I know about Johnny Cash, Mr. Middleton," Sawyer answered with his trademark grin complete with the dimples that made every woman in Grass Lake swoon. Too bad her brother had no intention of ever settling down. He had dated a few nice girls but never let anyone get too close.

Sawyer checked his hair in the mirrored backsplash and whistled for his buddy to bring him his guitar. Faith moved to the other side of the bar to cover for her brother while he performed. She had to admit, the kid had some talent. He wrote his own songs and played the guitar pretty well for a self-taught man.

Josie Peters leaned against the bar. A widow with a teenage daughter, Josie had moved to Grass Lake a few years ago and used some of the money she had inherited from her late husband's estate to buy the Sundown. She and Faith had become friends almost immediately.

Josie was the one who'd come up with the

idea to feature a drink-and-cookie special Friday nights. She'd begged Faith to help her out after tasting one of Faith's mudslide brownies at a potluck dinner, and since Faith had difficulty saying no, the treats were now a customer favorite.

"Did you get a look at what just walked in?" she asked, nodding toward the entrance.

The man Josie was ogling must have swum here. That or his clothes had just come out of the washing machine without going through the spin cycle. Faith would have bet that if he took off his shoe, he could fill a glass with the water that was inside.

"He must not be from around here." The dimly lit bar made it difficult to see his face.

"Maybe I can convince him to change that," Josie said with a wink.

Every able-bodied, single guy in Grass Lake had been on Josie's list of potential replacement husbands since she had decided to jump back into the dating pool. She had yet to catch one in her net, so this fresh blood made her absolutely giddy.

Faith couldn't blame her for staring at the newcomer. His red shirt clung to his chest and when he stepped further in, she could see his dirty-blond hair looked a little darker from being wet than the short, close-cropped beard he was sporting. With great effort, he shoved his hand in his jeans' pocket and pulled out his phone. The only way that thing was going to work was if its case was waterproof.

His frustration showed as he pressed the same button over and over without a positive result. Giving up, he headed in their direction. Josie readied herself for the big introduction by primping her hair with one hand and putting the other on her hip.

"You don't happen to have a pay phone I could use or maybe a cell phone I could borrow?" His voice was deep and husky. Now that he was close, his intensely green eyes made Faith's heart stop. She hadn't recognized him from afar, but those eyes...she would never forget those eyes.

"You can use my phone, stranger," Josie said, completely unaware of who she was talking to. She hadn't lived in Grass Lake long enough to know the man was no stranger. "You look like you've been standing in the rain all night."

"Something like that," he answered. "Got a flat on Highway 14 and had to walk here."

"Dean?" Faith choked out, her heart pounding like crazy.

Water from his hair dripped into his narrowing eyes. She could tell the moment he recognized her. She watched the muscle in his jaw tick before he exhaled her name.

She never thought she'd see Dean Presley again, and certainly not in Grass Lake. If there was one thing she remembered clearly, it was his desire to leave this town for good. Part of her had been relieved by his decision. It had saved her from having to face him after what had happened.

She forced herself to breathe as she pulled a clean dish towel out from under the bar and tried to act like there wasn't a heartbreaking history between them. With a plastered-on smile, she handed it to him. "This won't help all that much, but you can at least dry your face."

He tentatively took it and wiped his brow. "It's been one heck of a night."

Josie put a hand on his shoulder. "You two know one another?"

Faith and Dean exchanged a look. Faith had known a Dean Presley who was probably very different than the one standing on the other side of the bar right now. His sister had been the best friend she'd ever had. He had been her first love. She had lost them both one fateful night a dozen years ago.

"You could say that," Dean said, handing the towel back to Faith.

"Hey, Josie!" Bruce Gibson called from a table across the bar. He and his buddies were celebrating his fortieth birthday. "Another round!"

Josie glanced at Faith, silently checking if it was okay to leave them alone.

"I'll let you two catch up, then," she said once Faith gave her a nod.

Faith's throat was too dry to speak. For a fleeting moment she thought about how Addison would make fun of the two of them staring at each other like a pair of idiots.

"You look great," Dean finally said. "All grown up."

He had always treated her like she was a little kid. Faith and Addison had followed him around like puppies. He used to get so annoyed, but that changed the summer Faith was eighteen. That was the year he'd finally looked at her as someone other than his baby sister's friend.

"That's what happens. Time passes, we grow up."

Dean swallowed hard and nodded. "That's true for most of us."

She really was an idiot. Not everyone was lucky enough to grow old. Seeing him had caused her to lose her mind. She pulled the cordless phone out from under the bar. "You can use this," she said, setting it in front of him.

He thanked her and seemed anxious for their reunion to come to an end. She moved on to another customer and tried to keep her emotions in check.

Josie cut the music that played throughout the bar and welcomed Sawyer back to the tiny stage in the corner, barely big enough for the two of them to stand on. Josie stepped down as Sawyer strummed his guitar. He gave Hank a shout out before singing his version of Johnny Cash's "Ring of Fire."

For some reason the song seemed to give Dean pause. He hung up and set the phone down. Dean had always had a thing for country music. People used to tease him given his last name and his complete inability to carry a tune, but Dean didn't have to play music to love it. Addison used to call him obsessed. When Faith was a kid, she wished he was as passionate about *her* as he was about music.

Now, she'd give anything to go back in time and make sure he never gave her a second thought.

She realized she had been staring when Dean waved her over.

"Can I get you something to drink?" she asked him, his eyes returning to her brother.

"No, but you can tell me who that guy is." He pointed in the direction of the stage. Maybe he was as surprised as Hank that a young guy could make such an iconic country song his own. That was what Sawyer did best, take something old and make it new.

"That's my brother."

His wide eyes showed his surprise. He held a hand waist high. "That's your little brother?" Twelve years ago, Sawyer had been a scrawny middle-schooler.

"That's what my daddy told me when they brought him home from the hospital. Although, I often wonder if the doctors pulled a switcheroo." Her attempt at lightening the mood fell flat. Dean went back to watching Sawyer with intense interest.

After the cover song, Sawyer sang one of his originals about chasing fireflies. He'd never admit it, but that song had something to do with their mom. She had run off and left them behind when Sawyer and Faith were just kids, but before that she had been the one who would take them out on a hot summer night armed with a pickle jar and a lid poked with holes. He pretended to hate her. Maybe a little part of him did, but there was another part of him that missed her as much as Faith did.

"Can you reintroduce us when he's finished?" Dean asked when the song came to an end.

"Why? You want him to help you change your flat tire?"

"No," he answered as if she hadn't been kidding. "I want to make your brother a star."

CHAPTER TWO

DEAN SHOULD HAVE left the moment he realized he was sharing space with none other than Faith Stratton. At the very least, he should have stayed on the phone, begging his business partner to come rescue him so he could get out of this town before anyone else spotted him. Though, given their history, it was unlikely Faith would go running to his parents' house to announce his arrival.

Gone was the little girl who had been attached to Addison's hip and the sweet, doe-eyed teenager who had made him lose his mind and his sister in the process. In her place was a gorgeous, dark-haired, grown-up woman. Those warm brown eyes were still capable of stopping a man's heart, but everything else had changed...matured.

Seeing her stirred up feelings he preferred to avoid, bury, pretend he never felt. Dean was the master at hiding his true emotions. He also had a knack for keeping his personal life very separate from his business life, and this detour into Grass Lake had quickly become business.

Sawyer was the answer to Dean's prayers. It had been a long time since he had heard someone sing with such real emotion. He had noticed it during the Johnny Cash cover; he had *felt* it during the second song. Dean needed to talk to this guy and get him in front of Landon immediately.

With her hands on her hips and her chin tipped down, Faith frowned in confusion. "What's that supposed to mean?"

"He's amazing, Faith. I could introduce him to some people in the business. Does he write his own stuff?"

Her eyes gave away her wariness. She folded her arms across her chest. "Sometimes."

That was a plus and made the guy that much more desirable. "I have a legitimate record label with real artists signed to it. He could have a real music career."

"My brother helps me run the farm. Singing is what he does for fun, not for a living."

Before he could explain how that could change, Faith was called away by another customer. Dean had worked at the Strattons' horse farm and equine therapy center that last summer in Grass Lake. It was a worthwhile business, but Dean knew how much work went into it. Hopefully, Sawyer would be a little more excited about Dean's proposition than his sister was. He was exactly what Grace Note Records had been looking for— young, attractive and, most importantly, talented.

Bringing in a potential new artist would ease Landon's mind and keep him from giving up on their company. Without Landon, Dean would have to close up shop. He didn't have the capital to buy his partner out.

The rest of Sawyer's set finished strong. It didn't matter if he was singing a cover or an original, the songs all sounded as if every note belonged to him. He had a unique sound that would do well on the radio.

Faith approached her brother as soon he stepped off the tiny corner stage. She whispered in his ear and he immediately glanced in Dean's direction. The two siblings exchanged a few more words before Sawyer made his way to the bar.

"Dean Presley—long time, no see." Sawyer Stratton looked more like his father than the boy Dean had once known. He had big, brown, soulful eyes and chiseled features that would definitely make women swoon when he was on stage. There was nothing scrawny about him and he might have been an inch or two taller than Dean. "You got something against umbrellas?"

Dean could only imagine how ridiculous he looked as the two men shook hands. He ran a hand through his towel-dried hair and glanced down at the puddle of water that had collected under his bar stool. He was a wreck.

"I've got nothing against umbrellas. I would have *loved* an umbrella tonight."

"You in town for the weekend? Your mom didn't mention you were coming home when I saw her earlier this week."

Dean loved his mother, but he would have to convince Sawyer not to mention this visit. "I wasn't planning on being in town at all. I was headed back to Nashville after a scouting trip to Birmingham. If my car hadn't gotten a flat, I never would have heard you sing. You were a million times more entertaining than the band I saw earlier tonight. Did you write some of that set yourself?"

"About half."

"Ever post songs on the internet? Have any social media presence?"

"Nope. No time for that. Only place I play is right here," Sawyer said.

"What if I told you I could give you lots of time to play music?"

"Oh, yeah? You want to make me the next Boone Williams?" Sawyer snickered like it was a joke.

Country star Boone Williams had been the first to sign with Dean's label after the singer had a falling out with his record company. At the time, it had seemed like a huge win. Little had Dean and Landon known the problem was more Boone than it was his label.

It had been five years since the megastar recorded an album and three years of nothing but bad press. Stories of infidelity, drug and alcohol problems, divorce and a child custody war circulated ad nauseam. Dean had convinced Boone to go to rehab, but the guy was still in a fragile state, claiming with his sobriety had come a complete loss of creativity. There were no songs to record in his near future.

Lately all Boone did was cost Dean money. Sawyer would not become another Boone. Dean's gut told him he had a gold mine in front of him. "I want to make you the next Sawyer Stratton."

Sawyer called Faith over. Her hair was pulled back in a high ponytail. Her slender neck and apple cheeks were slightly flushed. She had always been pretty but that word no longer did her justice. Dean hated himself for drinking her in.

"Something tells me you put him up to this," Sawyer said to his sister. "If this is payback for telling Charles Hackney you like guys who wear tight jeans and big belt buckles, so help me…"

Faith poked her brother in the chest. "Don't you dare mention tight jeans and Charles in the same sentence. I'm not sure I'll be able to look at that man the same way ever again."

Sawyer's grin was wide and toothy. Something told Dean he was the same old troublesome younger brother he had been.

"Just tell the truth," Sawyer demanded. "Are you two messing with me?"

"I'm not joking," Dean insisted. "I need new artists and you're the first real talent I've seen in a long time. I would love to hear you sing again."

Sawyer gave him a light punch in the shoulder. "Well, flattery will get you everywhere."

"Your mom is going to be ecstatic," Faith said with a smile, leaving Dean to question what his mother had to do with this. If he was lucky, he'd be out of here before she even heard he was in town.

"She'll probably throw you a welcome home parade," Sawyer added.

Every muscle in Dean's body tensed. "Oh, I'm not staying. I was thinking you could come to Nashville. Meet some people. Nashville's where the magic happens."

"Nashville?" Faith's face drained of color. "Things are kind of busy at the farm right now. One of the paddocks needs the fencing along the east side replaced and Sawyer's in the middle of revamping the tack room."

"Nashville is where the magic happens," Dean repeated, looking at Sawyer in hopes of swaying him.

"I think what my sister is trying to say is I've got responsibilities here, Dean. I appreciate that you think I sound good enough to do more than play in this old bar, but with Dad gone, it's just me and Faith, and we have the farm to run."

Responsibilities? Didn't Sawyer have a responsibility to himself to do something he loved? And Dean didn't need to ask him if he loved making music; he'd heard it in every word the man sang.

The relief on Faith's face stopped him from pointing that out. She needed her brother, and Dean wasn't sure how he was going to handle that. He had to get back to Nashville. Once he was out of this godforsaken town, he'd find a way to lure Sawyer there.

Dean glanced at his watch. It was almost midnight. Too late to ask Landon to drive down here to get him. Going to his parents' house was completely out of the question. If he showed his face there, they'd never let him leave. There was only one option.

"I don't want to bother my parents this late at night and I need a place to crash. You think I could sleep on your couch? I'll be gone in the morning, I swear."

Sawyer glanced at Faith, who bit her bottom lip. It wasn't any wonder she'd be hesitant about inviting him into her house. The last time he had been there, he'd said some pretty horrible things.

"I'm sure your mom wouldn't mind being woken up because you were home," she said in her attempt to say no without actually saying the word.

"I don't want to make a scene, you know?"

"I get it," Sawyer said.

"What about Tanner's B&B?" Faith was quick to suggest.

"They don't take guests in the middle of the night, Faith. You know that," Sawyer argued.

Dean was desperate. "You won't even know I'm there."

"You can come home with us," Sawyer said. "I'll even let you borrow some dry clothes because I'm not only talented but kind and generous, as well."

"Right. That or you don't want me to ruin your couch."

Sawyer grinned. "That, too."

FAITH MUST HAVE misheard her brother because there was no way he'd offered to let Dean Presley sleep on their couch. She waited and cornered him while Dean went to hold his phone under the hand dryer for a minute.

"Have you lost your mind? You can't let him stay at our house."

"What else is he supposed to do?" Sawyer replied.

"He has family in town. Family that would probably love to see him." Not that he cared about the people he'd left behind. His parents visited him in Nashville, but he had made it very clear that he wanted nothing to do with this town…nothing to do with Faith. He had always blamed her for what had happened to Addison. Of course, no one blamed Faith as much as Faith did.

"It's late, sis. Have a heart."

He was so much like their dad, always willing to give the shirt off his back. Faith was really no different. Josie had warned them both that their generosity was their weakness. Kindness rarely helped pay the bills. He was also infuriatingly right. There really wasn't anywhere else Dean could go if he refused to wake his family. One night on their couch wasn't going to kill her.

"Fine."

Sawyer gave her a kiss on the top of the head. "You want to close up for me? His jeans are so wet, I'm starting to feel uncomfortable for him. Unless you want to take him…"

No way did Faith want to be alone with Dean. The last time they were alone at her house, he had ripped her heart out. It was almost closing time, anyway, and Josie wouldn't care who helped her lock up. "I'll stay. You go."

Dean returned from the men's room. His water-logged phone still didn't work.

"Let's go, Music Man," Sawyer said, grabbing his guitar case. "Let's get you dried off before you chafe something."

She watched Dean thank Hank for holding the door open for him and Sawyer. He still had his good manners. And broad shoulders. And green eyes that matched the color of the rolling hills that surrounded Grass Lake. Faith's chest burned. He also had a stone heart.

"Am I going to get the story on that one?" Josie asked when she came back to the bar with a drink order. "Or is this something I'm going to have to pry out of you with promises of chocolate and my child's free labor?"

"Your daughter already works for free," Faith quipped. Lily volunteered at the farm several times a week. "You can't bribe me with something I already get."

Josie's round face always wore a smile. Her blue eyes often had a mischievous glint. She nudged Faith with her elbow. "Then just tell me."

Faith let out a heavy sigh of resignation. "Dean is Marilee Presley's son. He's a big-shot record executive in Nashville. He thinks Sawyer should come to the city and start a music career or something." It sounded even more ridiculous when she said it out loud.

"That's amazing!" Josie lit up. "Does he work with anyone I listen to?"

"Boone Williams."

"Boone 'She Loves Me Better Than You' Williams?"

Faith wished Josie wasn't so impressed. "That's the one," she said.

Josie hopped up and down. "Our Sawyer is going to be famous like Boone Williams? This is better than winning the lottery! Why aren't you excited?"

"*Our* Sawyer runs Helping Hooves with me."

The Stratton siblings had been working under their father since they were old enough to hold a dandy brush. John Stratton had believed caring for horses was therapeutic. He had gone back to school after their mother left and gotten his master's degree in counseling with a certificate in equine-assisted therapy. Soon after, he'd opened up Helping Hooves.

Faith had always loved horses and couldn't wait to follow in her father's footsteps. She had imagined working side by side with her dad for years and years. Now that he was gone, Faith was the only licensed therapist while Sawyer assisted and did most of the heavy lifting. They weren't doing a terrible job running the place, but there was no way one of them could do it alone.

"We're trying to get accredited and there's a lot of work to do. Sawyer's place is here, not Nashville," Faith added.

"Oh, please! Your brother has more talent in his pinkie finger than everyone else in Grass Lake combined. If anyone has a shot at being something, at being *someone*, it's Sawyer."

Wasn't he already someone?

"How many people get discovered in small-town bars and become super famous?" Faith asked Josie, but answered first. "Not many. My brother is too much of a realist to get caught up in some crazy fantasy."

There was nothing to worry about. Faith would ignore the tightness in her shoulders and the way her stomach ached. Dean would leave. There was no way he would stick around long enough to convince Sawyer to go with him. Dean wouldn't be able to get out of Grass Lake quick enough.

Faith was annoyed at the way that thought stung. It made little sense. Addison would have been shaking her head in disgust. She hadn't understood how Faith could have *those* kinds of feelings for her brother. Oh, how

Faith wished she had never felt anything for Dean. Had she not, maybe Addison would still be alive today.

"Say what you want," Josie told her. "But I saw the way he listened to your brother play. It was like watching a snake charmer hypnotizing a cobra. It will be Sawyer doing the helping when he sells a million records for Mr. Presley's company."

Josie announced last call and slipped behind the bar to take over for Sawyer. Faith grabbed a dish towel and went to clean off one of the newly abandoned tables. Faith needed Sawyer's help more than Dean ever would. Her brother would stay loyal to the family. There was no doubt in Faith's mind.

CHAPTER THREE

DRY SOCKS WERE Dean's new favorite thing. Although it was possible hot showers ranked a little higher. Hot showers, dry socks and dry pants were definitely in the top three. It didn't even matter that the sweatpants were a little long.

"Feeling better?" Sawyer asked when Dean joined him in the Strattons' sitting room. The chocolate Lab at his feet lifted his head and gave Dean a once-over before probably determining they had already been acquainted. And by acquainted, Dean meant that Sawyer's dog, Scout, had stuck his nose right in his crotch and given him a good sniffing. Dean felt like maybe that made them more than acquaintances at this point.

"One hundred percent."

"Well, you look a million times better," Sawyer said, leaning back in his oversize upholstered rocking chair. "I think I might actually be able to be in the same room as you without laughing."

"Does that mean you might reconsider my offer to come to Nashville?"

A smile spread across Sawyer's face as he shook his head. "Not tonight. Faith says yes to a lot of things she'd rather say no to, and letting you stay here was harder than she wants you to know. I'm not going to push her buttons any more tonight."

Dean felt a little guilty for using the Strattons, given the way things had gone down between him and Faith after Addison's death. But one night and he'd be gone. This visit would be nothing more than a tiny blip on the screen of their lives.

"We can talk about music, though. No harm in that," Sawyer suggested.

Talking about music was easy. Dean had been in love with music since as far back as he could remember. Growing up, his dad had played banjo in a bluegrass band on the weekends and his mother had an unhealthy obsession with Garth Brooks. The first CD he'd bought was a George Strait album that his eight-year-old self had listened to on a constant loop for months.

The more he and Sawyer talked, the more

Dean could see the young man had a similar passion for great music. His eyes lit up when he told Dean a story about buying his first guitar. He had taught himself how to play by watching videos on the internet. Eventually he'd started writing his own songs as well as fooling around with the arrangements of some classics. Country music was his first love but he'd learned a couple Eagles' tunes for his old man.

"I was sorry to hear about your dad."

"He was a good man. An even better dad." Sawyer sat up and rested his elbows on his knees. His gaze fell to the floor. "It's been six months and I'm still not used to him being gone. It's like I keep waiting for him to walk through the door and tell me what needs to get done around here."

Dean knew that feeling all too well. It was a big reason for not wanting to be in this town. He imagined seeing Addison at every turn. She used to love hanging out at Gibson's Five and Dime, spending her allowance on candy and teeny-bopper magazines. How many times had she begged Mrs. Lam at the salon to dye her strawberry-blond hair a different color?

He'd never understood why she hadn't been

satisfied with the way she looked the moment she turned fourteen. Maybe it was a girl thing, but Addison hadn't been the kind of girl who needed anyone's approval. Addison had always done what Addison wanted.

"You okay?" Sawyer asked.

Dean nodded and shook off the memories of his baby sister. "I was just thinking about how hard you must have to work around here. If it's anything like the summer I was on staff, the work's never done."

"Faith and I have been working our butts off to keep Helping Hooves in business. It hasn't been easy," Sawyer admitted. "We're in the process of getting accredited by this equine therapy association. If we pass inspection, we'll have a better shot of paying our bills and expanding the services we provide. Faith understands it all more than I do. I just do what I'm told. Being a grown-up is a lot harder than I thought it would be."

"Is this what you see yourself doing the rest of your life? Keeping the farm running?"

Dean watched Sawyer think it over. It wasn't a simple yes-or-no question for him. "I haven't really thought that far ahead. I like to focus on one thing at a time or else it gets too overwhelming. Right now, the only thing

Faith lets me think about is the hundred pages of requirements we need to meet in order for Helping Hooves to get accredited."

Dean didn't like the sound of that. He needed Sawyer now, not later. "I get that the farm is your priority, but I have to believe you've thought about what it would be like if you could write and perform music for a living. You're too good not to have thought about it at least once."

Sawyer sat back. "I may have thought about it once or twice. But those were just daydreams."

"Well, I'm not here to make you any promises," Dean said, leaning in. "I don't make promises, I offer opportunity. I'd love to hear some more of your songs, and if the rest of them are as good as what I heard tonight, I'd love to offer you the opportunity to record some of them."

"But that would happen in Nashville?"

"Everything happens in Nashville. I can get you studio time there. I can introduce you to some other musicians. I'm telling you, once we get some things recorded, it can all move real fast. I'll have you singing in front of crowds a whole lot bigger than what comes into the Sundown."

Sawyer scratched the top of Scout's head. "That sounds like quite an offer."

"It is. I'm the guy who turns dreams into reality."

"I'm sure most people would say it was an offer they couldn't refuse." Sawyer paused. "But I'm going to need some time to think about it and talk to my sister. Just because I haven't thought about what I want to do with the rest of my life, doesn't mean I want to leap without looking."

"Fair enough." Dean could respect his need to make an informed decision. "Trust me, I don't want you saying yes and then backing out in a month, either. I want artists who are committed. If you sign with me, I can promise you that I will be committed to you."

"I thought you said you don't make promises." One side of Sawyer's mouth curled up. He was all too pleased with himself for catching Dean on that one.

"That's the only promise I'll make to you. Loyalty is that important to me."

Sawyer yawned and stretched his arms over his head. "I'm going to hit the hay. I'm not usually home this early and I think I better take advantage of the extra hours of sleep. I put a couple blankets and a pillow over there." He pointed to the chair in the corner. "The couch doesn't make too bad of a bed. I've fallen asleep there a few times."

"It'll be fine, I'm sure. Thanks again for putting a roof over my head tonight." Dean really did appreciate the kindness.

"Just don't mention any more of this Nashville stuff to Faith," Sawyer said, getting to his feet. "She never really recovered from losing Addison, and now with Dad gone… She puts on a brave face but I know she's having a real hard time. I'm all she's got right now."

Dean's heart lurched at the mention of his sister's name. He knew how close the two of them had been, but sometimes it was hard to find sympathy for Faith. Things could have been so different if she hadn't opened her mouth to Addison.

This wasn't about Addison or Faith. This was about Grace Note. Sawyer was exactly the kind of artist they were looking for. Bringing him to Nashville was imperative. Landon needed some proof that Dean could help the company rebound after the latest Boone Williams debacle.

Dean knew the music business and nurturing the talent in an artist was what he did best. In his mind, he was already booking shows in all the right places and setting up appearances that would benefit Sawyer and the label the most. He knew exactly who to hand off some demos to and which radio personalities to start buttering up.

Sawyer was going to be the next big thing. Dean just needed to figure out how to convince him that his dreams could be a reality.

DEAN WENT FROM dreaming about platinum records and big wins at the Country Artist Awards to fantasizing about chocolate-chip cookies. Why was he dreaming about cookies? They smelled so good. If they tasted half as good as they smelled, they'd be the best cookies he'd ever eat in his life. He rolled to his left and instead of being sprawled across his pillow-topped, queen-size bed, he fell like a ton of bricks to the floor.

"What the—?" Dean sat up and took in his surroundings. He hadn't fallen out of his bed. He'd fallen off the couch, a couch that belonged to Grace Note's next chart-topper.

The rain was still falling but the dark skies of night were now a cloudy-morning gray. Dean pulled himself up and sat back down on the couch. Rubbing his neck, he worked out a kink. The couch hadn't been his worst night's sleep, but it wasn't what he'd consider good, either. On the coffee table sat his clothes—clean, dry and folded in a neat pile.

Dean tried to come up with a plan for fixing his tire and getting out of town before his parents found out he was here. His thoughts were quickly interrupted by the beeping of a timer. The sweet smell of fresh-baked cookies meant that it was probably attached to an oven. His stomach growled, reminding him that he hadn't eaten anything since the fast food he'd inhaled in Birmingham.

Dean let his ears, nose and stomach be his guide. They did not lead him astray. The kitchen's soft butter-yellow walls were so much brighter in the hazy morning light that streamed in through the windows in the cozy breakfast nook than they were last night. On the kitchen table were cooling racks covered in dozens of perfectly golden-brown, chocolate-chip cookies. He could almost taste the melted chocolate, brown sugar and something else he couldn't quite identify.

The only thing that could pull his attention from these tempting cookies was the woman who'd made them. Faith slipped another cookie sheet into the oven. Her hot-pink apron was tied around her slim waist. Again, he was struck by how grown-up she looked. Where had the time gone? What would Addison have looked like at thirty years old?

He shook off thoughts of his baby sister. He couldn't go there. Not when they threatened to unleash feelings he had successfully boxed up and put away years ago.

"Do I smell whiskey?" he asked, finally putting his finger on the mystery scent.

Faith jumped, clutching her chest and shrieking loud enough to be heard for miles. Before he had the opportunity to apologize, she whacked him with her spatula.

Dean tried to protect himself. "I'm sorry! Stop. Stop!" he pleaded.

She gathered her wits and appeared remorseful. "Oh, my gosh, I'm sorry." Then quickly added, "But you really shouldn't sneak up on people like that."

Keeping a safe distance, Dean tried to explain. "I wasn't sneaking up on you. You didn't even give me a chance to say good morning before you went postal on me."

She pushed some stray strands of hair that had fallen out of her ponytail behind her ear. "I'm not used to people walking around the house like mice. Sawyer whistles everywhere he goes, so I always know when he's coming."

"Well, I apologize for not being a noisier guest. I'll be sure to stomp through the house so you hear me coming from now on." He reached for a cookie, figuring she owed him that much for attacking him. He was so hungry and the smell was so mouthwatering…

Faith smacked his hand with the spatula before he could grab one.

"Ow!"

"Sorry," she said, her cheeks turning red. "Just don't touch my cookies."

Dean was ready to wrestle that spatula from her hand. If she swatted him one more time, that thing was getting tossed outside as far as he could fling it. "You make cookies for breakfast, but I can't have one?"

"These are for Mr. Middleton and the church bake sale tomorrow. Not for you. If you want a cookie, you can buy one tomorrow at church."

"You made cookies that smell like whiskey for the church bake sale?"

There were dark circles under Faith's eyes. "It's my thing. I make cookies with a kick. I'll have you know that the people in this town love them and come to the Sundown every Friday night to get their hands on them."

"You sell cookies at the Sundown?" Temptation got the best of him and Dean reached for a cookie. Tennesseans sure did love their whiskey, and Dean was no exception.

Faith raised the spatula, but he gave a warning of his own. "Put that thing down before one of us gets hurt. And by 'us' I mean me or that spatula."

She set her weapon down and stepped back toward the oven. "My Salted Whiskey Chocolate-Chip Cookies happen to be my biggest seller. If you eat them, you are stealing from the church. You wouldn't want to do that, now, would you, Dean Francis Presley?"

Using his middle name was unkind. His mother was the only one who used it. When he was younger, it had been said quite a bit. Addison and Faith had thought it was *so* funny.

"That's a low blow. Maybe I want to steal one from Mr. Middleton. Come on, have mercy on your stranded houseguest."

Faith pursed her lips. Sawyer had said she often said yes when she wanted to say no. He hoped this would be one of those times.

"Fine," she relented. "You can have one cookie. But if I see you take any more than one, I'll charge you five dollars *per* cookie."

Dean was willing to accept any offer. He plucked the biggest cookie with the most chocolate from the nearest cooling rack and took a bite. It practically melted in his mouth. It was obvious these cookies were the ticket to heaven. One was not going to be enough now that he'd had a taste.

FAITH COULDN'T HELP but smile as she watched Dean share a moment with his cookie. He might have been falling in love. The expression on his face reminded her of Addison's after her first kiss with Kenny Gordon.

Dean dashed out of the kitchen and, as quickly as he had disappeared, he returned with a twenty-dollar bill in his hand. He closed the distance between them, leaving her no way to escape.

Clean and dry looked good on him. It smelled even better. He had the kind of hair that women needed to grab by the fistful when he kissed them and made their knees weak. She felt sixteen again, infatuated with the unattainable. Experience told her that when you played with fire, you got burned, and that was not something she wanted to experience again.

"That was the best cookie I have ever had in my entire life. I think you should change the name to Faith and Whiskey Chocolate

Chip, though. They're sweet with a kiss of sass. Just like you." He slipped the bill into the small pocket that was sewn on the chest of her apron. Faith held her breath as a devilish grin spread across his face. "I'll take four."

Stepping away, he snatched his paid-for cookies off the counter. His eyes closed when he took a bite.

Thankfully that left him completely unaware of the effect he had on Faith and her racing heart. Weak knees were nothing compared to her current state. Dizzy and hot, she felt like she had been knocked on the head and shoved in the oven. She spun and opened the refrigerator, letting the air inside cool her burning cheeks. *Faith and Whiskey.* She liked it. More than she should.

Dean wasn't going to be around long enough to eat or name any more of her cookies. He'd be gone and nothing but a memory, like his sister. Faith poured a tall glass of milk and set it on the kitchen table where he had taken a seat to finish his cookie breakfast.

"The milk is on the house."

"You are so much nicer without that spatula in your hand," he said with a mouthful of cookie.

"I know your mother taught you not to

talk with food in your mouth." She shook her head and went to check on her last batch. She needed to remember why he was here.

Dean had run away while she'd spent the last decade trying to make amends to a ghost. Now he was back and talking about making her brother a star. That was not happening. Sawyer didn't want to be a country music star. He was happy here, content to keep their father's farm running, like she was.

"What time does your brother usually get up?" Dean must have read her mind.

"Sawyer's already up. There are always chores to be done around here." Faith figured pointing out how much work her brother had to do would help discourage Dean from pursuing his crazy idea to lure Sawyer to Nashville.

"Oh, I was going to ask him for a lift to my car. I figure the sooner I get that tire fixed, the sooner I can get out of here."

The sooner the better, as far as Faith was concerned. No reason to delay the inevitable. "If you help me deliver these cookies, I'll get you to your car faster than a jackrabbit on a date."

Dean snorted a laugh. "See? Sweet and

sassy," he said with a shake of his head. "I missed you."

His confession seemed to shock them both. All the air left Faith's lungs and it was almost impossible to breathe more in. Dean's face flushed red and he stood to place his empty milk glass in the sink.

Faith couldn't believe how much three little words could affect her. He obviously didn't mean it the way she wanted him to. She knew all too well what it was like to really miss someone. Faith missed her mother and now her father on a daily basis. She missed Addison so much it hurt. She could even admit to missing Dean, but he hated her. He had said as much the last time they had stood in this kitchen together.

"I'll go get changed and then I'll take you up on your offer," he said, making his escape.

Faith could finally breathe again. She had often wished for just one more day with all of those people she missed. Now, standing in the kitchen with her stomach in knots, she realized one day would never be enough. Not when she had once wanted forever.

CHAPTER FOUR

"THANKS FOR WASHING my clothes. I assume that was you," Dean said, returning to the kitchen, ready to go.

"You're welcome," she replied as the oven buzzer went off. Effortlessly, Faith grabbed the fresh batch of cookies, set the baking tray on an empty cooling rack and went back to stacking cookies in travel containers. The woman had done this a time or two. She was in a zone.

Sleep was not something Faith apparently indulged in very often. How else could she have closed up the bar, done laundry and baked a hundred cookies all before eight in the morning? If this was normal for her, her work ethic rivaled Dean's.

She placed a bowl of uncooked rice in front of him. "I also dried your phone."

Dean fished it out. "In rice?"

"It's a little life hack I learned from my

friend Josie. Her daughter has ruined more than one phone in her short fifteen years."

Dean powered up his device and silently rejoiced when it came to life. Work was his life and had been since he'd graduated from college. Hired straight out of school as a member of the Artist Development team at one of the biggest record labels in country music, Dean's first job had been to nurture new talent and help them slowly build their careers with a string of album releases.

He'd been good at it, too, which was why his firing had come as such a shock. Apparently, product—not artist—development had become the company's focus. Forget about supporting the creative side of an act. Sell, sell, sell.

It had made Dean furious and even more determined to prove the big guys had it all wrong. Using every penny he had saved and then some, he'd teamed up with his best friend and started an independent label with a focus on finding a balance between fostering creativity and making a profit. Grace Note Records was supposed to be the solution to all that was wrong with the music business. Dean still had high hopes. Landon not so much.

"Did it work?" Faith asked.

He had three missed calls from Landon and one from Boone Williams. "It did. Thanks again." He jerked a thumb over his shoulder. "I'm going to make a couple calls while you finish up."

Faith pressed a lid on one of her containers. "I'll be ready in about ten minutes."

"Perfect." Dean headed back to the front room for some privacy and dialed Landon.

"You *are* alive!"

Dean chuckled. "Of course, I'm alive. My car got a flat in the middle of a downpour. My phone got soaked and I had to spend the night in some rinky-dink town outside of Nashville."

"Are you back? Because you have got to do something about Boone. I'm not talking to him anymore."

Landon Gilman and Dean had met in a business class at Belmont University and struck up an easy friendship. They both shared a love of music and had spent countless weekends at the local dive bars listening to all the undiscovered talent Nashville had to offer. While Dean's parents had fully supported his choice to study Music Business, Landon's parents had pushed him into accounting.

After graduation, the two had remained close friends. When Dean lost his job, Landon had been the one who planted the idea that maybe he could do this on his own. It hadn't taken much convincing to get Landon to quit his mundane auditing job and invest in the company. It had all been too easy. Until now.

Dean took a seat on the couch. Bad news should always be delivered to someone sitting down. "What's the matter now?"

"He's refusing to meet with Piper. Said there's nothing we can say to change his mind, and if we push, he's going to blow."

Piper Starling was young, talented and the world's biggest Boone Williams fan. She had a passion for country music and had been lighting up the charts since signing with Grace Note.

Piper also had a father/manager who imagined her to be the next Taylor Swift. Dean had a feeling that her dad was pushing her to write her own songs and try to cross over to pop music. He also feared that meant they were going to start looking for a bigger record company as soon as she fulfilled her contract with Grace Note.

Dean had hoped that a collaboration with Boone would encourage her to stay and reignite Boone's creativity. It would solve many of Dean's problems. He forgot that Boone never made anything easy.

"I'll talk to him," Dean promised. "He'll come around once he sees that it's in his best interest to cooperate."

"Cooperation isn't in that man's vocabulary, Dean. And Heath Starling is not happy either, by the way."

Of course he wasn't. Dean scratched at the back of his neck. "I'll handle it."

"You better, because I threw in the towel last night." Every time Landon said something like that, Dean's blood pressure rose to an unhealthy level. Landon had been re-thinking his decision to leave the security of a boring life as an accountant thanks to their constant issues with Boone. Dean needed Landon if Grace Note was going to survive.

"I'll text you when I get everyone on the same page. I still have to fix my tire, but I should be home by this afternoon," Dean informed him just as Sawyer strolled in the front door, whistling away. "And I have good news. I promise. Don't go job searching on LinkedIn again."

"The only good news that's going to keep me from looking elsewhere is that you've found another way to recoup the money we've invested in Boone so we can drop him."

Sawyer might be just that. "I'll talk to you when I get back in the city." Dean hung up and went to the kitchen, where Sawyer had been headed.

"I'll pick some up after I drop off these cookies," Faith said to her brother. She smacked his hand as he reached for a cookie. "Everything needs to be perfect. Don't cut any corners, because the people at NETA will notice, and you know how important this is."

"I know, and I'll get it all done before the visit next week. I promise." Sawyer held his hand out. "Can I please have a cookie now, boss?"

Faith set one cookie on his waiting palm. "I couldn't do this without you."

Dean's guilt resurfaced and so did his grief as he watched brother and sister sharing a moment. Would Addison have needed him? Would they have remained close?

"You could if you stopped doing everything for everyone else in this town," Sawyer said before devouring his cookie in two bites.

Sawyer stepped to the right and Faith noticed Dean standing in the doorway. "Are you ready to go?"

Dean pushed his feelings back into their hiding place. This was business, he told himself. Plain and simple. Sawyer was talented and could help get Grace Note out of the red. It wasn't personal. Faith wasn't Dean's problem, anyway.

"Ready when you are."

"It looks like they have the road blocked off." Faith pulled her car up next to the young deputy who was directing and diverting traffic. She rolled down the window. "Is there another way to get on Highway 14?"

Dressed in enough rain gear to protect him from a monsoon, the deputy pulled a whistle from his mouth. "We've been under a flash flood warning since last night. The highway's closed from here to Highwood. You can take Whispering Hills down and get on 14 off Brighton."

Brighton was a good fifteen miles from here.

"My car is no more than a mile down the road." Dean leaned forward so the deputy could see him. "I need to fix a flat and then I'll be headed north. Can you let us through?"

"Can't do that, sir. Road's closed. If you had a car out there, a flat tire is the least of your problems. Check back tomorrow." He stuck his whistle back in his mouth and blew it at someone making a U-turn behind them.

Faith could feel one heck of a headache coming on. Maybe Dean would be willing to go to his parents' now that he had to stick around a little longer. All she knew was that she needed to get him out.

"Take Whispering Hills but turn left on Rosewood," Dean said.

"That doesn't go all the way through to the highway. It dead-ends at the forest preserve."

He kept his eyes fixed out the passenger-side window. "I'll cut through the forest and come out right where my car is. I can't sit around all day waiting for the road to open up."

Faith figured she couldn't talk him out of his plan. Dean had always been a leader, not a follower. Besides, it was only drizzling now, nothing like the thunderstorm that had hit last night.

Dean grabbed the umbrella from the back-seat as Faith pulled into the parking lot. "Thanks again for taking me in last night."

"No problem." Faith opened her door as he stepped out.

"What are you doing?" he asked. The way

he looked at her made Faith want to climb back in her car and drive away.

"Going with you," she replied, pulling her hood over her head. "What if you need help?"

His eyes definitely rolled. "I got it, Faith. Don't worry."

"I either wait here for you or go with. But may I remind you that you can't change a tire and hold an umbrella over your head at the same time?" Faith could be stubborn, too.

"Whatever." Dean closed his door and stomped off into the forest.

Spring was in full bloom and the canopy of leaves provided some protection from the rain, but not enough to keep things dry. Faith was not wearing the right shoes to go traipsing through the wet brush. Instead of their footsteps crunching leaves and snapping branches, the only sound was the wet slap of their feet in mud.

Dean didn't wait for her or check to make sure she was okay. He barreled through to the other side, where the ground became so saturated it was more like a lake.

"You've got to be kidding me," Dean huffed with his hands on his hips. Faith trudged up next to him. Her shoes and socks were soaked.

They weren't far from the road and through

the trees she could see a car—a car that would be faring better if it was a boat. Water covered the tires.

"Is that—?"

Dean nodded and exhaled an exasperated breath. His car wouldn't be taking him back to Nashville today. Or tomorrow. Or…

He turned around and stalked off in the direction they had come. She could understand his frustration, but did he have to be so rude?

"I'm sorry about your car. I can take you to your parents' and I'm sure they'll be able to find someone who can help you tow it out of there," she said, desperately trying to keep up with him.

He stopped and Faith almost ran into him. "I'm not going to my parents'. Can you take me back to the farm?"

"You could be here a few days. Don't you think you should let them know you're here?" The thought of being around Dean for another day, possibly more, was enough to give Faith a full-blown panic attack.

"I can't. Please, Faith." He didn't have to explain. She could see it in his eyes, the pain the memories were digging up.

There was no way she could put him through that. "Fine."

His shoulders seemed to relax at her concession.

Instead of taking off and leaving her behind, he walked with her, even held out a hand to help her step over a fallen tree in their path.

Faith lifted her leg over the log but her foot stuck in the mud on the other side, throwing her off balance. She lunged forward, still gripping Dean's hand. He tried to steady her but she ended up pulling him down with her.

Her knee sank into the mud with a splat. She stuck out her hands to stop from falling face-first. Dean dropped the umbrella and landed on his behind. Not good. Faith tried to get up, but her feet couldn't get any traction and she fell again, sending splatters of mud everywhere.

"Great." Dean held his hands up, searching for a way to get up without touching the mud. It was highly unlikely in Faith's opinion.

She started to laugh because it was that or cry. They were both ridiculous and completely helpless.

"What are you laughing at?" he asked as he fought a smile.

Faith got up on her knees and lifted a

muddy hand, smacking it down on his shoulder. "We're hopeless."

Dean stared at the new mud print on his shirt. "That's going to cost you."

"I'm not scared of you," Faith said, making a second attempt at standing. "You look more afraid of getting dirty than I do."

The challenge had been presented and Dean Presley didn't back down from a challenge. Faith wasn't sure how she could have forgotten.

Dean used both hands to grab fistfuls of slop. "Not scared, huh?"

Faith's heart beat a little faster. If she didn't move, she would be washing mud out of her hair for sure. The twinkle in his eyes reminded her of the boy she once loved.

She thought she could escape, but standing on this sludge was worse than being on ice. Her feet went out from under her again. Dean smacked her on the forehead with one hand.

Game on.

CHAPTER FIVE

"I'LL PAY TO get your car detailed," Dean offered as he stood beside Faith in front of her car. Her *clean* car.

"It's not going to be cheap if we get in there like this," Faith replied. Her face was hidden under a mask of mud. Even her eyelashes had globs stuck to them.

"True. You should probably pay since this was all your fault."

"My fault?" She turned her head, her dirty hair flicking muddy water his way. "I slipped. *You* attacked me. We wouldn't be nearly this messy if it wasn't for you."

Dean smirked. Mud wrestling with Faith was the most fun he'd had in a long time. It was like they were kids again, back when neither one of them had any worries or responsibilities.

"Also true. I'll pay half. Can you unlock the doors now?"

They were both so dirty they'd be finding

mud in places they usually never thought to check for days. Getting in meant transferring all that sludge to the light gray interior of the car. Faith let out a heavy sigh and unlocked the doors. Dean quickly called dibs on the shower when they got back to the farm.

"Nice try. I'm going to have Sawyer hose you off before you step foot in my house."

Dean turned up the heat, smudging the button. "Oh, come on. You work on a horse farm. You've walked through that house dirty before."

"Not this dirty."

Dean tried not to lean back. Faith had scooped up a handful of mud and shoved it down the back of his shirt. It was cold and wet, and he wanted to keep the cleaning costs down. "Has *anyone* ever been this dirty? I don't think so."

One side of Faith's mouth quirked up. "Do you remember when Addison heard about that spa in Belle Meade where they charge people outrageous amounts of money for fancy mud baths, and she thought she could get the same effect by lying in a mud puddle in one of our flooded paddocks?"

The memory of Mr. Stratton calling Dean's parents to warn them that their daughter might smell like horse manure for a few days popped up and punched Dean in the gut. He could picture a thirteen-year-old Addison returning home wearing Faith's clothes, which were at least two sizes too small. Faith had always been the Laurel to Addison's Hardy. She had looked ridiculous and smelled even worse. Dean had teased her relentlessly for days after.

Faith laughed and the drying mud by her eyes cracked as the skin underneath it crinkled. "She told everyone at school that people in Europe bathed in the same stuff all the time because it detoxified the body of impurities. Jill and Veronica believed every word and asked when they could come over for a treatment."

That was a perfect example of who Addison had been. She could sell ice to a polar bear. She would have grown up to be someone amazing. The pain in Dean's chest made it hard to breathe.

"You probably don't remember," Faith said, mistaking his silence for a lapse of memory.

"I remember everything. Maybe I don't want to talk about it. Did you ever think of that?" he asked, his voice a bit harsher than intended.

Faith stiffened in the driver's seat. Her eyes stayed trained on the road. "Sorry. I shouldn't have brought her up. I won't do it again."

Dean doubted that was possible. Everything in this town reminded him of his sister. It surely did the same for Faith. Maybe it was a bad idea to stay at the farm. He couldn't go to his parents', but he could see if there was a room open at Tanner's. Of course, there was a greater chance he might run into his mother if he was in the middle of town. The farm was a safe distance from all the small-town eyes and ears.

A heavy silence fell between them as they made their way back. Sawyer waved from inside one of the paddocks when they pulled up. *Keep your eye on the prize.* Sawyer was the real reason for staying at the farm, the only reason Dean wasn't going to call Landon and ask him to come get him out of here.

Sawyer pushed back his cowboy hat and stared wide-eyed at the two of them as they got out of the car. His dog barked, probably thinking they were creatures of some sort. "What in the world…?"

"It's just me, Scout," Faith told the dog. She tossed her keys to Sawyer. "Highway 14 is shut down thanks to the rain and Dean's car is under water. I'm going to take a shower and then we can go over what you've gotten finished this morning. Jason's bringing Freddy by at eleven for his session."

She barely spared Dean a sideways glance before heading into the house. He had obviously hurt her feelings. He tried to not feel bad about it, but that wasn't working too well.

"Care to fill in the giant blanks?" Sawyer asked Dean.

"She slipped in some mud and dragged me down with her." Just like she'd done with her memories of Addison. "Do you think I could borrow some more clothes?"

"This relationship is becoming very one-sided, Music Man."

"I promise, it won't be like that for much longer." If Sawyer proved to be the performer Dean hoped he could be, the two of them would both be reaping the benefits of this relationship.

"There you go with those promises again. You said you don't make those."

This promise was different. This was one Dean was making to himself.

"GREAT, I'LL HAVE the tow truck drop the car off there as soon as they can get to it. Thanks again." Dean hung up with the auto mechanic who'd agreed to assess the damage to his car once it was rescued from its watery jail. He was praying he didn't have to trash it and get a new one.

Having done nothing but make call after call since getting out of the shower, he wandered down to the kitchen, hoping there were some cookies hiding somewhere. Faith had made herself scarce and maybe that was for the best.

He didn't find any cookies, so he settled for a Coke to satisfy his sugar craving. There was only one more call to make and Dean dreaded it, hence the reason he had saved it for last. Scrolling through his contacts, he stopped when his thumb hovered over Boone's name. He needed this man to cooperate. That usually meant Boone would try to be as uncooperative as possible. It was inevitable.

He pressed Call anyway. With each unanswered ring, Dean's desire to drop Boone, regardless of the financial loss Grace Note would incur, increased tenfold. Boone finally answered on the fifth ring.

"Save your breath, Dean. I don't have time to babysit your little princess. Find someone else."

"Boone…" Dean tried turning on the charm even though he wanted to wring the guy's neck through the phone. "Have I told you lately how much I respect your honesty?"

"I'm not collaborating with anyone right now. I've got nothing, absolutely nothing, to give. It's like the music disappeared from my soul."

Dean was thankful they weren't having this conversation face-to-face. His eye roll would not have gone over well. "I hear you, buddy. I'm taking this seriously. I talked to someone who heard that there's this place in California where Johnny Wilmett went to clear his head a few years ago when he was having similar issues. I'm still looking into it, but I think a retreat is exactly the kind of thing you need. Somewhere your soul can reconnect with the music. Know what I mean?"

A retreat that would include Piper Starling whether Boone liked it or not. He didn't need to know that right now, though.

"I'm not so sure. I'm trying to get my visitation rights back and Sara is being such a…"

Divorce was a killer. Fear of ending up like Boone was one thing that kept Dean cynical about love. Better to choose to be alone than to be left that way.

"We don't have to decide today. It doesn't have to be California. Maybe I can find somewhere closer to Nashville. We'll figure it out. I just need you to trust me. Can you do that? Can you trust that I'm on your side?"

"I'll trust you when you get me invited back to the CAAs. But they better not seat me anywhere near Blake Keller."

Dean didn't want to know what Boone's gripe was with Blake. That was his agent's headache, not the label's. The good news was that Boone had a goal Dean could help him move toward.

"I'll work on it," he said before adding, "Having a new album to promote would be a big help."

Boone responded by hanging up.

Dean took a deep breath and let it go. Boone hadn't agreed to anything, but he'd given Dean the right leverage. If being at the Country Artist Awards was important to Boone, he'd need new material for them to be interested in having him back after a less-than-stellar performance, an even more embarrassing attempt at presenting an award while intoxicated and a shoving match with an assistant producer a couple years ago. He'd have to cooperate and work with Piper.

Maybe Dean could even get them a shot at performing a duet on the show.

A teenage girl waltzed through the back door like she owned the place. "Oh, my gosh! You scared me." She held a hand against her chest. "Are you a volunteer? I told Faith I would be here. Did she not believe me?"

"I'm not—"

"I missed *once*. It's not fair of her to act like I'm going to blow it off every time. She's just like my mom," the girl said with a groan.

"I have no idea what you're talking about," Dean said, trying again to minimize the teenage angst. "I'm a family friend. I'm not volunteering for anything."

"Oh." Her cheeks pinked up. "Good. I knew Faith was cooler than my mom. Is she in here?"

"I think she's outside with Sawyer."

"Dean, could you—?" Faith came in from the front room and stopped short. "Lily, you're here. I was starting to worry. Freddy will be here any minute."

The teenager started rambling on about how she had slept over at a friend's and how they had stayed up all night because the other girl cried about how this girl's boyfriend was ruining their friendship. Then, when she got home this morning, she and her mom had fought.

Dean's eyes began to glaze over.

"I thought you had this guy come because you didn't trust me." Lily nodded in Dean's direction.

"I want to trust you, but you've been less than reliable lately. And this stuff with Kylie…"

"I won't let it interfere with my volunteering. You know I love the horses and the kids. I want to be here. I do."

Faith held out a hand and pulled Lily in for a hug. All was forgiven. "I hope you and Kylie make up. Never let a boy come between you and your best friend." Faith let her go and her gaze fell on Dean. "No one knows better than me that there's nothing worse than losing your best friend because of a boy who will probably break your heart anyway."

"DID SOMEONE GET a haircut since the last time I saw him?" Faith asked Jason Green as he helped his eight-year-old son out of the car.

"He's not happy about it. Told his mother he thought it made him look like a nerd."

"It does," Freddy said, gripping the handles of his walker. The white plastic braces on his legs had Nike symbols drawn on them with permanent marker. Cerebral palsy may have weakened his muscles but not his fashion sense.

"No way!" Faith helped get him on his feet. "You look very handsome. What do you think, Lily?"

Lily's opinion would matter more to him than all the adults' combined. Josie's daughter was gorgeous and attentive. She had all the little kids completely enamored.

"I like it." She crouched down so they were the same height and pulled out her phone. "Smile," she said, taking a picture of the two of them. "I'll post this to my Instagram and you'll see how cool you are by how many likes we get."

Freddy's face lit up the way it did when he saw his favorite quarter horse, Winston. The girl wasn't always reliable, but she had great instincts when it came to the kids, always knowing exactly what they needed to hear and relating to them one-on-one. She often reminded Faith of Addison.

They walked Freddy down to the stables and let him greet Winston there to do some grooming and stretching before heading to the covered arena. Someday, Faith hoped they'd be able to build an indoor arena to make it easier to give lessons year-round. Getting the accreditation from NETA, the National Equine Therapy Association, would help ease some of the burden and make it easier for potential clients to come to Helping Hooves because insurance would then defer some of the cost.

"All right, who's ready to ride?" Faith asked once they were in the arena. Winston was saddled up and ready to go. The four-year-old bay gelding was as gentle as they came. He obeyed commands like a champ and walked more politely than any horse Faith had ever owned.

"Me!" Freddy shouted with his arm raised. Sawyer helped Freddy mount the horse while Lily adjusted Winston's halter. Today, they were going to work on motor planning as well as posture control. Faith handed Freddy some plastic rings in an array of colors and explained that he would have to put the correct colored ring on various posts spread out around the arena.

Sawyer and Faith walked alongside as Lily held the lead rope and guided Winston though the course. Freddy struggled but was determined to complete the task.

"Next up, red," Faith said. Out of the corner of her eye she noticed Dean had ventured out and was catching up with Jason. She had forgotten they had both graduated from Grass Lake High the same year and would have known one another.

His presence made her uneasy. It was obvious he still held her responsible for what had happened all those years ago. He had good reason. Addison never would have gone to that party, never would have gotten in the car with someone like Aaron Evans, if she hadn't found out her brother and her best friend had been sneaking around behind her back all summer.

Faith shouldn't have told her the truth, but the secret had been eating away at her, at their relationship. She should have known Addison wouldn't take the news well. Dean had warned her. By the time she had admitted to him that she had told, it was too late. Addison had already made the choice to get in the car, a choice that had ended her life.

"Last one, Freddy. You can do it." Sawyer encouraged the little boy. Freddy would have to move the green ring from his right hand to his left and lift it up above the post so it would fit around it.

"I'm tired," Freddy said, his head drooping forward.

"You've got this." Faith put a hand on his lower back to remind him to straighten up.

Freddy fought through the fatigue and lifted the ring up and over the post. His dad cheered for him like he had hit a home run in Little League.

"I knew you could do it," Faith said, patting his leg. Lily led the horse back to where Freddy would dismount.

"Great job today, bud." Lily held up a hand for a high five. Even though he was exhausted, Freddy didn't pass up the chance to celebrate with the lovely Lily. She took her phone out of her back pocket. "And look, thirty likes for that haircut while you were working. I bet we hit a hundred by the end of the day."

Freddy's smile was wide and proud. That haircut would never be thought of as nerdy again.

Jason brought over his son's walker. "Come meet an old friend of mine, bud." He introduced Freddy to Dean, who stuck out his hand to shake. Freddy gripped the handles of his walker tightly. He wasn't going to be able to let go if he wanted to remain upright.

"I need Freddy to keep both hands on his walker until we get to the stables," Faith said so the little boy felt like he shouldn't—instead of couldn't—let go.

"How did you get this guy to come back to Grass Lake?" Jason asked her as they returned to the stables.

"I had nothing to do with it. He only has his car to blame."

Dean explained what had happened the night before, but quickly steered the conversation in another direction. He seemed more comfortable talking about Jason and what he'd been up to than himself.

"How amazing is this woman?" Jason said, putting an arm around Faith's shoulders and pulling her against his side. "I owe everything to her and this place. When Freddy was four, he was wheelchair-bound. My wife and I weren't sure we'd ever see him walk, but thankfully Faith suggested we come out and work with her dad and his horses. She's the reason my son walks today."

Faith wished the conversation hadn't turned to singing her praises. Dean had no reason to do so.

"She's always been pretty incredible," Dean said with his gaze fixed on her burning face. "That's why Addison loved her like a sister."

CHAPTER SIX

THERE WERE NO oven timers to wake Dean up Sunday morning. Instead of the sweet smells of baking cookies, it was dreams of Addison that had him up bright and early. He couldn't even blame Faith. She had held to her promise and hadn't uttered his sister's name once since the muddy car ride.

Sunlight glinted off the aerial photograph of the farm that hung opposite the window. The rain had ended and the promise of some drier days lay ahead. Dean tried to focus on the possibility of retrieving his car instead of the painful memories of his sister. Getting out of Grass Lake was becoming more of a necessity than a simple desire.

He picked up his phone to call the towing company to check the status, but it rang instead. His mother was calling. Word must have gotten out. Thanks to his reunion with Jason Green yesterday, there was no way to stop the news of his return from spreading like wildfire. It had always been a matter of when his mother would find out, not if.

"Hi, Mom."

"Imagine my surprise when I walked out my front door this morning to get the Sunday paper and Caroline Hughes tells me she hopes to see you at church today since you're in town."

"I was going to call you," he said, knowing she wouldn't believe him.

"Where are you?"

"I'm at the Stratton farm. I ran into Faith and Sawyer at the Sundown after my car broke down." Leaving out the fact that two days had passed since then seemed like a good idea.

"And you didn't think to call me and your father? You decided to stay out there instead of coming here?" The hurt in her voice made him feel guiltier than he already did.

Dean rubbed his forehead in an attempt at easing the headache that was sure to stick around all day now. "I'm sorry, Mom. I planned to come see you today."

"Good. I'll be at church in an hour. I expect to see you there."

Before Dean could tell her he really didn't want to go to church, especially not the church he hadn't set foot in since Addison's funeral, she hung up.

Marilee Presley did not mess around when it came to going to church on Sundays. Dean and Addison had been taught early on that no excuse other than illness got them out of their religious obligation. It wasn't until after Addison died that attending Sunday services started to seem pointless to Dean.

What kind of God let people like his sister die? Not one he wanted to pray to.

Having nothing to wear would have been a decent excuse, except his freshly laundered clothes sat on the coffee table. Faith was some kind of laundry fairy who delivered clean clothes while people slept. There wasn't a trace of mud on any of them. His socks were whiter than he remembered them ever being. Not even his dry cleaner in Nashville was this good.

Faith came tiptoeing down the stairs and grimaced when she noticed he was up. "Did I wake you? I tried to be quiet while I got ready."

She had avoided him all day and evening yesterday, even after he'd tried to make amends for his moodiness. Here she was still walking on eggshells around him.

"You didn't wake me up. My mom called. She heard I was in town."

"I swear I didn't say anything to anyone," she argued unnecessarily. Dean knew she wasn't to blame.

Faith had always been honest and trustworthy, even as a child. She had been the good one while Addison had been wild. Whenever those two had been up to something, Dean's mom only had to give Faith a look and the poor girl would spill her guts. It had driven Addison crazy, which was probably why she hadn't taken the news that Faith had been lying to her that summer very well.

"It's not like I've been hiding. Anyone could have seen me at the Sundown on Friday. I talked to the towing company and Dwight from the auto shop. I caught up with Jason yesterday. She was bound to find out sooner or later."

Faith seemed to relax a bit and smoothed out some invisible wrinkles on the skirt of her pale yellow sundress. Her dark hair was down, loose curls falling over her shoulders. Her pink lips were glossed and those brown eyes needed no help drawing attention.

"I guess that means there's no reason to sleep on our uncomfortable couch anymore."

The hair on the back of his neck stood on end. At least the dreams of Addison last night had been of her alive and well. He could only imagine the nightmares he'd have sleeping under his parents' roof.

"Would it be a huge inconvenience to stay here on this perfectly comfortable couch, if that's the way things played out?"

Sawyer came bounding down the steps in a shirt and tie, followed by Scout. The dog always seemed to be right on Sawyer's heels. "The couch is yours, but it's time to go shopping so my sister doesn't have to do your laundry every night and my clothes can stay in my closet where they belong."

Faith looked like she wanted to say something but bit her bottom lip instead.

"You two headed to church?"

"Well, we don't dress like this to shoe the horses," Sawyer said, checking his hair in the mirror above the couch. He had just the right amount of ego to become a star.

"Can I catch a ride with you? My mother may disown me if I don't show up for Sunday services."

"We leave in ten minutes," Sawyer replied. "Faith likes to get there early."

Always the good girl. Until she had fallen

for him. No mistake had been bigger than giving in to his feelings for Faith. It had cost them both more than they were willing to lose.

"LET'S HOPE HIS mother won't take no for an answer." Faith's arms were folded across her chest as they waited in Sawyer's pickup for their guest. It had been fifteen minutes since Sawyer had said they needed to leave in ten.

"I don't get why he won't go home. What's he hiding from?" Sawyer asked, honking the horn for the third time.

"Addison." Faith's voice broke a little.

"I don't get that, either."

"People grieve in different ways." Faith scooted to the middle of the bench seat as Dean approached. No one in Grass Lake went to church in jeans, but at least his were clean and dry. His blond hair was finger-combed and his beard needed a trim, but the sight of him still made Faith's heart skip a beat.

"I need to make a quick stop before church," Sawyer said, backing out of the driveway. Faith was thankful her brother was taking credit for their detour. She didn't want to have to explain where they were going or why.

"The longer the better," Dean mumbled. His arm felt warm against hers even though she was trying her best not to make contact. Such a different story from twelve years ago when she couldn't get close enough.

That last summer they'd spent together Dean had insisted Addison finally learn how to drive, and Faith had always tagged along. While Addison had been focused on the road, Dean would brush his fingers against Faith's thigh or throw his arm over the back of the seat and play with her hair. It had been a dream come true to have his attention and affection, even though they'd had to be sneaky about it.

Faith didn't dare mention those days or Addison's horrendous driving skills. Dean had buried his memories along with his sister, and it was clear that was where he wanted them to stay.

Sawyer pulled into the spot in front of Harriet's Flower Shop and Faith waited for him to climb out so she didn't have to ask Dean to move. Nothing downtown was open on Sundays this early except the Cup and Spoon Diner. Some people needed their morning coffee before their day could really begin.

Iris Hackney and her son stepped out of the diner and spotted Faith. Mrs. Hackney had been Faith's fifth-grade teacher. Her red hair was now gray, but she still wore pink glasses on the end of her pointy nose.

"Good morning, Miss Stratton!" She waved a gloved hand and pulled her son in Faith's direction. Dressed in her Sunday's best, Mrs. Hackney looked more like the wife of a politician than a former grade-school teacher. Her navy blue dress was paired with white gloves and a belt that cinched her thin waist.

"Good morning, Mrs. Hackney. Charles," Faith said, nodding in his direction.

"I was just telling Charles we should give you a call. Wasn't I, dear?"

Charles smiled sheepishly. With a round face like his father's and red hair like his mother's, many people forgot he wasn't the Hackneys' biological son. Mr. and Mrs. Hackney had adopted Charles as a baby when they were in their forties. He was the same age as Faith even though his parents were much older than hers.

"I heard that you have some experience sewing drapery, and Charles is in desperate need of some new window treatments. Would you be willing to help him out? I've chosen some lovely fabric, but I've never been very good on a sewing machine."

If by experience she meant the one time

Josie roped Faith into helping sew drapes for the high school drama club, then, yes, Faith had experience.

"My last clients weren't very discriminating. I'm not sure I'm the kind of seamstress you're looking for." Faith had a difficult time coming out and saying no to people, but that didn't stop her from hoping they would change their minds if she gave them an out.

"You did a wonderful job! Everyone raved about how beautiful and realistic the sets were for the fall play."

Mrs. Hackney would not be changing her mind. For years the woman had been playing matchmaker for her son. He was a nice guy, but not someone who made the butterflies in Faith's stomach come to life. Shouldn't the man she was going to marry at least make her heart beat a little faster? Charles and his ho-hum personality were more likely to cause her to flatline.

Always the pleaser, Faith agreed to help and Mrs. Hackney was overjoyed. Charles shifted uncomfortably and said nothing. His mother suggested they talk after church to set up a time to meet and go over the design.

Faith glanced back at the pickup as the Hackneys got in their car. Sawyer gave her a thumbs-up and Dean was definitely smirking. Seeing him smile was almost worth the embarrassment.

The sign outside the flower shop clearly said Closed, but Faith knocked on the bright green door like she did every Sunday. The window boxes were filled to the brim with a beautiful mix of verbena, petunias and white snow mountains. It smelled like heaven.

Faith heard the lock slide open and was greeted by Harriet herself. "Good morning, Sugarplum. Come on in."

Harriet Windsor had been Faith's mother's best friend. When their mom left, Harriet had stepped up and done her best to fill the hole she'd left in the kids' lives. Her sage advice had been the only way Faith had survived puberty in a house with two clueless males. Sawyer still had the picture of the two of them in his room from when Harriet had gone as his date to the Boy Scouts' Mother/Son Dinner and Dance.

"I set aside some arrangements I thought you might like, but go ahead and look around while I finish getting ready." Harriet's cheeks were rouged but her eyes and lips were bare. Not to mention, her caramel-colored hair wasn't nearly big enough. There was still plenty of teasing and hair-spraying to be done.

Faith spent a minute poking around but settled on two of the bouquets Harriet had put together. She was the expert, after all. Faith found her upstairs in the bathroom of her small apartment above the shop.

"I'll take the ones you picked out."

Harriet smiled at her through the vanity mirror as she applied her mascara. "Good choice. How are you doing?"

Faith's eyes fell to the baby blue tiled floor. "Fine."

Harriet knew better. "Missing your daddy or stressed out about the return of one Mr. Dean Presley?"

"You heard, huh?"

"I'm sure half the town has heard by now. No one thought he'd ever come back here. Are you worried about seeing him at church?"

"He's been staying at the farm," Faith confessed.

Harriet set down her applicator brush. "He's what? You've seen him already? Has he been nice to you?" She was the only person who knew how horribly things had ended between Faith and Dean. Faith had cried on her shoulder more times than she could count.

"It's been awkward. It's like nothing and everything's changed since the last time I saw him. And he wants Sawyer."

"What?"

"Dean wants him to come to Nashville with him to record some music. He heard him sing at the Sundown on Friday."

"Sawyer wouldn't leave you."

"I know." Faith swallowed down the lump that had formed in her throat. "He's not going to go. We have NETA coming to do the accreditation visit next weekend. Summer camps start in a month. He can't go—I can't do this without him."

Harriet went back to her makeup. "You don't need to worry about any of it. Everything is going to work out. You got two angels up in heaven looking out for you."

Faith wanted to believe that. "Thanks again for the flowers."

"Anytime, sweetheart. Can I still count on you to help me out on Tuesday?"

Faith didn't feel right taking the flowers for free and Harriet refused to take her money, so once or twice a month, Faith helped at the shop in exchange for the bouquets. This Tuesday was busier than usual, but Faith couldn't say no.

"I'll be here." She started to go. "Sawyer and Dean are waiting for me. I'll see you at church."

"Hey," Harriet said to get her attention one last time. "Don't let him feed that guilt of yours. You understand me?"

Faith nodded and gave Harriet a reassuring smile even though deep down she knew it wasn't possible. Dean had been home less than forty-eight hours and her guilt was back with a vengeance and a voracious hunger.

CHAPTER SEVEN

"IT'S FUNNY HOW this town can seem familiar and yet so foreign at the same time," Dean observed as he and Sawyer waited for Faith.

"It's *not* funny how long my sister takes when we need to be somewhere."

"Be happy you have a sister to be annoyed with."

Sawyer stopped complaining. Chagrined, he took a deep breath and apologized. Dean couldn't be mad. He knew firsthand how easy it was to take people for granted.

Dean's gaze drifted back down the street. He wasn't surprised the bank where his father had worked for the last thirty years hadn't changed. There was a new gas station on the corner. The old-fashioned gas pumps were a nice touch and made it look like it had been there forever. The movie theater had gotten a facelift and the sign above the hardware store was new. The barber shop where his mom had taken him to get his hair cut as a child had closed and a nail salon stood in its place.

"Here she comes," Sawyer said, pulling Dean's attention away from comparing this Main Street to the one in his memory.

Dean knew who the flowers were for the moment he saw Faith making her way to the truck with bouquets in her arms. A familiar unease settled in his stomach.

What could his mother really do to him if he didn't show up for church? She had nothing to hold over him. She couldn't ground him or take away his phone. He didn't live under her roof or have to follow her rules. He was a grown man who could decide where he wanted or didn't want to go.

He didn't want to go to the church. He didn't want to be within a hundred feet of the cemetery. Even sitting in the parking lot would be too close. He'd have to walk back to the farm. He didn't care how far it was.

"Did you tell Harriet you couldn't help her on Tuesday because you rescheduled Freddy's therapy?" Sawyer asked his sister as he got out of the truck so she could get in.

"I don't want to cancel on her. She asked me to enter the inventory information into the computer. I'll run over there at lunchtime and get it done quick."

Dean was again reminded of his sister. Addison had worked at the flower shop all through high school. She had wanted to become a botanist. Dean hated that she'd never got the chance to live out any of her dreams.

Sawyer groaned as he started up the truck. "You have a full day of therapy scheduled. All the horses have to be prepped."

"I'll be back in time to help with the horses," Faith assured him.

"And you're still going to go to Lily's award ceremony, aren't you?"

"I promised her. She got into National Honor Society. That's a big deal."

"Can you skip Bible study then?"

Faith looked down her nose at her brother. "You don't skip Jesus, Sawyer."

"You're burning the candle at both ends, Faith." He sounded sincerely worried about her.

Dean wondered how often she stretched herself so thin.

"I'll be fine. As long as I have you to help me out."

She relied on him, but Faith needed Sawyer more than he needed her. If he was going to get Sawyer to follow him to Nashville, Dean needed to find a way to break their co-dependent relationship.

The potent scent of the flowers started to make him nauseous as they drove to the church on the outskirts of town. There had been so many flowers at Addison's funeral they had overwhelmed the small space. Dean remembered wanting to rip all the arrangements apart and crush every petal. A funeral wasn't a joyous occasion no matter how it was dressed up. There was nothing to celebrate, and no sweet-smelling rose could make up for the hole in Dean's heart.

As soon as the towering white steeple of Grass Lake Community Church came into view, Dean thought about jumping out of the moving vehicle. He felt trapped and escape was the only solution.

"I want to talk to Pastor Kline before the services start," Sawyer said. "Dean, can you help Faith carry the folding tables out back for the picnic?"

The tension in Dean's shoulders was so great he feared he wouldn't be able to move once the truck came to a stop. He needed to man up; he couldn't succumb to this anxiety.

"I'll take care of it," he replied in a voice

that sounded much more composed than he felt. The parking lot was half full and his father's Buick was parked right up front. Dean's mom was probably in charge of the picnic today.

He focused on the task at hand and not the way the rolling hills surrounding the church looked exactly the same as they had that late-summer day twelve years ago.

With Faith's help, he unloaded the two tables. Stacked on top of one another, they were bulky but not impossible to move. Faith left her flowers in the truck and lifted her end.

As they came around the side of the building, the first person they bumped into was Dean's father. Ted Presley was a huge hulk of a man. A former Olympic weightlifter, his neck was as thick as a tree trunk.

"I never thought I'd see the day." He greeted his son with a side-hug before taking the tables from them and carrying them behind the church by himself. "Look who I found, Marilee."

Dean's mother stopped what she was doing to throw her arms around her son. Even though they visited him in Nashville all the time, there was something about being together in this place that made this reunion more emotional than it needed to be.

She let him go and gave him a quick once-over. "Jeans? Really?"

"I'm working with what I got here, Mom. I drove down to Birmingham for a show Friday and was supposed to sleep in my own bed that night, but my car had other ideas."

"Perhaps there was an even higher power at work." Marilee turned her attention to Faith and pulled her in for a hug like she had Dean. "Hi, honey. Thanks for taking him in and for baking cookies for the picnic. I may have sampled one already."

"I hope you donated," Dean said, wishing he could have another one of those chocolate-and-whiskey-flavored bites of joy. "She doesn't give those away for free."

His mom swiped her golden brown bangs out of her face. She was the complete opposite of his father. Where he was thick, she was thin. Her dark brown eyes and tanned skin were in complete contrast to his fair skin, blond hair and blue eyes. "I think the weeks of organizing I've done for this picnic are worthy of one cookie, Dean Francis."

Faith smiled wider than he had seen the whole weekend. "She can have as many cookies as she likes. I'm going to change the flowers. I'll see you inside."

Dean watched as Faith walked away. He knew where she was going and it made his heart heavy. How did she survive in this town, surrounded by constant reminders of what was lost? She had more reasons than he did to leave it all behind. Yet here she was setting out to put flowers on his sister's grave.

"She brings Addison flowers every Sunday without fail," his mom said. "Now, she does the same for her dad. What I wouldn't give to take away some of that poor girl's grief."

Something that felt very much like guilt settled on Dean's shoulders. He tried to shake it off. It wasn't his fault Faith was in mourning. A voice in his head reminded him that he hadn't ever done anything to ease her pain, either, but that was because he was much too good at exacerbating it.

"Can I help you set something up before services start?" he asked his mom, pushing all those feelings back into the box where they belonged.

She put her hand on his face and gazed up at him with nothing but love. "It makes me happy to have you home." She gave him a little pat on the cheek. "Even if I have to sit next to you in church when you're wearing jeans."

"HARRIET OUTDID HERSELF this week, don't you think?" Faith said as she slipped the mix of wildflowers into the granite vase beside Addison's headstone. "I hope you aren't mad I gave my dad the ones with the red tulips. Red's his favorite color and these purple ones remind me of the bluebells we used to pick."

She brushed debris off the headstone and ran her fingers over Addison's birthdate. It wouldn't be long before Addison would be gone longer than she'd been alive. It was so hard to believe that a dozen years had already passed.

"So…your brother's here. I know. I can't believe he showed up, either. I'm pretty sure he still hates me. He tries to be nice, but the hostility is always there just under the surface."

Faith often wondered if Addison would have been glad that Dean wanted nothing to do with Faith after the accident, or if she would have regretted being so angry about their relationship. She supposed it didn't really matter since she'd never get an answer anyway.

"He likes Sawyer, though. Thinks he could be 'a star.' Feel free to laugh about that for a second." The whole thing was ridiculous. Dean had shown up and was quickly upending Faith's life. "Can you picture Sawyer's face on a tour bus? Or his songs on the radio? Goofball Sawyer? The same guy who still thinks fart jokes are funny. I cannot imagine what your brother is thinking."

He thought Sawyer was talented, which he was. But he neglected to see how important Sawyer was to the farm and to the children who came to Helping Hooves.

"Oh, and Mrs. Hackney wants me to sew Charles's drapes and marry him and have his redheaded children. Go ahead and enjoy a good laugh over that, too."

Anything that caused Faith to want to crawl under a rock and run away in fear would have made Addison giddy. Faith liked her comfort zone and Addison had a rebellious streak. She'd always pushed Faith's limits, getting her to do things she never would have risked otherwise. Faith's role in their relationship had been to make sure rebellion didn't turn into recklessness. They had balanced each other out that way…until that one night.

The church bell rang, signaling it was time

for the service to begin. "Wish me luck this week. I think I'm going to need it." Faith stood and shook the grass from her dress. "And if you have any influence up there, maybe put in a good word for me?"

She had asked the same from her father. As Harriet had pointed out, Faith had two people up in heaven looking down. A little help would be nice.

The choir's joyful hymn welcomed everyone who entered through the doors of the white-clapboard church. Lined up behind the choir, along the back wall, were the enormous golden organ pipes. The long and sharp notes of the organ complimented the singers beautifully.

Faith slid into the pew with Sawyer and Harriet. The Presleys sat across the aisle. Happily sandwiched between her two men, Mrs. Presley gave Faith a smile and a wink. Dean, on the other hand, was pale as a ghost. He wrung his hands as his leg bounced.

Pastor Kline led everyone in an opening prayer from the pulpit. Faith bowed her head but her gaze kept sliding over to Dean, who sat with his eyes closed and his jaw clenched tight. He seemed to get more agitated by the second until he finally stood up and bolted down the aisle.

Against her better judgment, Faith followed him out the doors and into the parking lot. She spotted him by Sawyer's pickup, bent over with his hands on his knees. He righted himself as soon as he saw her.

"Try breathing through your nose. It'll help slow things down." Even though it wasn't very hot outside, his shirt was wet with sweat.

He cleared his throat. "I'm fine," he said, placing his hands on his hips and not looking the least bit fine.

Faith remembered the first time she'd shown up for church after Addison's funeral. Every song on the organ had sounded like some ghoulish lullaby and her imagination had played tricks on her. She had thought she'd heard Addison calling her from the cemetery.

With time, however, the church became a place of comfort again. Faith had found herself looking forward to attending services and speaking with Pastor Kline. When her dad died, everyone in the congregation came to support her and Sawyer. It had meant the world.

"How do you do it? How do you come

here every Sunday? Doesn't it eat you up?" he asked.

"It did right after Addison died, but it's gotten easier over time. Eventually, I moved past the painful memories and embraced the good."

Time wasn't something Dean seemed to want to give Grass Lake, though. His absence made Faith feel responsible for the Presleys losing both of their children. Dean was alive and a short drive away, but never home where Faith knew his parents wanted him to be.

He kicked a rock across the pavement. "The only thing I want to move past is this stupid town."

Faith wasn't surprised. Dean had avoided this place for so long that he was still in the earlier stages of grief. By running away, he was stuck somewhere between denial and anger.

"Pretending this place doesn't exist doesn't make what happened here go away," she said.

His chest heaved with a deep breath. He rubbed his bearded jaw. "I know, but being here reminds me that some wounds haven't healed."

"They didn't heal because you ignored

them," Faith reasoned. "If you don't do something, they're going to get infected."

"Oh, yeah? And what exactly should I do?"

"Mourn her so you can finally accept she's
gone."

"This coming from the woman who brings
flowers to her grave every Sunday?" he
snapped. He apparently didn't like her suggestion. The vein in his forehead bulged. "Is
that how you show everyone you've accepted
she's gone?"

Faith refused to let him rattle her. "I bring
Addison and my dad flowers because it
makes *me* feel better. They're for me, not for
them."

Dean dropped his arms to his sides. "We're
the reason Addison's in that cemetery. Maybe
that's why I can't find peace. We don't deserve to feel better."

He might as well have punched her in the
stomach. There was nothing Faith wanted
more than to be redeemed for what had happened and her part in it. Dean reminded her
that perhaps she'd never be worthy of it.

"Maybe that's true," she choked out. "All
I know is that pretending she never existed
isn't honoring her memory. Addison deserves
to be remembered."

Those green eyes bored into hers and his hands balled into fists. There was so much he tried to bury inside that the emotion came off him like steam, leaking from his pores. For once, all the anger didn't feel completely directed at her. Faith could see that he'd saved some of his contempt for himself.

"Come back into the church with me." She extended a hand. "Come listen to what the pastor has to say and then let the people of this community welcome you home at the picnic."

Dean glared at her for a full minute before he took her hand and walked back into church without a word.

CHAPTER EIGHT

"YOUR MOTHER BRAGS about you all the time."

"I don't brag."

"Well, you gush. Excessively."

"You ask me how he's doing and I tell you. I can't help that I only have amazing things to say. He's a successful record executive. There's no way to answer your question without gushing."

"I ask to be polite, not to hear you name-drop."

"Name-drop?"

Dean put an arm around his mother before she could lunge at Mrs. Hackney and make a scene. The older woman hadn't changed much since Dean was in grade school. Mrs. Hackney was the only teacher at Grass Lake Elementary who didn't believe in things like gold stars or Student of the Month. She was a staunch observer of "spare the rod, spoil the child," and looked down her pointy nose at people who didn't share in that child-rearing philosophy.

"She's a proud mother. Can't fault her for that. Right, Mrs. Hackney?" Dean asked in a sugarcoated tone. "I'm sure you're very proud of Charles. I heard he's very…competent at his job."

Charles worked at the same bank as Dean's father. Charles was supposedly good with numbers but not people. They had moved him to Collections, last Dean had heard. No one liked people in Collections, so a sparkling personality wasn't a prerequisite.

"Charles is doing fine. He'll make someone an excellent husband someday. In fact, you've just reminded me of something. It was good to see you, Mr. Presley. I'll see you at mah-jong on Wednesday, Marilee."

"Where I'll beat you and brag about it later," Dean's mom grumbled after Mrs. Hackney walked away.

She made Dean laugh, which felt nice to do until he noticed his former teacher heading straight for Faith. Charles might make an excellent husband someday, but his wife was not going to be her.

"Can you believe that woman?" his mom

continued. "I swear, she wouldn't know polite conversation if it punched her in the face."

Mrs. Hackney waved her son over to the table where Faith was selling her delectable cookies. Dean had already purchased and eaten ten.

"I don't brag, by the way." Marilee couldn't let it go. "I simply tell people what you've been up to, and you have a very exciting job. It's not name-dropping when I'm simply referencing the people you work with, right?"

Faith's flaming-red cheeks and the way she wrapped her arms protectively around her, like she was giving herself a hug, were dead giveaways that she needed to be rescued.

Mrs. Hackney had pulled her away from the desserts she was selling. Sawyer was too busy filling his plate with a second helping of Mrs. Brookstone's famous corn dip to help. Faith's friend Josie was over there but too distracted by the long line of people waiting to buy cookies to notice Faith's predicament.

"I appreciate that you're happy for me." Dean kissed his mom on the top of her head. Hopefully he'd still have a company in a few months for her to gush over. "I think I'm going to buy a couple more cookies."

Everyone brought food to share at the picnic. The church provided the hot dogs and buns while the congregation divided up the paper products, drinks, salads and casseroles. The women's club was in charge of desserts, which were sold to raise money for the church's outreach programs. Baking all those cookies seemed like one more in a long list of things that Faith did because she never said no.

"Tuesday it is!" Mrs. Hackney exclaimed. "Charles, maybe you could make Faith dinner in exchange for her help. Wouldn't that be nice, Miss Stratton?"

Dean knew Faith's plate was already full on Tuesday. He interrupted before she had a chance to say yes to yet another responsibility.

"My mom sent me over here to make sure you have enough help selling cookies. How many are you buying, Charles?"

"Uh…"

Mrs. Hackney frowned and answered for him. "We'll take two. Maybe you can bring some more when you and Charles have dinner on Tuesday."

"Tuesday?" Dean questioned. "You can't have dinner on Tuesday. We're going to Lily's

NHS ceremony and then I promised her we'd take her out for pizza. Remember?"

Faith's forehead scrunched up in confusion. "Pizza?"

Dean nodded, encouraging her to play along. "You were standing right there when we made the plans."

"Pizza." It took a second for the realization to hit. One corner of her mouth curved up when it did. "Right, pizza with Lily. I can't believe I forgot. I'll have to come after dinner. Maybe I can stop by for a few minutes to get the drapery measurements and fabric," she said to Charles, who stood there with a puzzled expression.

"I bet Charles can write down the measurements for you and drop off the fabric on his way home from work," Dean suggested. "That would sure save everyone some time and trouble. Right, Charles?"

"Uh…"

Mrs. Hackney was so enraged, Dean imagined steam coming out of her ears. "I'm not quite sure why you're part of this conversation, Mr. Presley."

"You're right. I'm sorry." *Not sorry.* "These two are capable of figuring this out without our help. How about you and I go over here so I can get you your cookies?"

She didn't seem to like that suggestion any more than Dean's intrusion. Sadly for her, he'd set her up to look like the meddling nuisance she was if she didn't remove herself from Charles and Faith's conversation.

Mrs. Hackney paid for her cookies, scowling at Dean the entire time. "I didn't realize you and Faith were friends."

"We grew up together. I've always thought of her as family." His admission made him feel guilty again. Faith had been like a sister until he hadn't been able to stop thinking about kissing her. The desire to press his lips to hers was one of those things he had buried away that had frustratingly resurfaced since arriving back in town.

"Well, the protective big brother act was a little much, don't you think?"

Dean placed two cookies on a paper plate for her and decided to play dumb. "I'm not sure what you mean."

Mrs. Hackney lowered her voice as she glanced in Charles and Faith's direction. "Her father's gone. It's about time she settled down with someone who can provide for her. A woman like her needs a man to take care of her, give her a family. If you really cared about her, you would want her to have those things."

Her 1950s' mentality rubbed Dean the wrong way, as did her assumption that Faith would fall for someone like Charles. Dean couldn't kiss her anymore, but he wouldn't let her settle for someone like Charles Hackney, either.

"Faith is perfectly capable of providing for herself, Mrs. Hackney. I don't think she needs a man to take care of her. In fact, from what I've seen in the last couple days, she seems to be doing most of the caretaking in this town. So, shoving your son down her throat was a little much, don't you think?"

Mrs. Hackney bit her tongue and turned on her heel, leaving without her cookies. Dean took a bite of one; they were paid for, after all. No reason for them to go to waste. Charles chased after his mother and Faith rejoined Dean and Josie at the dessert table.

"You didn't have to do that."

"I know I didn't. *You* did." Dean didn't remember her being such a pushover. It seemed like every time someone asked her to jump, she not only ask how high, but if she could also bake them some cookies while she did it.

She pushed her hair over her shoulders. Her sun-kissed skin looked soft to the touch. Dean resisted the urge to brush his fingers along her collarbone, to cup her face in his hand, to cover those pink lips with his.

"Well," she said, "maybe you aren't the only one with things to work on."

"THAT WILL BE one dollar and one song. You can choose what you sing. But you gotta sing."

Dean had been working the dessert table with Faith and Josie for the last half hour. His dark mood from earlier had lifted and he was all sunshine and silliness. He had guys singing for brownies and ladies doing the two-step with him for a piece of pie.

It was like spending time with the boy Faith had known and loved. He was the Dean who used to make her and Addison laugh until their sides hurt. The Dean who loved life and wanted everyone around him to love it, too.

"I'm not a very good singer, young man," Mr. Middleton said in an attempt at getting his treat without the tune.

"I didn't say you had to sing well."

Mr. Middleton frowned then said, "'Hound Dog.'"

"A little Elvis! Love it. Sawyer?" Dean had roped Sawyer into the fun. Faith's brother and his guitar were the musical accompaniment.

"Let's hear it, Hank," Sawyer said, strumming a couple of chords.

Mr. Middleton belted out the first few lines with the dance moves to boot. Faith laughed and Dean happily handed over the cupcake Mr. Middleton had wanted.

Sawyer kept playing and took over the vocals. A crowd gathered and clapped along, encouraging Sawyer to sing a medley of Elvis songs. Faith was so caught up in watching, it wasn't until the end that she noticed Dean had taken out his phone and recorded it.

A sinking feeling came over her. He hadn't brought up Sawyer coming to Nashville yet today, but that didn't mean he wasn't thinking about it.

"Your brother is really talented," Josie said, bumping shoulders with Faith to pull her out of her head. "It's one thing for him to sing a set at the Sundown, it's another to sing something off the cuff like that."

"Yeah," Faith replied halfheartedly.

"More! More! More!" was the chant from the crowd, and Sawyer happily complied. He put a on a concert in the middle of the church lawn. A few of the choir members acted as backup singers while the crowd clapped the percussion. Bruce Gibson pulled out his harmonica and joined the makeshift band. Dean recorded every song.

"Dance with me." Ty Hanson didn't ask Faith, he just pulled her out from behind the dessert table. Ty worked for his dad on their dairy farm. He was big and burly with an infectious smile. For a large guy, he could move. He twirled Faith around and had her laughing in spite of herself.

Just over his shoulder, she spotted Dean watching them with as much interest as he had been showing Sawyer. She could feel his eyes on her even as Ty spun them around. It made her self-conscious and her face warmed.

When the song came to an end, Faith found herself scanning the crowd for Dean but he wasn't where he had been. Maybe she had been wrong about thinking he was still staring.

"You mind if I cut in, Ty?" Dean said from behind her. Faith's heart stuttered at the sound of his voice.

Always the gentleman, Ty thanked Faith for the dance before handing her over. Dean's palm rested on the small of her back, setting loose the butterflies in her stomach.

"I didn't need you to step in," she insisted. "Ty isn't like Charles."

"Good to know," he replied without loosening his hold on her.

This close, his eyes reminded her of green glass. If she looked hard enough, maybe she could see into his head and figure out what he was thinking.

Sawyer hadn't started the next song; he was busy taking requests. There was no reason for Dean to be holding her the way he was, but she couldn't find it in her to step away and wait for the music.

"Thank you for telling me to stay." His words sank right into her heart and made it swell.

"You're welcome." Faith tried her best not to think about the way he held her hand or the small sliver of space that separated her body from his. She didn't dare dwell on the rapid beating of her heart.

"Addison would have ditched this picnic a long time ago."

Faith smiled, knowing he was right. "She'd be spending a day like this by the lake, working on her tan."

Dean nodded in agreement just as Sawyer and his band found one last song to play.

He started strumming his guitar, slow and serious. The melody took shape and Faith realized it was "Amazing Grace." Once he began singing, it took everything Faith had not to cry.

Slowly, with his eyes never leaving hers, Dean led her in a dance. It was as if everyone else at the picnic disappeared, her brother's voice the only sound in the world. Faith felt Addison's presence in that moment. Observing. Listening. Forgiving? Faith couldn't be sure. All she knew was that she hoped Dean felt it, too.

When it was over, Dean didn't let go even though he'd stopped moving. He swallowed hard, his Adam's apple sliding up and down his throat. Faith couldn't hear the applause her brother was surely receiving. She felt like she was in a bubble, protected from everything but the way Dean made her feel.

For a moment she thought he was going to kiss her. Instead he let her go and stepped away without saying a word. The reality of the world came rushing back. There were people everywhere around her. Their chatter so loud, she wasn't sure how she hadn't heard it before.

"Your brother is amazing," someone said as Faith watched Dean disappear around the side of the church.

CHAPTER NINE

"I'M GLAD YOU decided to stay here." Dean's mom smoothed down the cream-colored top sheet on the guest bed. "Do you need anything else? Toothbrush? Oh, please tell me you've been brushing your teeth for the last couple of days. I paid a lot of money to make sure those choppers were in tip-top shape. The least you can do is brush them regularly."

"I bought a toothbrush, Mom. Your investment is safe."

Nothing about his childhood bedroom was the same except for the Little League baseball trophies that cluttered the top of the bookcase in the corner. He wondered if his mom had taken everything out of Addison's room, as well, but didn't have the nerve to check it out.

"Okay, you're all set," his mom said, giving the pillow an extra fluff. "I'll see you in the morning."

He gave her a kiss on the cheek. "Thank

you. It's nice to have someone make the bed for me. Can I hire you permanently?"

She smiled but waved her hand dismissively as she left the room. "You couldn't afford me."

"I can nearly afford her. She keeps raising the rates." His dad poked his head in. "Nice to have you home, son," he added.

They had both mentioned that several times since he'd shown up there. He had left the church picnic and walked to the high school, the one place in town that didn't remind him of Addison or Faith. Being three years older than them, they'd only gone to school there together for one year.

Faith Stratton. Somehow she'd managed to have the same effect on him today that she'd had that summer everything changed. It wasn't because she was beautiful—there were beautiful women everywhere. Beauty was easy to come by. It was the way she laughed, the goodness that dwelled in her heart. There was something about it that sucked him in and wouldn't let him go.

"It's good to be here," Dean lied. It was torture, but better than fighting this pull Faith had over him. Hopefully he'd only have to stay here one night. His car had been towed to the auto shop but they wouldn't get to it until Monday.

Left alone in his room, Dean pulled up the videos from the picnic of Sawyer singing. The boy knew how to command a crowd. He was a born entertainer. Dean picked the best song and sent the clip to Landon.

How does this guy have no social media presence? Landon sent back.

That was what Dean needed to do tomorrow while he waited for his car—talk to Sawyer about setting up a YouTube account and uploading some videos. It was the best test market around. Once Sawyer had some things out there, Dean could talk to the right people and ask them to share the videos on their social media. With some buzz, Dean could easily convince Landon to let him sign Sawyer to the label.

It had been an emotionally draining day and getting some sleep seemed like the best medicine. Dean tried hard to keep his mind on Sawyer and where Grace Note could take his career. If only that other Stratton would stop finding a way into his thoughts…

"WHAT'S THIS?"
  "It's your birthday present."

"*My birthday is in October.*"

"*I know—I'm early.*"

Faith stared at the box for a minute more before taking it from him and giving it a little shake. She needed to open it before Addison got off work and headed over to the farm to hang out.

"*Why do I feel like I'm going to open this and be disappointed by something gross?*"

She really had no idea. They had spent almost every day together for the last three weeks thanks to the summer job her father had given him at Helping Hooves. It had taken less than one week for Dean to confirm his feelings weren't brotherly anymore.

Winter break was when he'd first noticed. Gone was the silly little girl and in her place was this gorgeous and sweet young woman. When she had laughed, he couldn't wait to hear it again. When she had sat next to him to watch a movie with Addison and innocently rested her head on his shoulder, his thoughts had been anything but pure.

"*It's not gross. You're going to like it,*" he said. *She narrowed her eyes and contemplated whether to trust him or not.* "*I promise.*"

She bit her bottom lip and his desire to

kiss her grew. As she carefully peeled off the wrapping paper, he admired her self-control. Faith wasn't like his sister, who would have torn it away with reckless abandon, letting it drop to the floor, discarded. Faith opened a gift like every part of it was special, even the paper it was wrapped in.

"You better not be tricking me, Dean Francis Presley."

He didn't even mind it when she used his middle name, a sure sign that things were different. Her hair was up in a ponytail and she had hay stuck to her T-shirt from helping him clean the horse stalls. He scooted a little closer to her on the bench where he had her sit to open her gift. Their legs touched ever so lightly, but it felt like a very big deal.

"Hurry, open it." Once Addison got there, the moment would be lost.

Faith set the paper next to her on the bench. The skin on her neck was splotched red. Maybe he had the same effect on her that she had on him. This was bound to be embarrassing if she had no interest in him at all. She took the top off the box and pulled back the tissue paper.

Her eyes lit up. "Are you serious?"

He couldn't help his cocky grin. "If you're asking if they're real, they're real."

Faith lifted the concert tickets out of the box—the tickets to the show that was sold out. The show she wanted to go to more than anything in the whole world.

"You got me and Addison tickets to Ryan King?"

He knew that was what she'd think. Ryan King was the hottest pop star around. Dean would rather stab a fork in his ear than listen to him, but to watch Faith smile for two hours straight, he'd do just about anything.

"They aren't for you and Addison."

Her shoulders slumped and head tilted to the side. "I knew you were teasing me. I'm going to make Addison kick your butt for this."

Addison was going to want to kick his butt for an entirely different reason. Faith was her *friend. Her* best *friend. Dean would have to convince Faith to keep this a secret. Maybe after the two girls spent a year apart while at different colleges, Addison would be more understanding, more willing to share Faith with him.*

"They're for you and me," he revealed, then waited for her reaction.

"You?" One eyebrow raised in disbelief. "Okay, this has to be some kind of joke."

"I want to take you. I want to take you... on a date."

"Me?"

"Yes, you."

"Why?"

There was no turning back now. He hoped she didn't laugh at him when he confessed his true feelings.

"Because I want to kiss you. I've been thinking about kissing you for a really long time."

The look of surprise on her face was expected. The kiss she planted on his lips was not. It was as if she had been waiting to kiss him for a thousand years and he had finally given her the permission she needed. It wasn't rushed, not a quick thank-you-for-the-gift kind of kiss. This one made him wonder who she had kissed before and hope she would only be kissing him from now on.

"WHY SO GLUM, SIS? Sad you didn't have the honor of washing Dean's clothes this morning?"

Faith rolled her eyes while refilling Winston's water. If Sawyer wasn't nice, she wasn't going to make him breakfast when they finished their chores. "Are you going to trim Duchess's and Winston's hooves this morning?"

"That's on the agenda," he replied, placing Sassy's fresh hay net in her stall.

The morning routine on a horse farm sometimes felt never-ending. It was the time of day Faith missed her dad the most. He used to talk to the horses, tell them jokes and sing them songs to start their day.

The old horse barn had six horse stalls, feed storage and a large tack room that had a space for grooming. It was in good shape for its age. Their dad had been a stickler for keeping things tidy and fixing things when they needed fixing. A trait he had passed on to his children.

"Uh-oh." Sawyer stood in front of Duchess's stall. She was the oldest horse on the farm at twenty-four. "She didn't eat all her hay. Or drink her water."

"Take her temperature." Duchess hadn't been eating well for over a week. Not eating or drinking overnight meant she could be sick. Faith prayed that wasn't the case.

They had been watching Duchess. Besides not eating, she hadn't been as social.

Sawyer had noticed her wandering in circles and pressing her head against everything and anything. All of that could mean something major was wrong, but Faith was in denial. Duchess was probably depressed. Faith and Sawyer weren't the only ones missing their dad.

Faith finished feeding and watering the rest of the horses and, one by one, led them out to the larger paddock near the stables, where she gave them a quick brush-down.

"Her temp is normal but at the high end," Sawyer reported when Faith returned to the barn to check on Duchess.

Faith stroked the horse's forehead. "What's the matter, Duch?"

Duchess snorted and shook her head up and down. Faith tried to soothe her with kind words, but it didn't help. If only horses could talk. Duchess was Faith's favorite and she hated thinking the mare was in pain.

"Let's take her outside. Maybe she needs some space," Sawyer suggested.

Faith wanted to believe that would do the trick. Duchess gave her some trouble, though. She refused to follow commands, which was unlike her. Sawyer took the lead rope from his sister and got the horse to move out of the barn.

Faith was frustrated with her inability to fix this. Their dad would have known what to do. He was a self-proclaimed horse whisperer. As much as she loved the horses, Faith hadn't inherited that particular skill. She'd have to call the vet, even though money was tight; extra expenses would make things tough.

"Come on," Sawyer said. "We need to muck these stalls before the morning gets away from us."

"What would I do without you?" she asked, putting on her work gloves.

"You'd die of exhaustion because I do most of the work."

Faith used her stable fork to pick up a chunk of manure and tossed it at her brother. He dodged it with ease.

"See, there you go, adding to my workload."

"Hilarious, little brother. You make a list of all the things you do and I'll make a list of all the things I do, and we'll compare. I think you'd see that we do a darn good job of splitting responsibilities down the middle."

They both got busy cleaning the stalls. The metal forks scraping the cement floors and the soft rustling of dry straw were the only sounds to be heard. Outside, as the morning sky brightened, the natural light cast a warmer glow than the fluorescents overhead.

"Honestly, you could hire someone to do the stuff I do," Sawyer said. "You're the one this place couldn't survive without."

Faith stopped what she was doing, breathing heavy from the physical exertion. She stepped out of Winston's stall and joined Sawyer in Sassy's. He was much farther along than she was—as usual.

"What's that supposed to mean?"

Sawyer startled, unaware she had come up behind him. Jabbing the fork into the straw, he turned to her. "I'm just saying you're the one with all the business sense and the one with the degree in occupational therapy. All I do is the heavy lifting."

"You do more than that," she argued.

He had put on a baseball cap instead of his cowboy hat this morning. It made him look younger. "Not really. I help with the horses. I do some maintenance work. I'm convenient but not irreplaceable."

"I need you, Sawyer. I could hire people to fix the fences or help me muck these stables, but I need you to keep me balanced, to remind me when I'm biting off more than I can chew. You're the only one who can do that."

His lips curved into a small smile. "That's true. You need all the help you can get when it comes to that. And I'd starve if I didn't have you. Guess I need you, too."

Faith's stomach growled; Sawyer wasn't the only one who was working up an appetite. "Let's finish up and I'll make us some bacon pancakes for breakfast."

He got right back to work. "No one motivates me the way you do. You had me at bacon."

Back in Winston's stall, Faith's smile faded. There was an uneasy feeling she couldn't shake, no matter what Sawyer had said about needing her. Truth was he didn't need her half as much as she needed him.

"I WAITED FOR HER outside the school, but she never showed. She hasn't answered any of my texts, which probably means she's with *him*." The sneer on Kylie's freckled face made it clear how she felt about Lily's boyfriend.

Lily was late. *Again*. Faith stood on her wraparound front porch and checked her phone one more time to see if she had missed a call or text.

No messages. No texts.

Kylie wanted to believe the worst, but Faith was trying to give Lily the benefit of the doubt. Maybe she had to meet with a teacher after school and hadn't turned on her phone yet.

"What do you want me to do?" Sawyer asked.

"We'll have to ask Roseanne to be a side walker." Faith didn't see another alternative. She needed Kylie to clean out the paddocks because there wouldn't be time for it tomorrow.

They'd had parents participate in therapy sessions before. Roseanne's daughter, Hayden, was autistic and had benefited greatly from the work she did at Helping Hooves to improve her trunk strength and social skills. She loved having her mom there, so including her shouldn't cause too much of a problem like it could with kids who were less flexible thinkers.

"Maybe Lily will get here before we go to the arena. Hayden can brush Sassy first." Sawyer's optimism was commendable. "I'll get her ready in the tack room."

Faith contemplated calling Josie but didn't want to get Lily in trouble…yet. This was between Faith and Lily. Getting Josie involved might backfire and Lily could quit. Helping Hooves needed all the volunteers it could get, and the teenagers in town were more interested in hanging out down by the lake than working for free at the horse farm.

"They sneak around because she doesn't want her mom to find out," Kylie said. "I bet they're in the woods behind the school."

She was probably right. Best friends just knew. Faith and Addison had always known what the other was up to, even when they weren't together. Well, until Faith had snuck around with Dean.

As if he'd heard her thinking about him, Dean pulled up in his mom's bright yellow VW Beetle. Mrs. Presley had a deep affection for her car. There was always a fresh Gerbera daisy in the flower vase, and whenever there was the slightest bit of dirt, it got a wash. Mr. Presley was not allowed to drive it because he tended to roll stop signs and his wife was sure this was going to lead to a fender bender one of these days.

Dressed in something other than the red shirt and jeans she'd seen him in the whole weekend, he stepped out of the car. Today he was sporting khaki cargo pants and a pale blue button-down shirt. His facial hair had been trimmed so it was more like a shadow than a beard. He took Faith's breath away.

"Is your brother around?"

"You're talking to me again?" She wasn't going to lie—it hurt her feelings that he'd not only left the picnic without saying a word, but had called Sawyer, not her, to say he wasn't coming back to the farm. After making such a big deal about not being able to stay with his parents, it stung that being around her was obviously worse.

His chin dropped and his gaze fell to the ground. When he looked back up at her, there was genuine remorse there. "I'm sorry. I haven't been intentionally not talking to you."

It sure felt that way. She didn't have time to hash things out with him, though, because Hayden and her mom had arrived. Their white minivan pulled into the makeshift lot they had by the stables.

"My brother and I have a client. If you want to talk to him, you're going to have to volunteer."

"Volunteer?"

"Kylie, run ahead and see if Sawyer needs anything." Faith made her way down the porch steps and headed toward the stables, away from Dean.

"Faith," he called after her.

"You heard me." She glanced back over her shoulder. "You do remember how to lead a horse around the arena, don't you?"

CHAPTER TEN

WHY DID SHE have to make everything so difficult?

Dean begrudgingly followed Faith to the horse barn where she greeted a little girl and her mom. She went ahead and introduced Dean to them as one of the volunteers, even though he hadn't agreed to anything. This was not the plan.

"This is Hayden," she said to Dean. "She just turned six. I heard you had a super-fun birthday party, Hayden. Your mom told me there were lots of cupcakes."

"Lily!" the girl shouted from behind her mother.

"I know how much you love Lily. She's going to be sad she missed you. Dean used to work here years ago, so don't worry. He knows how to lead a horse better than anyone," Faith said, giving him the most passive-aggressive smile he'd ever seen. She was daring him to say he couldn't help.

Hadn't she learned during their mud wrestling match not to mess with him?

"I'm an expert at leading *people* where I want them to go."

"Well, I can only speak to your expert walking skills," Faith returned, that unpleasant smile still plastered on her face. "You walk away really well."

Dean's shoulders tensed. She was pushing all the right buttons. His only defense was to shift the focus to someone else. "Do you have a favorite horse, Hayden?"

Six-year-old Hayden refused to make eye contact. "Lily! Lily!"

"Are you ready to see Sassy?" Faith asked, garnering a much more positive response. Hayden took her hand and led the way to the tack room.

Instead of leading, Dean followed. Again. Thankfully, Sawyer was in the barn, refilling hay nets with the redheaded teenager.

"Look who's back." Sawyer took off his work gloves to shake hands. "What are you doing here?"

"I wanted to—"

Faith cut in. "He's volunteering. He's going to fill in for Lily. Come on, Dean. You can help us with grooming."

"Is she always this bossy?"

Sawyer snickered. "That's nothing. If you want to see her get bossy, stay out here talking to me instead of doing what she says."

Dean considered being petulant. It was tempting, but in the end it seemed in his best interest to do this for her so she'd feel obligated to let him have a few minutes with Sawyer when they were done.

SOME THINGS WERE like riding a bike: easy to pick back up. Working in the arena with the horses was one of them. It had been a long time since Dean had heard the huffing of horses, the rattle of the harnesses, the clomps of hooves on the dirt.

He held tight to the lead rope and guided Sassy around the obstacle course Faith had set up for Hayden. There were stops along the way that required the little girl to throw balls through hoops. Faith and Sawyer walked on either side of the horse, providing support and encouragement.

"Last one, Hayden," Faith said. "You can do it. Can you throw the blue ball through the hoop?" She offered her two balls, one blue and one orange.

Dean stopped Sassy and gave her head a

pat. "Good girl, Sassy. Did Faith give you that name?" he whispered. Wouldn't that be the pot calling the kettle black?

Tired after a full workout, Hayden's behavior began to deteriorate. She purposely took the orange ball and threw it in the dirt. Maybe Hayden was the sassy one.

Faith pushed. "Come on, Hayden. It looks like you're getting frustrated. Back straight, head up. Blue ball through the hoop."

"One more ball and you're all done," Sawyer added. "Then you can feed Sassy a carrot."

Hayden lifted her head and focused on her posture. With a little encouragement, she reached up and tossed the ball through the hoop.

"Awesome!" Sawyer gave Hayden a high five. The pride on the little girl's face was priceless.

Faith told Dean to move Sassy forward. She placed her hand on Hayden's leg. "Victory lap for doing so well today."

The one summer Dean worked at Helping Hooves, Faith had been the one in charge of leading the horses while Dean and various volunteers were side walkers. It was different without Big John Stratton running the show, but Dean was impressed with how well Sawyer and Faith worked together.

Sawyer had been such a little kid last time Dean was here. He didn't remember much about him except that he'd loved to annoy Faith and Addison when they'd hung out on the farm. All grown up, he and his sister had a mutual respect for one another and a real partnership. It made Dean wonder once again what things would be like if Addison was around.

"Would you take Sassy back to the barn for me while I stretch Hayden?" Faith asked her brother.

"Sure." He loosened the girth strap on the horse and took the lead rope from Dean. "Come on, Music Man. You can help me."

Faith looked like she wanted to protest but held back. Dean had to take advantage of this chance to get Sawyer alone.

"So, I sent some of the videos I shot of you singing at the picnic to my partner back in Nashville," Dean said, tying Sassy up in the tack room.

Sawyer undid the girth strap and folded it over the seat of the saddle. "Oh, yeah? I didn't realize you were recording me. That was pretty rough stuff, not polished at all."

"He loved it. Thinks the same thing I'm thinking."

Lifting the saddle off Sassy, Sawyer was sure to raise it high enough so it didn't hit her back. "What are you thinking exactly?"

Dean did his part by removing the saddle pad. "We think there's a ton of potential. It would help if you had a little social media presence, though. Would you be willing to start a couple accounts? I could help you set everything up. Even post a few things for you until you get the hang of it."

Sawyer had moved to the other side of the room in search of a brush. "I'm not real big into social media. Faith set up a Facebook account for this place and neither one of us knows what to do with it."

"That's why I'd help. I'm not talking about having to send out Tweets every five minutes. I'm thinking something simple to showcase your sound. Get some feedback from the public, build an audience."

Sawyer thought it over while giving Sassy a brush-down. Dean offered to check her hooves to be helpful. The horse kicked a little when he tried to put her foot between his knees. This part of working with horses didn't come back as easily as the others.

"I've got a lot of connections in the music business," Dean continued. He couldn't stand Sawyer's silence. "If you let me, I can help you. Once my partner sees there's a buzz around you, he'll be on board with signing you."

"I'll think about it, but I'm going to be honest—my sister needs me here. If I go off to Nashville, I worry she's going to kill herself trying to keep this place running alone. She's not real good at asking for help or saying no to someone who needs hers."

Dean could picture Faith working herself into an early grave because she felt like she had to do everything—for herself, her clients, her horses, her friends, her neighbors… The list went on and on.

"We can talk to her, together, when it comes time. I think you should make this decision based on what you want, though. Not what's best for Faith."

Sawyer stopped brushing and seemed to be weighing his words. "No offense, I know you haven't had a sister to worry about for a few years now, but that's not the way things work in this family. We don't have anything but each other. That means something to me. It means something to her. Decisions are made based on what's best for the both of us. Always."

FAITH HELD HER BREATH and pressed her back against the wall outside the tack room. Her heart beat so hard, she feared it would alert Dean and Sawyer to her presence.

"I respect that," she heard Dean say.

Did he?

She had no idea what they were talking about before she'd heard her brother assert that they would always have each other's backs no matter what, but assumed it had to be about going to Nashville.

She was proud of her brother for not being blinded by Dean's big promises. And she wanted to strangle Dean for making them. He must have forgotten how important this place was to their family. Without Sawyer, she'd never manage.

Just as Faith was about the reveal herself, Lily came storming into the barn. "I am so sorry for being late, Faith. I have no idea why I thought I didn't have to be here until four thirty."

The boom of her voice startled the horses

in their stalls and added to the noise. Faith jumped. She often had this fear that one of these days she was going to fall over from a heart attack like her dad, and getting sneaked up on was not helping ease that concern.

Sawyer stepped out of the tack room. "You guys scared the living daylights out of us."

"I'm real sorry for freaking everyone out, for being late, for everything," Lily said in a rush.

"Why don't you help Sawyer put Sassy back in her stall and then grab a shovel to help Kylie in the paddock? You and I can have a talk about what's really going on later."

"You're making me shovel manure? I said I was sorry," Lily whined.

"'Sorry' doesn't clean my paddock."

Lily glowered at Faith but went to get Sassy in the tack room. Josie was a saint. How parents survived the teenage years, Faith would never know.

Dean stepped out into the wide aisle that ran the length of the barn. The wariness in his eyes led Faith to believe he was worried about what she had overheard.

"How long were you standing out here snooping?"

He raised her hackles. "I don't think walking through my barn is snooping. Is there something you were talking about that you didn't want me to hear?"

"I have nothing to hide."

"Oh, good to know. I think we both know how things can go downhill real fast when there are secrets between siblings. I sure hope you aren't putting Sawyer in a position to have to keep stuff from me."

Dean moved toward her with enough fire in his eyes to cause her to step back. "He's not a kid. He doesn't need your permission to do things."

"What do you want him to do, exactly?"

"Hey, can you two take your little spat somewhere else?" Sawyer asked, leading Sassy out of the tack room. "You're making Duchess anxious."

In the far stall, the horse snorted and shook her head. Faith walked down there to check on her. Duchess was unhappy, to say the least.

"It's okay, girl. Everything's okay," Faith tried to reassure her.

Duchess shook her head as if to say, *No, it's not.*

"Isn't that a bad thing when she shakes like that?" Dean asked, coming up behind Faith.

He'd worked there for one summer twelve

years ago and he thought he was some sort of expert. "She's flustered with you—like I am."

"Remember when Big John used to sing to the horses? Duchess used to whinny the loudest when he'd do that."

Suddenly, Faith understood what it was like for Dean that day in the car when she'd brought up Addison unexpectedly. Faith's emotions were already heightened and thinking about her dad wasn't helping.

"Just because I remember doesn't mean I want to talk about it," she said, using his own words against him.

She went to move past him but he grabbed her arm to stop her. "I deserved that."

Faith closed her eyes and willed the tears to stay away. She hated being mean. Behaving this way didn't make her feel better, only worse.

"It's a fresh wound."

Dean dipped his head close to hers. "I know. I'm sorry," he said in a low voice that sent a shiver down her spine. He smelled like expensive cologne. He had always had a love for the finer things in life. "Your dad was a good man. I have nothing but respect for who he was, and he was good with these animals. I learned a lot from him when I worked here."

She opened her wet eyes and chewed on her lip. Her dad had been the best. It couldn't have been easy, raising two kids on his own, but he'd never used being a single dad as an excuse. He'd sacrificed and went out of his way to be present and available for Faith and Sawyer.

"He was a terrible singer, but the horses loved it," Sawyer chimed in. "They don't respond to me the way they did him. Maybe they're tone-deaf."

Dean let go of her arm but stayed close.

Faith wanted to move but couldn't. Her feet stayed planted and her body leaned toward his like it didn't care what her brain thought was best.

"What song did he used to sing?" he asked.

Sawyer replied, "Anything Garth Brooks."

Faith had lost the ability to speak. The knot in her stomach had moved up and become a lump in her throat.

Dean laughed through his nose. "Good ol' Garth." He turned from Faith and rested his arm on the stall door. "Got any requests, Duch?"

As off-key as her dad, Dean broke into song until Duchess relaxed and let out a soft nicker. Faith had thought she'd had all her feelings for him under control until he serenaded her horse. Everything went right back to complicated.

CHAPTER ELEVEN

DWIGHT ANDERSON'S COVERALLS had more grease on them than could have possibly been in one car. He wasn't the cleanest auto mechanic around, but he was the most trusted. Dean's mother swore by him.

"Since you only have a little over 30,000 miles on it, your insurance company is opting to fix it rather than junk it, but you pretty much need the guts of this car replaced."

"How long will something like that take?"

Dwight scratched his head, his fingernails as black as his coveralls. "Well, we need to remove the door panels and trunk liner, clean the carpets and floor mats, replace the seat bottoms, get a new engine since there's water in the cylinders, drain the rear end and transmission, and replace the brakes. Of course, there's also that tire that needs fixin'. I'd say it'll take a month."

Dean's precious BMW had paid the price for his bad luck. He loved that car, though, and if they needed a month to get it back in tip-top shape, then Dwight and his grease would get their month.

Dwight snatched a set of keys from the wooden key rack that hung next to his register. "Good news is that they pay for a rental car while it's in the shop."

Dean wasn't sure driving around in a 1995 green Ford Taurus was good news. The old car had more miles than all the vehicles he had ever owned combined. It was the only car for rent in all of Grass Lake, so Dean didn't have a lot of options. Only problem was, he wasn't confident it could make it all the way to Nashville.

One month was a long time to be away from home. Heading back to Nashville seemed like the best thing for him to do. He had survived a second night in his parents' house, but surviving wasn't the same thing as sleeping. Another night of dreams that were more like flashbacks led to restlessness. Strangely enough, it was still Faith who starred in the dreams, not Addison.

He parked his "new" wheels in one of the open spaces along Main Street. Dean planned to meet his mom for lunch at the Cup and Spoon. The black lampposts lining the street were decorated with red, white and blue bows for the upcoming Memorial Day parade.

A bell rang above the door to Harriet's Flower Shop. Flowers would soften the blow that he would be leaving town as soon as possible. The scent of roses hit him the second he stepped inside.

"Well, well. Look who's here." Harriet, dressed in bright purple from head to toe, was putting together an arrangement at the counter. Just behind her sat none other than Faith.

Her dark hair was pulled back from her face and a loose braid was draped over her shoulder. Those big brown eyes were framed in lashes so thick she didn't need to wear any makeup. The apples of her cheeks matched the color of the pink peonies Harriet stuck in the vase.

"How are you doing, Harriet? You're looking lovely as always." He walked over and gave her a hug.

"I roll out of bed looking fabulous. What can I say?" she replied, making Faith laugh. "What? I do. And then I do my hair and my makeup and I go from fabulous to unforgettable."

She wasn't lying. Harriet had a way of drawing all eyes on her. At least that was usually true; right now, Dean's eyes were locked on Faith. She was another reason to hightail it out of Grass Lake. She was as infuriating as she was alluring. One minute he wanted to scream at her, the next he wanted to kiss her until it erased all the hurt between them.

"Helping with the inventory?" he asked her.

"I'm horrible with computers," Harriet said, bringing the attention back to her. "I know how to turn them on and that's the extent of my abilities."

"I'm meeting my mom for lunch. I thought it'd be nice to get her some flowers."

"Isn't that sweet?" Harriet's hand covered her heart. "Let me pull something together for you."

While she glided around the store gathering a variety of blooms, Dean stepped up to the counter. Faith shifted her focus back on the computer screen.

"Your mom will be pleasantly surprised."

"I wasn't planning on getting flowers, but when I got out of the car, the shop was right there, calling me in. I forget what it's like to be in a town where everything you need is on one street."

"Small towns have some advantages," she said, running her finger down a list of numbers.

Dean cleared his throat and shifted uncomfortably. Carrying on a conversation with Faith shouldn't be so difficult. It didn't help that this was the place Addison had spent so much time the last few years of her life. He could picture her sticking flowers in her hair and making daisy chains to drape over everything.

"So, my car isn't going to be a total loss."

"That's good."

"Dwight has to basically replace everything, but hopefully it'll be good as new when I get it back in a month."

Faith stopped what she was doing and glanced back up at him. "A month?"

Harriet returned with the perfect mix of flowers for his mother. She wrapped them in her signature gingham kraft paper and tied them up in a pink bow.

Handing them over, she said, "You tell your mom that I said hello, okay?"

"How much do I owe you?"

Harriet waved him off. "On the house. Such a sweet gesture deserves a reward."

Dean shook his head and pulled out his

wallet. "I can't do that. Let me pay you something."

"Return the kindness when you get the chance," Harriet replied. "That's how you can pay me—by paying it forward."

Arguing wouldn't get him anywhere. He gave her a nod and said his goodbyes. Faith chewed on her lip and didn't spare him another look.

It was a short walk to the Cup and Spoon Diner. His mom was already seated at a table when he got inside. She sipped coffee and read the *Grass Lake Gazette*, unaware of his arrival. The diner hadn't changed in the twelve years he'd been gone.

The glass display case filled with fresh-baked pies, cakes and cookies was the first thing customers saw upon entering. Five booths big enough to sit four people each lined one wall of the narrow space while the counter on the other side sat another seven patrons. The red-vinyl-and-chrome stools gave the place a pop of color. Dean noticed the daily specials were still painted above prep stations on the other side.

He set the flowers on the table where his mom was seated.

"Are those for me?"

"They are," he said, bending down to kiss her on the cheek. He took a seat across from her.

Picking them up, she inhaled their sweet scent. The smile that spread across her face was worth every awkward minute he had spent in the flower shop.

"Harriet put them together. I can't take any of the credit."

"She does beautiful work, doesn't she? I always imagined her doing the flowers for your sister's wedding," she said wistfully. "You know Addison, she would have wanted flowers, flowers and more flowers."

Addison had loved everything about nature. Since Harriet was so close to the Strattons, she had taken Addison under her wing, as well, teaching her everything she knew about flowers and plants.

"She would have." Dean took the menu from the holder on the table. He didn't want to dwell on yet another thing Addison would never get to experience.

Even the menu was the same since the last time he had eaten at the Cup and Spoon. Not only did they still have the same daily specials, but customers could order breakfast all day long and the featured kid's meal was the smiley-face pancake with chocolate chips.

"So, what did Dwight say about the car? Is it totaled?"

Dean explained the car situation. When he got to the part about it taking a month to fix, his mother nearly jumped out of her seat.

"You're staying for a month! This is wonderful!"

That wasn't how he wanted this to go. The flowers were supposed to help lighten the blow of hearing he was leaving. "Mom, I have to get back to Nashville. I have to get back to work."

Her face fell. "You can't do work from here? What do you do there that you can't do from here for a little bit?"

"Meet with artists, attend important budget meetings. Not to mention I'm wearing clothes that I bought at Hugo's."

Hugo's was the town's makeshift department store. Growing up, they'd gone to Hugo's three times a year—in the fall to buy new clothes for school, at Christmastime to see Santa and shop for gifts, and in the spring to get all the summer essentials.

"My computer—my life—is back in Nashville. I need to go home."

"Couldn't you have an assistant bring you some things? Or I could drive you up there right now and you could pack for a real visit while Dwight works on your car."

He hadn't expected her to be so insistent. Before he could tell her he didn't want to do any of those things, the waitress came by to take their orders. His mom ordered the same thing she always got when they came here: the BLT with fresh-cut fries. She was so much like Faith; both of them somehow found comfort in surrounding themselves in the past.

"When are you leaving?" she asked.

"Today." He knew she'd hate hearing it, but there wasn't a good reason to stick around.

"Today? I was hoping you'd be here long enough to help your dad trim that tree in the backyard. I'm nervous about him climbing a ladder and doing the work himself. His back hasn't been the same since he slipped this past winter." She sighed and glanced out the window. "But I guess we'll just have to hire someone."

Guilt made his stomach ache more than hunger. She had never really made him feel bad about not coming home. Of everyone, his mom seemed to understand why he had to exile himself. His unexpected visit had obviously given her hope that things were different.

Were they?

A little girl and her dad were seated at the counter. They had been eating when Dean came in. The waitress brought over a sundae with two spoons for father and daughter to share.

When Dean was a kid, his mom would bring him and Addison downtown in the summer and they'd pick up their dad at the bank. The teller would let them each have a lollipop before they left to the have lunch at the diner. If they finished everything on their plates, their dad would buy them ice cream or a slice of pie. Addison always got a hot-fudge sundae.

The memory left more of a warm feeling in Dean's chest than the sharp pain that usually accompanied his thoughts of Addison. Maybe things *were* a little different.

His mom picked up the flowers he had given her and gave them another sniff. Harriet's request that he pay forward her kindness sank in.

"I guess I could stay to help dad with whatever he needs to get done," he said. Her eyes lit up like it was Christmas morning. "But I have to go back eventually."

"I know, honey. Thank you for giving me a little more time with you." She reached over to cover his hand with hers. "I'll try to remember that when you leave this time, you'll be back. That's something."

"WE COULD CLOSE UP for lunch and head over to the Cup and Spoon," Harriet offered.

"I need a few more minutes to finish things up for you." Faith's focus had been scattered since Dean had showed up. Why was he everywhere she was lately? One of the disadvantages of a small town.

"I can't tell you how much I appreciate you."

Harriet looked like a plum today. She was even wearing purple shoes. Her quirkiness always made Faith smile. "Well, I appreciate you, so we're even."

"I shouldn't have been so nice to our friend Mr. Presley. I guess I was hoping he'd pay the kindness forward to you."

"What?"

"He broke your heart. Even though you can't seem to hold a grudge, I could have."

Faith had to laugh. "I don't want you to

hold that against him. He lost his sister. I can't blame him for being angry and hurt."

"You lost your best friend. I lost my protégé. His parents lost their daughter. We were all devastated by losing her. His emotions don't excuse his behavior."

It was a good point, but Faith wasn't sure what to do with it. She had tried venting her own frustration and it had only made her feel worse. Their relationship was forever scarred by what had happened. It was clear that neither one knew how to proceed.

Faith had less than an hour to eat lunch once she finished her work for Harriet. She searched her purse for her sunglasses. The cloudless sky provided no relief from the heat they were experiencing lately. She worried about Duchess in this weather. They had put a call in to the horse vet this morning.

"If we get breakfast food, we should be able to get in and out," Harriet said, holding open the door to the Cup and Spoon.

Dean lifted his head the moment Faith stepped into the diner. He acknowledged her with a wave, causing his mom to turn around to see who had walked in.

"Hey, sweetheart," she called out. Faith

raised a hand, knowing exactly what Mrs. Presley was going to say. "Come join us!"

They had their drinks but no food. "I don't want to bother you. It's not often you get your son to yourself," Faith said. It was valiant attempt but shot down immediately.

"It's fine. We were just talking about your brother. Come, sit." Instead of offering the seat next to her, she motioned for Faith to slide in next to Dean.

Harriet and Mrs. Presley exchanged greetings and Mrs. Presley called the waitress over to get their orders.

"Do you want to look at a menu?" Dean asked.

"Regulars like us don't need the menu," Harriet said, jumping right into her omelet order.

Faith tried to ignore the way her body seemed to respond to sitting so close to Dean. She made a concerted effort to keep space between them. When he had touched her in the stables last night, it was like going back in time.

The conversation between the four of them was strained. Mrs. Presley asked how things were going on the farm. She promised to come volunteer one of these days, which led to a discussion about the joys of retirement. Mrs. Presley had been retired from her job as the elementary school nurse for almost a year.

"I guess I thought I'd be more bored, but there's always something to do, some project to take on at the house. My closets have never been so organized."

"That's really sad, Mom," Dean said before finishing off his Coke. "If the only thing I have to look forward to in retirement is an organized shoe rack, I think I'd rather work until I die."

"Well, hopefully when your father retires, we'll travel."

"Josie has been to every country in Europe at least once," Faith said. "She promises to take me to a place in Italy called the Cinque Terre someday. You should go there."

"Remind me to look that up when we get back to the house," Mrs. Presley said to Dean.

"How is Josie these days?" Harriet asked.

"She's good. Lily's getting inducted into the National Honor Society tonight. I'm sure she's feeling like a proud mama."

"Oh, my gosh, remember the year you and Addison were inducted?" Mrs. Presley laughed so hard the man at the counter turned around to see what was so funny.

Faith's shoulders tensed. Talking about Addison was a no-no around Dean. She waited for him to ask his mom to change the subject.

"Was that when she cartwheeled across the stage?" he asked instead.

"In her dress." Mrs. Presley cried, she was laughing so hard. "Your father was mortified."

Faith decided to go with it. Maybe the longer Dean stayed, the more he could handle. "*My* father was mortified. We drove home and he made me promise to never to show my underwear to a room full of people."

Mrs. Presley wiped under her eyes. "That girl was crazy."

Everyone else nodded. Faith felt her throat tighten. She glanced at Dean, sure his jaw would be clenched. He turned and smiled at her.

"Remember the time I let you two come with me to the library and after being there like, a half hour, she stood up and asked if someone could turn up the music because she needed to dance?"

"And there was no music." Faith clearly remembered her best friend "getting jiggy with it" in the middle of the young adult section of the Grass Lake Library.

"I was studying for a really tough history final, too," Dean said. "I was ready to strangle her."

"I was so embarrassed. I think I hid in the bathroom."

"I think you did. We couldn't find you and I wanted to leave," Dean said with a smile on his face. "You two were such a pain in the butt."

Faith wasn't sure what was happening, but it felt good to reminisce with him. She tried not to overthink it. He had to be leaving Grass Lake soon and they'd go back to being strangers.

CHAPTER TWELVE

"We should tell her."

"We will...later."

"She keeps asking me why I'm so happy lately."

He grinned so wide he thought his face might split in two. "Do I make you happy?" He kissed her in that spot just under her earlobe.

He could feel her melt in his arms. They had been hiding in the hay stall for a while. Her father might come looking for them soon, but Dean couldn't bring himself to leave this place. Propped up by hay bales, he held his girl close. She sat between his outstretched legs and leaned back against him.

"You make me the happiest."

He could say the same, and making her happy was all he wanted. There was something about Faith that made him want to protect her. He wanted to shield the goodness inside her from every bad thing there was in the world.

It was different than wanting to take care of her. Faith didn't need him to do that. She was strong. She took care of her dad and the horses. She watched over her brother. Without her mother around, she'd had to grow up fast. Maybe that was why their age difference didn't bother him. Faith was more mature than most of the girls at Belmont.

"Telling Addison will make you unhappy because my sister won't understand and she won't want me to be the reason you're happy."

"It's just so hard. I met this guy and he's perfect. He has the prettiest eyes and a nice car. He has big biceps and is the best kisser I have ever kissed."

"How many kissers have you kissed?" He tickled her sides when she refused to answer, making her squirm and giggle.

She turned her body to face him. "Not many, but enough to know you're the best." She pressed her lips to his. The kiss was soft and innocent, like her, until it quickly turned heated.

He had to stop before they went further than either of them was ready to go. "So ev-

erything you like about me is completely superficial. Is that what you're telling me?"

She gave him a look that said she took exception to his observation. "What I'm trying to say is that I want to tell my best friend I'm in love with this amazing guy and I can't even tell her that there is a guy."

They'd been sneaking around for two months. Stealing moments here and there while they worked on the farm. Hanging out whenever Addison had to work. Showing their affection for one another in subtle ways and tiny gestures. They hadn't labeled what they were to one another or told each other how they felt.

Love.

She had said it first, but that didn't mean she'd been the first one to feel it.

"You love me?"

Faith hid her face in the crook of his neck. "Did I say that out loud?"

"Look at me," he said, coaxing her to show him those eyes.

Warily, she lifted her head and grimaced. "Go ahead, tell me how I'm too young and I don't know what I'm talking about. Tell me you think I'm really sweet, but I shouldn't get my hopes up that this could be something real."

Instead of telling her what he was thinking, he showed her. He cradled her cheek in his hand and he kissed her so she felt it from head to toe. He pulled back just enough to whisper the words against her lips.

"I love you, too, silly girl."

"DEAN!" HIS MOTHER'S words jarred him from his late-afternoon nap. He almost fell off the couch. "Were you asleep?" she asked, coming around the other side of the couch so she could see him.

Dean sat up and scratched the back of his head. He hadn't meant to fall asleep. He was trying to watch some YouTube videos and the combination of lack of sleep and a full belly had knocked him out.

"I can't remember the last time I took a nap in the middle of the day. This town is seriously detrimental to my work ethic." He yawned and pulled his phone out from in between the seat cushions where it had fallen while he was passed out. The flowers he had given her were sitting in a vase on the antique side table.

"You deserve a little break from work.

When was the last time you took a vacation?" his mom said, fluffing the couch pillows he had knocked onto the floor. There was no time for vacations. There was only time to find the next big thing. There was only time for making sure Piper was happy and helping Boone find a way to get the music back in his soul where it belonged.

"How long was I out?" The room was full of shadows and he was quickly reminded of his dream. He rubbed his lips to make sure they weren't as swollen as they had felt when he was kissing Faith. Those kisses had happened, only they'd happened a long time ago.

"I don't know, but it's late. Your dad will be home anytime now. Any dinner requests?"

"Pizza."

"You want me to order pizza?"

Dean shook his head. "No, I need to run out. I'm going to grab dinner on my own, okay?"

His mother's concern creased her forehead. "Are you all right?"

That was debatable. "I'm good." He kissed her cheek. "I'll be back."

GRASS LAKE HIGH SCHOOL's auditorium seated eight hundred people, which was almost the entire population of the small town. It was great for the school play performances but made the group of family and friends there to cheer on their honor student look pretty tiny.

Faith browsed the program she'd been handed when they'd arrived. Josie leaned over and whispered, "When you see her after the ceremony, could you please tell her that her dress is beautiful? She changed eight times before we got here and wanted to put on something else one minute before we left and I wouldn't let her. She's sure I'm the devil who wants her to look horrible."

Lily, like nearly every teenage girl, never saw herself the way everyone else did. Faith was certain she knew she was pretty, but often felt she wasn't pretty enough. It reminded her of Addison, who'd had all the confidence in the world except when it came to her appearance.

"I'll make sure to slip that in. Not that my opinion matters much."

"Oh, are you kidding me?" Josie huffed. "What you think carries way more weight than what I think. You're young and gorgeous. She thinks you can do no wrong, while I'm an old hag who knows nothing."

"I can't wait to have teenagers." Faith

laughed before adding, "And you're hardly an old hag. Look at you—you've got a good… three years before you hit old-hag status."

Josie elbowed her friend hard and they both giggled like the teenagers, garnering the attention of another parent in front of them. Faith apologized as the lights dimmed, signaling the start.

Faith had forgotten how boring these types of things were. She found her mind wandering right away. She thought about Duchess and the way she seemed to be getting worse, not better. She thought about the new mounting ramp Sawyer was building and hoped he was following NETA's specifications to a tee. But her thoughts dwelled longest on Dean and how good his laughter had sounded and how handsome he was when he smiled.

When the kids were called up to the stage, tears welled in her eyes as she imagined Addison doing cartwheels. Sharing memories with the people who loved Addison today had been therapeutic. She hoped Dean had walked away feeling the same.

When it was all over, Faith handed Lily a small bouquet of flowers Harriet had helped her put together. "I'm so proud of you even though I can take no credit for how smart and beautiful you are. That dress is adorable, by the way."

Josie gave her a thumbs-up and mouthed a thank-you from behind her daughter.

"Thanks for coming, Faith. I really appreciate it."

Faith knew what it was like to not have two parents. Having Harriet show up to important events and the Presleys in her corner had meant the world to Faith growing up. She was happy to return the favor. Paying it forward, as Harriet would say.

"Did you see Kylie? She said she was going to come." Lily stood on her tiptoes and surveyed the crowd of parents and siblings scattered around the hall outside the auditorium.

"I didn't see her," Faith said. "Maybe her parents couldn't drive her over here. I'm sorry I didn't check. I could have picked her up."

Lily shook her head. "This is her way of telling me she's still mad. She didn't like my picture on Instagram, either. She's always the first like I get."

Social media added a whole new level of communication that Faith would never understand. It broke Faith's heart to see two best friends in a similar situation as her and Addison had been in at the very end.

They headed outside to the parking lot. Faith needed to get home, make dinner and get to bible study on time.

"Faith!" someone called out.

Dean pushed off the car hood he was sitting on and strode toward her like the hero from a romance movie. He had his father's broad shoulders and long legs. She had always thought of Dean as the perfect alter ego for a superhero.

"What are you doing here?" She stepped away from Josie and Lily, trying to meet him halfway.

"Pizza."

She stopped short. "You're picking up a pizza in the school parking lot?"

His crooked grin made her heart skip a beat. "No, we told Charles we were going to get pizza after the ceremony. You know how people in this town talk—I wouldn't want it getting back to him that we didn't go."

Faith's head felt fuzzy. Maybe she was imagining this. "You want to go out for pizza? With me?"

"I mean, Josie and Lily are welcome to join us."

Faith glanced back at Josie, who was standing at her car door. "You okay?" Josie asked.

"Stay here," Faith said to Dean. She needed to talk to Josie and didn't want him close enough to hear. Heat crept up her chest. "He wants to take us out for pizza."

"You. He wants to take you," Josie said with a smirk.

"Why would he want to take me to dinner?"

Josie put a hand on Faith's shoulder. "From what you've told me, I think he was a guy who didn't handle his sister's death really well. Maybe he wants to make up for it."

That seemed unlikely, but the best explanation. She wouldn't let her anxiety get the best of her. She held her head high as she walked back over to where he was waiting.

"Meet me at Sam's?"

"Is there anywhere else to get pizza in this town?" he asked rhetorically.

PIZZA SAM WAS the only pizza joint in Grass Lake. Luckily it had the best pizza in the county. People from neighboring towns often drove through just to order some pies for carryout.

Dean had already grabbed an open table when Faith arrived. Without the buffer of

Harriet and his mother, she wasn't sure how this shared meal would go.

The front room at Sam's was quiet and quaint. There were half a dozen tables and a counter where people picked up their carryout orders. The walls were decorated with window murals that made it look like you were gazing out at the streets of Rome. The tables were covered in red-and-white-checked tablecloths, and the lit candle in a red glass holder on each added to the ambience.

Dean got to his feet and pulled out her chair. "Is this okay? I can ask if they have something in the back if you want."

"This is fine. We're here to be seen, right?"

"Right." His voice was soft.

The back room at Sam's was where families with younger kids usually sat. White lights were strung across the ceiling and video-game machines lined the back wall. There was one of those claw games that Addison had always seemed to win on her first try. Faith would burn through five dollars' worth of quarters and that darn stuffed animal would slip out every time.

"Still like pepperoni?" he asked, picking up a menu.

"Pepperoni is fine."

Faith grabbed a menu, too. Pretending to read it was better than sitting there not knowing what to say. The squat, teenage busboy came over with ice water.

Being with Dean was like spending time with both the person she knew best in the world and a complete stranger. She knew how old he had been when he got braces and what kind of car he drove when he was sixteen, but she had no idea if he currently lived in a house or an apartment, if he had a girlfriend, what he did in his free time.

"It's weird, right?" he asked, peeking over his menu.

Faith set her menu down. That was a loaded question. Everything between them was weird. "What?"

"That we've hung out in public more times in the last couple days than we did the entire summer we were dating."

"A secret relationship usually means the couple doesn't go traipsing around town together," Faith pointed out.

"Did I ever make you feel like I didn't want to be seen with you?"

Faith had to reflect back on that. It had been such a short period in their lives. A whirlwind romance. "I thought everything we did was because of Addison. I never thought about how anyone else would feel about us. Did you?"

"I worried about your dad. I wasn't sure he'd want you to be with me because I was older. I know I'd be wary of some twenty-one-year-old and my eighteen-year-old daughter. His intentions would be questionable."

"*Were* your intentions questionable?" Faith leaned forward and rested her elbows on the table.

"Being respectful of you was always my intention, but that doesn't mean I didn't think about doing things with you that would have made your dad chase me off his property with a shotgun."

Faith's face was aflame. She took a sip of the ice water. She wanted to steer the conversation as far away as possible from what those thoughts could have been. "Maybe part of me thought you were a little embarrassed to be with someone who hadn't been to college yet. I heard what your friends would say when we all hung out at your parents' house."

"What did they say?"

"Why are we talking about this?" Faith had bible study in an hour and rehashing the past wasn't going to change what happened or even what the future held for them. There was no future for them. "Why are we having pizza together? Why do you care if Charles Hackney makes me dinner?"

Dean seemed taken aback by her bluntness. He shifted in his seat and rubbed his knuckles against his bearded jaw. "Do you want Charles to make you dinner? Do you want his mother setting you up constantly?"

"No." She didn't want to be set up with anyone. Her time and energy were better spent on Helping Hooves. The horses and her clients needed her more than she needed a man.

"Then why were you ready to do whatever Mrs. Hackney wanted?"

"Because giving people what they want keeps everyone happy," Faith said with a shrug.

"What about you?"

"What about me?"

"What makes you happy?"

Faith couldn't keep up with his opinions on how she was supposed to be living her life. "You're the one who said we don't deserve to be happy."

"I never said that."

"Fine, I think you said we don't deserve

to feel better. To me, that's the same thing as being happy."

"I was out of control after Addison died."

"You said it in the church parking lot two days ago!"

Dean threw his hands up. "Of all the things I've ever said to you, that's what you're going to hang your hat on? Something I said in the middle of an anxiety attack?"

"No, what really sticks with me is that I was stupid for loving you and *really* stupid for thinking you could care about me after what happened."

Dean frowned and exhaled deeply. "I said that?"

"I might be paraphrasing." She wasn't. Those words weren't ones Faith could forget.

"I know I said that after she died." He sat back in his seat. "And I wasn't in my right mind."

"Just tell me what we're doing here." Faith was drained. She didn't have any more patience for this. He needed to be clear now because she had thought he'd been very clear twelve years ago.

"Well, if you're so good at remembering the things I say, remember this—you deserve better than Charles Hackney, Faith. Don't settle for less than you deserve to make other people happy."

Faith's heart was pounding hard enough to break through her chest. "That's funny. I thought that was what I was doing the night Addison died. Telling her was my way of not settling for stolen moments. And we both know where that got me."

"That's not what happened. I had put you in an impossible, no-win situation. You deserved better than me, too."

"We might have to agree to disagree on that one," she said, feeling a bit light-headed. Dean had a way of knocking her off kilter. "I'm not sure you know me as well as you think you do."

"I will agree to disagree about that," he replied.

"I don't like pepperoni," she admitted. It felt like the whole room went silent, although no one was really paying attention to what she said except for Dean. "I've never been a fan. I used to eat it because I knew you liked it. I prefer sausage and mushroom."

Dean blinked and, with his elbow on the table, rested his chin on his palm. He seemed to be trying to see inside her brain, wanting to know what else she was hiding inside there.

When the waitress came to take their order, he didn't hesitate.

"We'll take a medium—half pepperoni, half sausage-mushroom, please."

CHAPTER THIRTEEN

"ONLY CUT THE branches that are touching the house," Dean's dad said from the ground below.

The large yellow poplar had grown several feet taller in the last decade. Dean definitely didn't remember it reaching the upstairs bedroom window. The Presleys' backyard was immense and sprinkled with a variety of trees with branches that provided lots of shade under all those green leaves. They lived on a three-acre lot that Dean used to hate to mow even on a riding mower.

Dean took another step up the ladder. Trimming trees was not something he ever had to do back in the city. He spent most of his life on the phone or in the studio. Today, he'd been on the phone for hours, much to his mother's dismay.

"I don't know if I can reach the ones at the top."

"We might have to get those from your sister's room."

An unexpected wave of panic hit Dean and he had to hold on to the ladder so he didn't fall. Every day it had gotten easier to talk about Addison, but the thought of going into her room and possibly seeing her things made his stomach ache.

"You okay?" his dad shouted up.

Dean nodded, hoping his dad could see, because no words were coming. He took a couple deep breaths and tried to shift his focus back to the task at hand.

"So what's this I hear about you having pizza with Faith last night? Word around the bank was you and she were spotted at Sam's with your heads together. Charles Hackney didn't seem too pleased."

Dean shouldn't have, but he smiled at the thought. It didn't surprise him that he was right about small-town gossip. It had taken less than twenty-four hours for the rumor to spread.

"I needed to clear the air a little bit." His attempt at empowering her pretty much backfired. He hadn't realized how much she cared about what he thought—back then and now. He hadn't gotten her to agree she deserved to be happy, but he *had* gotten her to be honest about her favorite pizza toppings. It was progress.

"Since when have you had a problem with Faith Stratton that needs working out?"

Dean had never told anyone what had happened between him and Faith. Addison hadn't had the chance to spill the beans to their parents about it and, after she'd died, he'd felt too guilty to admit that she had gotten herself into that situation because he was off at a concert with Faith.

Dean clipped every branch he could reach and climbed down. He handed his dad the pruners. "That summer—" Dean didn't have to clarify it was the one that changed everything for their family "—Faith and I were seeing each other behind everyone's back."

"Yeah," his dad said, like he was already aware of this information. But that was impossible. Unless…

"Faith told you," he guessed.

"No," his dad said with a chuckle. He folded up the ladder. "John Stratton called me about a month after you started working for him that summer and told me he saw you two making out in the horse barn. Wanted me to know that he wouldn't shoot you as long as you got your work done and it didn't go any further than kissing."

Stunned, Dean didn't even notice his dad was trying to hand him the saw to cut up the fallen branches.

"Son, can you please take this while I put the ladder away?"

He took the saw. "Wait, you're saying you guys all knew Faith and I were together?"

"I thought I needed to have a man-to-man chat with you, reminding you how important it is to treat a girl with respect and not to do anything that could lead to responsibilities you two weren't ready for—or her dad wanting to shoot you—but your mother said we needed to trust that you two were good, responsible kids."

"Did you know Addison didn't know?"

"I suspect that's part of the reason your mom didn't want me to talk to you. You all must have thought your sister was going to blow a gasket over you dating her best friend."

Dean's head was spinning. All this time he was sure his parents had had no idea. It had been a secret that was still tearing him up inside.

He couldn't bring himself to tell his dad that Addison did find out and wasn't happy.

She was so unhappy about it that she ran off to a party she never would have gone to if she had been with Faith that night. She was so angry that she got in a car with someone who had been drinking, instead of calling Dean to come get her like she would have if she didn't think her brother was trying to steal her best friend from her.

He couldn't tell his dad that it was his fault his sister was dead.

"I think Addison would have been mad for a day and then she would have gotten over it," his dad continued. "She would have been planning your wedding because, let's be honest, the thought of Faith being her sister would have had her over the moon."

They'd never know for sure. She never got the chance to get over it.

"Cut these up and meet me upstairs. We'll try to get the ones at the top from Addison's room." Dean's dad didn't wait for him to reply. He lifted the ten-foot ladder with ease and carried it to the garage.

Dean did as he was told. He stood outside the closed door to his sister's room and prayed it was like his old bedroom, completely unrecognizable. If his mother had busied herself with updating his room, she wouldn't have stopped there. His parents had no trouble talking about her; they were obviously much further along in the grieving process than Dean was.

He had himself convinced as he grasped the doorknob, turned it and pushed. Reality smacked him in the face hard. It was like walking through time. On one side of the door, it was present day and on the other it was as if the millennium had just begun.

The purple walls were still covered in hundreds of pictures of Addison, Addison and Faith, Addison and the family, Addison and anyone she was friends with over the course of her life. Where there weren't photos, there were flowers—paper flowers, fabric flowers, plastic flowers. Her tiny twin-size bed was covered by the flowered quilt their grandmother had hand-stitched for her.

His dad came into the room like there was nothing odd about the fact that they were standing in a time warp. "Hopefully we can reach them all from here. Help me with the screen."

Dean's lungs constricted. It felt like there wasn't enough air in the room. His feet were cemented to the floor.

His dad's hand came down on his back

with enough force to jostle him out of his head. "I forget you haven't been back here. Do you need a minute?"

"You left it like this for all these years?"

"Your mom went through her clothes and donated a bunch of things about a year after she died. She let Faith come in and take whatever she wanted. We talked about packing up the stuff on her dresser and desk, but seems like your mom has gotten to every other room in this house first."

Dean wanted to sit down, take a moment to process what his dad had said, but he couldn't bring himself to sit on anything in this room. Addison's smiling face was everywhere.

His dad picked up a framed picture of Addison and Faith. "Everyone grieves in their own way and at their own speed. Some take longer than others." He set the photo down and gave Dean's shoulder a squeeze. "You and your mom are more alike than you think. Maybe the two of you need each other to put this behind you instead of letting it hold you back."

FAITH AND SAWYER both paced the aisle outside the horse stalls while the vet examined Duchess. Scout sat at attention, watching the two of them. The dog had no idea what they were worried about but seemed to be aware of their anxiety. Faith said a prayer that it was nothing or at least something that could be treated with a change in diet or maybe some medicine.

Rebecca Fielding came out of the stall wearing an expression that didn't bode well. Faith's stomach was twisted in knots and there was a ringing in her ears.

"What is it?" Sawyer asked.

Rebecca pulled her latex gloves off one at a time. "Her eyes are yellow. She's underweight. You've reported the circling in her stall, head-pressing and shaking. My guess, without seeing the blood work, is liver failure."

"That's treatable, right?" Faith needed to hear something good.

"Often, yes," Rebecca answered with some hesitancy. "But Duchess is an old horse."

"So, what are you saying? You won't help her?" Faith said, feeling her heart pounding in her chest.

Sawyer put his hand on her shoulder to hold her back.

"No, of course I'll help her. But I want you to be aware that she might not respond to treatment. I don't want you to get your hopes up, that's all I'm saying."

"We understand, Bec," Sawyer said. He was always better at reining in his emotions than she was.

"I took some blood. I'll run some tests and come up with a treatment plan as soon as I can."

Sawyer and Scout saw her out while Faith opened the door to Duchess's stall. The pain in her chest intensified. She stroked the horse's head and made Duchess promises she knew she wouldn't be able to keep. It didn't take long for the tears to start flowing.

"Come on, you can't stay out here. Let's go inside and watch a movie," Sawyer suggested when he returned.

"I don't want to watch a movie." She ran her hand over Duchess's mane. She was such a patient and tolerant horse. How many times had Faith and Addison played horse beauty shop and tied flowers in her mane and tail? Duchess was such a sweet, social horse. It was unbearable to imagine this farm without her.

Sawyer opened the door and gave Duchess a pat. "Let's see how things go. Rebecca isn't saying we have to put her down."

"I can't put her down, Sawyer. I can't lose her so soon after Dad." She wiped her face with the back of her hand. The emotions hit her like waves that were trying to knock her over.

"I know."

"I can't lose you, either." The words tumbled out. She'd been holding them back since the last time they'd talked about Dean's proposition. "I'm barely holding it together. You realize that, right?"

Sawyer sighed and dropped his head. With his hands on his hips, he stared at the ground. "I don't want to talk about this."

"I hear you. I hear you in your room, playing the guitar, writing new songs, practicing old ones. I hear you all the time. I know why you're doing it, too. I know it's not to play at the Sundown."

Sawyer's head came up and he looked his sister directly in the eye. "What do you want me to say, Faith? You want me to promise you that I'm going to work on this farm until the day I die? Is that what you need to hear right now?"

The frustration in his voice took her aback. Faith wasn't trying to pick a fight. "I'm sorry."

"I'm sorry, too. I'm sorry Duchess is sick.

I'm sorry Dad died. Don't make me feel guilty for sitting in my room playing guitar. It's how I de-stress. It's how I unwind. Maybe all that's going on is hard on me, too."

Guilt created another pit in her stomach. "I know it has been. That's why we have to stick together. I'm not trying to make you feel bad. I'm just so sad."

He wrapped his arms around his big sister and held her tight like their dad used to do when she was having a bad day. "Come inside with me and let's find something to take our minds off all the negative stuff."

"Maybe you can play me one of your new songs," Faith suggested, trying to show her support. He could enjoy playing music. It didn't mean he was going to run off to Nashville with Dean.

Sawyer agreed and they went back to the house. Faith popped some popcorn while her brother went upstairs to get his guitar. He returned with Scout following behind him and his phone in his hand, texting up a storm.

"You got a secret girlfriend I should know about?" she asked when he smiled at something he read.

"That's one thing you for sure don't have to worry about. You're the only woman I am willing to put up with and that's because we share the same blood. If you tell me I'm adopted, I'm out of here."

Sawyer sounded like a guy who had had his heart broken by someone he had been madly in love with. The truth was he rarely dated. All through high school, he hung out with girls, but no one stuck around for very long and he was never really sad to see them go.

Faith suspected that the heartbreaker was their mother. When Faith was ten and Sawyer was four, their mom had decided that Grass Lake wasn't right for her. Being a mother and wife was too much responsibility. She had tried. She had put in ten years' worth of effort, but the world had been calling and she'd needed to get out there and see what it had to offer.

"Who has you giggling like a girl over there, then?" she asked, pouring the popcorn into a big bowl.

"You don't want to know."

"I wouldn't have asked if I didn't want to know." Not telling her made her that much more curious. She was ready to grab his phone and steal a look.

"It's Dean. But I swear I'm not plotting my escape to Nashville, okay?"

The man was going to drive her insane. He disappeared for years and years only to come home and flip her world upside down, all the while making it very clear that they could never have any sort of relationship because they either didn't deserve to be happy—at least not happy with one another—or because Faith deserved better than him. She couldn't be sure which it was anymore. He was more than confusing.

"I trust you," she said, trying her best to sound convincing.

"What's your deal with him, anyway?" Sawyer asked, setting his phone aside and sitting down with his guitar. "I thought you and him were close. I remember you guys getting along when Addison was alive."

Faith hadn't told Sawyer anything about her relationship with Dean. He had been twelve when it had happened and she'd had no desire to share her personal heartbreak with an adolescent. Harriet had been the only one she'd confided in.

There wasn't a good reason not to tell him now. "Remember how Dean worked here the summer Addison died?"

"Yeah."

"We kind of dated." She hadn't expected it to be so embarrassing to say out loud.

Sawyer's face scrunched up in disbelief. "No, you didn't."

"In secret. We dated in secret so Addison wouldn't know."

"Are you kidding me? You and Dean Presley snuck around behind Addison's back? Did you make out in the stables while he was working or sneak out in the middle of night for a secret rendezvous?"

Faith said nothing because both were true.

"No way," Sawyer said with a shake of his head. "No. Way. Dad would have killed you if he'd caught you sneaking out of the house to meet a boy."

"Dad never caught me. It was only for a couple months, and it ended the night Addison died."

Sawyer thought it all over for a second or two. "Because Addison died?"

"Yes."

"I am so confused right now." Sawyer set his guitar down and grabbed a handful of popcorn, and tossed a piece to the dog at his feet. "But this is more interesting than any movie we could have found on TV."

"He blames me. He blames both of us, but mostly me."

The popcorn in Sawyer's hand fell back into the bowl. "Blames you for what?"

"For Addison going to that party. For her getting in that car."

"How is that your fault?"

"I told her the truth. I told her I was going to a concert with Dean and we were in love with each other." Faith shuddered at the memory of the hurt emanating from Addison's eyes. She had never seen her friend so angry, so disappointed. Faith had told her because she'd thought maybe, just maybe, Addison would be happy for her. "Dean had warned me that she wouldn't take it well. He told me over and over again that we should wait until we went away to school. I thought I knew her better than he did. But I was wrong."

Sawyer's face hardened. His lips fell into a straight line. "It was not your fault, Faith."

She shrugged, unwilling to give up the blame.

"It was *not* your fault."

"She wouldn't have gone to that party if I hadn't told her and made her so mad." That was the truth and something no one could convince her wasn't the reason for the tragic events that occurred that night.

"Faith, listen to me." He stood in front of her and put both his hands on her shoulders like he was going to shake some sense into her. "It was not your fault. Aaron Evans drank a case of beer, got in his car, let Addison get in with him and hit that tree. Aaron Evans killed her. Not you."

"I know."

"No, say it. Say you didn't kill her." The intensity of his stare made her look away. "Tell me whose fault it was."

"I didn't drive the car. Aaron was driving the car. But she wouldn't have been in that car—"

"Faith!" Sawyer shook her once. "You are not the reason Addison is dead." He let go of her and paced in front of the kitchen table. "This is why you do what you do. It's why you never say no. Why you think you need to take care of everyone you meet. You're atoning for a sin that's not even yours."

His anger was unexpected and Faith didn't know what to say to make things better. He was right, that was what she did. She hated to upset anyone. She didn't want to be responsible for anyone's unhappiness.

"Do you think it's your fault that Mom left?" he asked. "Or that Dad died? Do you think you're the reason Duchess is in liver failure?"

"No." Although she often wondered if she had made sure her dad ate better or pushed him to go for a yearly physical, could they have prevented his heart attack? Now didn't seem like the right time to confess those thoughts, however.

"No. Because you can't control the bad things that happen in the world by being nice or putting other's needs in front of your own. Please tell me you understand that."

"I get it," she assured him.

"Good, because you can't fall apart. I need you to hold yourself together no matter what happens to Duchess or what Dean Presley thinks happened twelve years ago when you were a kid. We need to stay focused on getting this place ready for NETA. We have to make Duchess as comfortable as possible for however long she has."

He was right. Faith needed to put her emotions aside and put all of her energy toward Helping Hooves. Her brother was invested. She couldn't be the weak link because she was holding herself responsible for things that weren't in her control.

She was not the reason Addison died. Faith would keep telling herself that until she believed it.

CHAPTER FOURTEEN

FAILURE WAS NOT an option. Too much work had been done. Too many years spent making something out of nothing.

"Boone, listen to me. Kevin and I have talked about this. We're on the same page." At least they were after a dozen phone calls and three strongly worded emails had been exchanged. Boone had said he wouldn't agree to anything until Dean had his agent on board.

"I need to hear it from Kevin. Last I checked, he thought it was a better idea if I go to meetings around here."

AA meetings weren't going to help sustain Boone's sobriety. One nasty interview with his ex had sent him on his most recent bender. Dean needed to get him away from it all, so he could get his head clear and his life together.

"Let's call Kevin. We'll call Kevin and you can hear it from *Kevin* that the best thing for you to do is to go to this facility in California."

Dean's mom walked past the entryway to the kitchen where Dean was seated at the table. She gave him a look that expressed her concern. He waved her off. He was fine. Or he would be as soon as Boone agreed to go back to rehab.

"I thought you said it was a retreat. Now you're calling it a facility. I'm not going back to the hospital. No more rehab."

Dean cringed and wanted desperately to punch a hole through the tabletop. "Don't get worked up over semantics. It's a facility that offers retreat for people in your situation. That's all."

"'People in my situation'? You mean people who have a crazy ex-wife who goes on record about things that happened in the privacy of their own home and exaggerates facts to make her look innocent when she is *far* from innocent? In fact, she is the reason 'people in my situation' drink!"

This was not going well. This was going the exact opposite of how it was supposed to be going. Dean blew out an exasperated breath. Doing an intervention over the phone was a bad idea. It was another prime example of why he needed to get back to Nashville. His dad had guilted him into staying a bit longer.

"Boone, I understand what you're saying. I hear your frustration. I hear that you feel betrayed by what Sara did. All the more reason to go on this retreat."

"I will talk to Kevin. But don't get your hopes up," Boone said before hanging up.

Maybe it was time to let him go. Boone didn't understand that the world didn't owe him any favors and that his attitude was going to cost him everything his talent had earned him. As much as Dean respected his talent, his behavior was ruining this relationship.

Dean needed Sawyer. If he had any chance of cutting Boone loose while keeping Grace Note afloat, he was going to need someone who sold more records than tabloid magazines. Boone's drama would never make Dean any money.

"Off the phone?" his mom asked, poking her head back in.

Dean rubbed his tired eyes. "I'm off. At least until Kevin Phillips calls me and wants to know why Boone thinks he's going back to rehab instead of an artistic retreat."

"Sawyer Stratton is here to see you. Want me to send him back?"

Dean laughed at her. "Are you trying to get a job as my secretary? Can I get some coffee? I like it black."

"Ha, ha. You can get your own coffee. It's right over there on the counter. But I will tell Sawyer you're off the phone."

Signing Sawyer was meant to be. His visit was proof of it. Sawyer followed Dean's mom into the kitchen. She was quick to offer him something to drink. Dean got up to greet his soon-to-be superstar properly.

"No, thank you. I just need a minute of Dean's time and then I have to head back to the farm. We have a horse who isn't doing real well. I need to get back and attend to her."

"Duchess?" Dean asked. Faith would be beside herself if anything happened to that horse. He remembered how she used to favor her over all the others.

"She's sick. Took a real turn for the worse this morning."

"I'm so sorry to hear that," Dean said, and his mother relayed the same sentiments.

"I wanted to ask you a couple questions." Sawyer glanced at Dean's mom, who quickly took the hint that it was private. She excused herself and left them alone.

"Sit, please." Dean motioned to the chair across from where he had been sitting.

"No, I'll stand. Did you tell my sister she's the reason your sister died?" Sawyer didn't waste any time cutting to the heart of the matter.

"What?"

"Did you tell my sister that she's the reason your sister got in Aaron Evans's car twelve years ago?" Sawyer's eyes were hard and his jaw ticked with anger. "It's a simple yes or no question."

"There's nothing simple about that question," Dean replied as the tension in his shoulders somehow managed to increase twofold. "Nothing about my sister's death was simple."

"Just answer the question, Music Man," Sawyer demanded, his patience obviously thin. "I really don't have time to debate every aspect of the accident and the little love affair you were having with my sister when she was barely an adult."

Dean's "love affair" with Faith had been about as little as Addison's death had been simple. He had so many conflicting emotions at the moment, he wasn't sure he could give

Sawyer what he was looking for without coming to blows. His aggressive questions made Dean defensive and it was hard to be compliant.

"Faith and I have always agreed that our choices and our relationship are the reason Addison wasn't thinking clearly that night."

"So, yes. Your answer is yes, you told my sister that she killed her best friend." Sawyer jumped right into his next question. "Are you trying to bait me into going to Nashville to get back at her or to hurt her?"

"What? No!" Dean moved around the table to put some distance between them so neither one of them did something they would regret.

"Are you sure? You don't think that maybe there's part of you that wants to take her brother away since you think she took your sister from you?"

Dean's sat down, unable to stay on his feet. Holding his throbbing head in his hand, he tried to put himself in Sawyer's shoes. This was the most outrageous accusation he'd ever heard, but as a brother, how would he have felt if the tables were turned?

"Does Faith think that I'm trying to lure you away to get back at her?" He hoped not, because he thought he had made it clear to her that he wished her the best. Even if that wasn't him.

"My sister thinks that she killed her best friend. My sister thinks that she needs to make everyone happy at whatever cost to her own well-being because if she upsets someone and they die in an *accident*, she'll be at fault."

When Sawyer put it that way, it made Dean feel like a horrible person. He didn't want Faith to spend her life trying to please the world, but if he let her off the hook for what happened to Addison, he'd have to absolve himself, as well. He wasn't sure he was ready to do that.

"I want you to come to Nashville because you are talented enough to make it in the business. That's it," Dean said.

Sawyer glowered at him, seemingly unconvinced. After a few seconds of staring Dean down, he took the seat across from him. "I opened a YouTube account. I want to upload those videos you took. I had Lily make me an Instagram account, too. I don't know what to put on there, but I figure you do."

Progress. "I can help you with both of those."

"If you want me to come to Nashville, you

need to help me make sure Helping Hooves passes the test to be accredited with NETA."

Dean's eyebrows pinched together. "I don't have any influence with that particular organization. I don't know how to help you there."

"I don't need your influence. I need your muscle and your time. I need to get the new mounting ramp finished and every building on the property has to meet all these requirements for accessibility. I think my dad built the place to be accessible to anyone, but there's a really long list and I need to go through everything on it one by one to make sure. You can help me with that."

"How long do we have?"

"Not long. The visit is scheduled for Saturday."

It seemed like a fair trade, and something told him he should be grateful Sawyer was still willing to consider working with him. There was only one major concern.

"What about Faith? She's okay with this?"

"I'll handle my sister. When I'm ready to tell her what I want to do, I will. Can I count on you or not?"

Dean wasn't sure how to feel about that answer, but getting Sawyer signed to the label and in the recording studio was the only way to get the company back in the black.

"When do we start?"

FAITH HAD SPENT the morning calling everyone she could think of to help her with the fund-raiser she'd decided she'd put together as a way of covering the expenses the NETA accreditation had created. Now she needed to find out from Sawyer how many volunteers he needed to help him fix the paddock fencing.

Her brother had left a half hour ago to run a mystery errand and wasn't answering any of Faith's texts. She was beginning to worry when she heard his truck pull up to the house.

As she stepped out onto the porch, it was the man getting out of the passenger side of Sawyer's pickup who got all of her attention. Dean in his now-infamous red T-shirt walked to the back of the truck and got to work unloading the feed bags.

"What is he doing here?" Faith asked Sawyer as Dean headed to the barn with two bags of feed on his shoulders.

"He's here to help," he replied. Scout nudged his hand, eager for some attention. Faith hadn't been the only one wondering where he'd been. "We're going to go through the accessibility list, make sure everything is good to go. Then he's going to help me knock out the east-side fence of the grazing paddock."

"I guess a better question would be *why* is he doing all that for us?"

Sawyer shrugged. "He wants to. Let's not look a gift horse in the mouth, right?"

Faith and Sawyer unloaded the rest of the feed bags and started carrying them to the barn. Dean came running out in a panic. Faith's stomach dropped along with the bag of feed. He didn't have to say anything for her to know what was happening.

"Something's wrong with Duchess."

"Call Rebecca!" Faith shouted to Sawyer as she ran past Dean and into the stables.

Duchess was on the ground. Her breathing was labored and her eyes rolled around in her head. Faith knelt down and sat behind Duchess's head.

"It's okay, sweet girl. We're going to get you some help. Everything is going to be okay." She stroked the horse's head, her heart in her throat. She didn't hear Dean enter the stall but he was suddenly there beside her.

They had moved Duchess into the foaling

stall to give her more room and to reduce her anxiety. She had been unusually aggressive with the other horses earlier this morning when Sawyer had turned her out. For her safety, they had decided to keep her inside until they heard from Rebecca regarding the blood tests.

Duchess had lost so much weight over the last few weeks, Faith could count her ribs, which were rising and falling at an alarming rate. Duchess let out a cry Faith had only heard one other time, when they'd lost Winston's mother a few years ago. The hair on her arms stood on end.

"Don't give up, Duch. Come on, I need you to hang on until Rebecca gets here." The tears streamed down Faith's face as all the cracks in her heart that had begun to heal broke wide open.

Faith felt Dean's hand on her back as she bent over to press her wet cheek against the dying horse. "Maybe it would be best to tell her it's okay to go," he said softly.

Closing her eyes, Faith searched inside herself for the courage to do what was right and not what would be easiest, not that any of this was easy. She ran her hand down Duchess's once strong and steady back.

"I love you, Duch. You are a good girl. Such a good girl." Faith's voice broke, but she carried on. "I don't want you to suffer. You can let go, sweet girl. Let go."

Duchess's rapid breathing began to slow. Faith kept stroking her neck and whispering her love for the beautiful and brave horse Duchess was. Faith lost all track of time. It felt like seconds but was probably much longer. Duchess began to take fewer and fewer breaths until she took her last.

CHAPTER FIFTEEN

WATCHING FAITH SAY goodbye to Duchess had been the second most gut-wrenching experience of Dean's life. If he could have taken her pain away, he would have done it. Instead all he could do was offer comfort and his condolences.

Sawyer joined them in the stall after calling the vet, who couldn't have arrived in time. With tears in his eyes, Sawyer pulled his sister off Duchess and into his arms where she let out the most heartbreaking wail. There had been so much loss in this family, Dean didn't know how they managed it.

Feeling like an intruder on a private moment, Dean got up and left Sawyer and Faith to mourn. He brought the rest of the feed in and was the first one to greet the horse vet when she arrived. He waited on the Strattons' front porch while they spoke to Rebecca.

"Thanks for your help," Sawyer said when

he finally emerged from the barn. "I'm sorry you had to be here for this."

"Don't be sorry. I'm glad I could be of some help. How's Faith?"

Sawyer shook his head. Not good, would be Dean's guess. It took all of his self-control not to go back into the barn and take her in his arms and hold her until she stopped crying.

"Duchess was Dad's first therapy horse," Sawyer explained. "She was Faith's baby. This one is going to sting for a long time."

"What can I do to help?" Dean needed to feel useful or the sadness would become too overwhelming and he'd have to leave.

"I need to dig a hole," Sawyer answered. "I also need to figure out how I'm going to move her body."

"We'll figure it out," Dean assured him. Whatever he had to do, he'd do.

Faith and the vet came out of the barn together. The sight of her caused him to lose all control. Her pain was suddenly his. The only thing that would make him feel better was helping her and easing her burden.

Dean didn't care if it was awkward or their relationship was messy; he took Faith into his arms. She began to sob and fresh tears wet his shirt. He didn't let her go until she was finished.

It took the majority of the day to bury Duchess. Dean and Sawyer were sweating up a storm, but they had managed to borrow a neighbor's backhoe to dig a hole big enough and cover her back up. When it was finished, Faith joined them for a final goodbye.

Harriet came over and unsurprisingly brought flowers with her. Her presence seemed to calm Faith more than anything else had all day. Sawyer led the four of them in a prayer and Faith was the last one to leave the gravesite.

The others were walking back to the house when a car pulled up. Sawyer didn't recognize it, and neither did Harriet. A woman got out and spotted them in the distance. She waved and waited for them to get to her.

"Hi, I'm Molly Medina from NETA." She extended a hand to Sawyer who shook it with confusion creasing his face. "I have had a crazy day and I know we had you guys scheduled for Saturday, but my college roommate is coming in from out of town and we were going to drive up to Nashville, so I was hoping we could do this today. I should have called, but I figured, what's a couple days? No biggie, right?"

Dean and Sawyer exchanged a look. Which one of them would enlighten her about a crazy day? Sawyer took a swing at it. "Actually, today isn't really going to work for us."

Dean glanced back at Faith who wasn't close enough to hear what this woman was doing there yet. The last thing Faith needed today was to have the farm put under a microscope.

"I just drove an hour to get here," she said, digging around in her bag for her phone. Ms. Medina had tightly curled hair that sat on her head like a helmet. She wore dark lipstick and ran her tongue over her coffee-stained teeth. "I can be in and out in a couple hours. Otherwise, we'll have to reschedule and I don't know when I could do it. It could delay things months." She scrolled through her phone's calendar. "Maybe all summer. Wouldn't you rather get it done?"

"You have to understand," Sawyer began, but Faith interrupted him.

"I've got this, Sawyer," she said, coming up beside her brother.

Dean wished he had led her into the house. Faith was too much of a pushover. If she heard that the visit could be delayed months, she'd give in and let this woman collect her information today.

"Faith, we don't have to," Sawyer said.

"Won't it be nice to have a stress-free weekend?" Ms. Medina chimed in.

"You're from NETA?" Faith asked for clarification.

Ms. Medina nodded and her hair jiggled like a Jell-O mold on her head. "Molly Medina. You are?"

"I am very sorry you drove all the way here without giving us the courtesy of a phone call, but we will not be participating in the walk-through today. We lost a horse this afternoon. Your appointment is scheduled for Saturday. We'll see you then or I'll be sure to call NETA headquarters and let them know you couldn't make our appointment and request they send another evaluator. Good day, Ms. Medina."

Without waiting for a reply, Faith turned and walked toward the house with Harriet right behind her wearing the proudest grin. Dean and Sawyer made eye contact. It was clear that Sawyer was as shocked as Dean. Faith had found her backbone and it was stronger than steel.

"Have a great day," Dean said, following the ladies into the house.

"Drive safe," Sawyer added, jogging a couple steps to catch up to Dean and leaving Ms. Medina with her jaw on the ground.

FAITH SHOULD HAVE been freaking out. By dismissing the NETA evaluator, she could have created an enemy she didn't want. But Faith didn't let those things get her down. She was actually proud of herself for finally telling someone no.

"Did you hear yourself out there?" Harriet asked when they were safely inside the house. "That was pretty amazing."

The boys were right behind them. Faith worried Sawyer might have been mad at her for choosing this moment to take a stand, but he had the same look on his face that Harriet did.

"Wow, where has this you been all my life?" he asked.

"Did she say anything after I walked away?" She said a silent prayer that the woman hadn't threatened to fail Helping Hooves because of her behavior.

"She didn't say a thing. You pretty much put her in her self-centered, inconsiderate place. I'm proud of you." Sawyer gave her a hug.

"What if I just ruined everything by being rude?" The worry crept in.

"You didn't. She was wrong to assume she could come here unannounced. And by her expression when you said you'd call NETA to reschedule, I think she's not going to mess with us," Sawyer reassured her.

Faith glanced at Dean for his reaction. "What do you think?"

He seemed stunned she was asking. "I think you handled yourself perfectly. You were assertive, not rude. It was awesome. Anyone trying to get you to do something you don't want to do better watch out. The Faith who tells everyone yes might have been replaced with the Faith who isn't afraid to say 'no, and go jump in the lake.'"

She smiled for the first time all day. It felt good. Harriet offered to make some tea and headed to the kitchen to put on a pot. Tea sounded good. Faith's throat felt a little raw from all the crying she'd done earlier.

Her chest ached. Poor Duchess. Faith couldn't imagine what it was going to be like to walk into the barn later and not have Duchess there to say good-night to.

She couldn't dwell on things that hadn't happened yet. She needed to stay in the present if she was going to get through this. She encouraged Dean to come with her to have some tea. She promised cookies, as well.

"Thank you for your help today," Faith said, taking out the small stash of cookies she had from last Friday and placing them on the table. "I don't know what Sawyer and I would have done without you."

"I didn't do nearly as much as I wish I could have. I'm so sorry about Duchess."

"She had a good life. I know that's what I need to focus on. She wasn't like Dad and Addison, taken too soon. She lived a long, happy life."

"That's a good way to look at it, sweetheart," Harriet said as she pulled some mugs from the cupboard.

Faith had some tea then made calls to all the volunteers to let them know Duchess had passed. Lily was the hardest hit. Josie's daughter had a way with the horses. She planned to go to school to become a large-animal vet. Faith promised to take her out to the grave the next time she volunteered.

Once she finished all her calls, she went outside to see if Sawyer needed help before she made them dinner. Even after everything that had happened today, Dean was still there, working on the paddock fencing. A light sheen of sweat covered his skin. The muscles in his arms flexed as he lifted one of the railings.

Faith's focus since graduating high school had always been on Helping Hooves. She'd been so single-minded that there was no time for romance. She'd dated, but in truth, she was no different than Sawyer, putting everything else ahead of connecting with another person.

Watching Dean, she couldn't help but be affected by the way his body moved. Her attraction unsettled her because the last person she needed to want a connection with was him. But when she thought about how it felt to be in his arms and to have him comfort her in her time of need, the desire for that connection only grew. It scared her because it felt as reckless as getting into Aaron Evans's car.

"Everything okay?" he asked when he noticed her staring.

She folded her arms across her chest like a shield, as if that could guard her from his bulging biceps. "Just checking to see if you guys need anything. Sawyer could put me to work."

Dean nodded toward the horse barn. "He's in there cleaning up the stall. Why don't you stay out here with me?"

"Can I help you?"

"No, just keep me company," he said, giving her one of those grins that her shield was defenseless against.

"I'm stronger than I look."

He stopped what he was doing and said, "You're stronger than everyone I know."

The compliment made her blush. It meant something that he didn't think she was fragile because she'd broken down earlier. Being sad was part of the process, she had to remind herself.

"I haven't been to a funeral since Addison's," he said, setting the railing down and moving closer to her. "I didn't even think about it until Duchess's was over."

"I wish it had been my first since then."

Six months had gone by in the blink of an eye. Faith still missed her dad every day and nothing had been harder than burying him. His funeral had been even more traumatic than Addison's. He had been Faith's rock through all the difficult times in her life.

He was her constant, the one she could rely on not to leave her. The thought of facing all the challenges life was sure to bring without him was unbearable.

Dean leaned against the corner post of the paddock fence. "I should have come home when my mom told me about your dad. I could have at least paid my respects."

"Another thing to add to the list of should-haves, huh?"

He took off his work gloves and wiped his forehead. "Seems so. Your dad always treated me well. He always made me feel welcome, which surprises me now that I know he knew about us."

"Knew about us? Knew what about us? He didn't—"

Dean nodded. "He called my parents about it. Told them he'd spied us making out."

Faith covered her face with her hands. How mortifying. Thank goodness he'd never admitted to knowing anything when he was alive.

"Guess we weren't as good at sneaking around as we thought," he said.

"Not much got past my dad on his farm," Faith said, dropping her hands. "I'm not as surprised as I am embarrassed that he saw us. I hope all he witnessed was innocent kissing."

Sawyer slid open the doors on the side of the horse barn. He pushed out a wheelbarrow filled with dirty straw. The ache in Faith's chest flared back up. Knowing her dad was up in heaven with his arms around Duchess's neck and that Sawyer was here for her was a bit of comfort.

Her brother didn't realize what an asset he was to Helping Hooves. He was loved by all the kids who came there and he worked harder than any volunteer ever would. She didn't tell him enough how much she appreciated him.

"Do you want me to help you two with the fence? Or should I make dinner?" she asked him as he walked by.

"Looks like you're helping Dean take a break. Anything would be better than that."

"My fault. I told her to hang out and keep me company while you did all the work," Dean said, putting his gloves back on.

Sawyer was breathing heavily from the exertion. "That wasn't part of our deal, Music Man."

Faith glanced back and forth between Dean and Sawyer. "What deal?"

Sawyer set the wheelbarrow down and wore the same guilty expression as a kid caught with his hand in the cookie jar. "There's no deal. I was joking."

More like lying, but now wasn't the time to confront him. Curiosity got the best of her when Dean was quick to return to the fence railing, though. What deal would Sawyer have made with Dean? Why would it include Dean helping on the farm?

"What's going on with you two?" She put her foot on the piece of wood Dean bent to pick up.

"Your brother seemed to know a bit about our relationship when he came to talk to me today. I got the feeling that, unlike your dad, he only recently learned we used to kiss in the hay stall."

"We talked about it last night." Faith didn't want to talk about how they used to kiss. His answer only created more questions. "That doesn't help me understand. Why are you here and why are you fixing our fence?"

"He asked me to help get things ready for that lady who showed up today."

"In exchange for what?"

"You should talk to your brother, Faith.

Can I fix the railing now so when Ms. Medina comes back, we're ready?"

Faith took her foot off the wood and watched Sawyer out in the far field where they usually dumped the dirty horse bedding. They had talked last night. He wasn't going to leave. But the knot in her stomach told her that whatever deal Sawyer and Dean had made, it wasn't good. She'd had enough bad news for today; confronting Sawyer would have to wait.

CHAPTER SIXTEEN

"HOW MANY HITS?" Dean asked.

Landon had texted several times while Dean was working at Helping Hooves Friday morning. The last one warranted a return phone call.

"Over 15,000. In one day. How did you do that?"

Dean had shared Sawyer's video on his own accounts and nudged a couple Nashville radio stations to share it, as well. He was hoping for a positive result. Fifteen thousand hits was exactly the response he was looking for.

"He's singing tonight. I'll shoot some of the show and we'll upload those before night's end. How many of the views turned into subscribers?"

"A couple hundred," Landon said. "He's good. He's got the right look. But I'm not convinced you don't have a lot of work to put into him before he's going to sell a million records for this company, Dean."

"I'm willing to put the work into the ones I think are going to pay off. We found Piper when she was nobody. She had less than a hundred subscribers, most of whom were girls she went to school with. The right artist just needs a little help. Trust me, Landon."

"There have to be more sure things out there. People who have been putting their time in. I'm not sure I want to risk it all on a complete unknown."

This was the battle they had been fighting since even before Dean had found Sawyer. What Landon didn't understand was that there were no guarantees in the music business. How many winners of those television singing competitions garnered millions of votes every week but only sold a handful of records? More than those who became chart-toppers.

To make it, you had to have something that no one could label. Something that drew people in and didn't let go. Sawyer had it. Even when he wasn't singing, he had it. People wanted to be around him.

"When I get him to come to Nashville, we'll set some shows up," Dean said, checking over his shoulder to make sure Faith was nowhere to be seen. He didn't want to answer any more questions about what they were up to. "You'll see. You just better hope that no other record companies take an interest while he's trying to prove himself to you. I don't want to lose this one because you were afraid to take a risk."

"I don't want to sink a lot of money we don't have into another lost cause," Landon shot back.

Boone was an obvious thorn in Landon's side. Sawyer wasn't going to cause the same trouble. Not if Dean had anything to say about it.

Hanging up, he headed back into the arena where Sawyer was putting the finishing touches on the mounting ramp. They had been working nonstop all morning to get things in tip-top shape. Faith had a checklist and they were knocking the items off one by one.

Sawyer's head popped up from the other side of the ramp. "Everything good?"

"Things are real good." Dean did a quick check for Faith. Satisfied they were alone, he continued. "I need you to sing a cover tonight of something big right now. Something close to your style but popular across the board. We'll post that and see what happens."

"I'm not sure I like having to overthink things when I play. I want it to come off natural, not like I'm trying to perform a certain way."

"That's the key to show business—making it look like it's easy and effortless. You got to learn to fake it so you can play what you want someday."

Sawyer was quiet while they finished their work. There seemed to be a lot going on in his head today. Dean wasn't sure if it was losing Duchess, the secret he was keeping from Faith or the choice he had made. Maybe it was something completely different, but Sawyer was definitely distracted.

Dean decided the kid might need someone to confide in. "Did you and Faith have a conversation last night about what you're doing?"

"No, she didn't ask me anything, which sort of surprises me. I thought for sure she'd be all over me about what you were getting out of this arrangement." He set down his hammer. "But she went to bed pretty early. That's also not like her. Can't tell if it was because of Duchess or something else."

"Maybe it was because she's got that new backbone. She decided to take care of herself and get some sleep," Dean suggested.

Sawyer found that comment funny, at least. Some of the tension seemed to ease.

A moment later Faith and her clipboard came flying in to give the mounting ramp a good once-over. She consulted her clipboard. "Did you double-check the measurements?"

"Check," Sawyer replied. This was the way they had communicated all day. She asked if something was done and he replied with either a "check" or a "not yet."

"When will you be ready to do a run-through?"

"After we clean up here."

Faith gave a stiff nod and was back on the move. She was a ball of nerves and Dean felt it was best to be quiet and stay out of her way. He did as he was told and tried to get everything done.

"She's intense today."

Sawyer's eyes widened as if to say, "I know."

"I hope you guys pass the test."

"Me, too," Sawyer said. "She needs this more than she needs me."

IT HAD BEEN A long day and it wasn't over yet. Sawyer made Faith promise she wasn't going to spend the whole night fretting about the

NETA visit tomorrow. He expected to see her at the Sundown, and if she had a drink to relax, he'd be really impressed. She wasn't allowed to use her new superpower. She couldn't tell him no.

"The Sundown?" Kylie asked. "I didn't know we were going to have dinner at the Sundown."

Faith had decided she was holding an intervention. It was about time Lily and Kylie cleared the air once and for all. She might have had to trick Kylie to make it happen, but desperate times called for desperate measures.

"I need to drop off cookies for Ms. Josie. Can you help me carry them in?"

Kylie reluctantly got out of the car and walked to the back to pick up some of the containers Faith had in the trunk. Faith made sure Kylie's pile was tall enough that she wouldn't be able to bolt when she saw Lily inside the bar and grill.

Josie greeted them on their way in. She was in charge of getting Lily there. She had better have done her part.

"Yay! Cookies are here. What's on the menu tonight?"

"Margarita cookies. They've got that salty-sweet tequila glaze on them." Faith handed her two of the containers. She mouthed, *Is she here?*

Josie pointed to the booth in the far corner. The back of Lily's blond head could be seen over the seat.

"Let's bring the rest of them over here, Kylie." Faith guided the teenager to the table where Lily was unknowingly waiting for them. She had Kylie set the cookies on the table beside the booth.

"Faith?" Lily said, setting down her phone.

"Hey, look who's here! Can we join you? We're here for dinner. Awesome," she said without waiting for an answer. She gave Kylie a gentle but firm nudge and made her sit down across from Lily. Faith sat next to her so she couldn't run away.

Lily frowned. "You guys were going out to dinner without me?"

Faith folded her hands on the table. "No, we planned to meet you."

"We did?" Kylie asked.

"Well, I did. I decided it's time you two sit down and figure out what's wrong and make it right. So, I tricked you into coming here by telling you I wanted to talk to you about volunteering more and I had your mom tell you she needed you to help out here tonight."

"My mom didn't say she needed help." Lily scowled at her mother as Josie came by to pick up the cookies. "She told me I was grounded because I missed one night of volunteering this week. She is the meanest mom in the world."

"Don't forget it," Josie said with a smile. "I plan to put that as a tagline on my business cards. And you're not grounded unless you refuse to talk this out with Kylie."

Faith thanked her for helping out then turned her attention to the girls. "Okay, let me start by telling you guys something. I had a best friend my whole life. We were as different as different could be, but we both loved Johnny Depp movies and chocolate-covered raisins."

"Ew," both girls said at the same time.

Faith tried not to be offended by the fact that they were grossed out by something she found absolutely delicious. At least they were finding common ground. That was good.

"We liked the same music and no one made me laugh harder than Addison. But we let stupid things get between us. Things we chose not to talk about. Things that I'll never get to talk with her about because she died."

Lily played with the napkin on the table in front of her, tearing it into little pieces. Kylie bit her lip.

"What is going on with you two? When you started helping out at the farm, you two were the best of friends. In fact, you reminded me of me and Addison. You supported one another and I think you still care about each other. What happened?"

"Nothing," Kylie said, folding her arms across her chest. "She stopped being my friend."

"*I* stopped being *your* friend? You're the one who stopped liking my statuses and wouldn't like any of my photos even when I tagged you."

"I stopped because why did it matter if I liked your stuff, you didn't act like I existed when we were at school. The only person you care about is Jonah."

"Shh!" Lily glanced around to make sure her mom wasn't in hearing distance. "Please don't say his name when we're around my mom."

"I told you that it hurt my feelings that you seemed to choose him over me. You said you wouldn't do that anymore, but you did," Kylie accused her.

Faith let the two of them hash things out. The hurt feelings, the lies, the secrets. They told each other how much they meant to one another. In the end, the two girls were crying and holding hands and promising to do better, to be better friends to each other.

"There's one more thing you two need to talk about. If I could go back in time, I never would have let a secret ruin everything. I would have told Addison that I could love her as my best friend and love—" Dean's name almost popped out, but since they had both met him, she thought better of it "—the boy, too. Had I been honest and open about my feelings from the start, things could have been so different."

Lily turned all the way around this time to make sure her mom wasn't close. Kylie sighed loudly. "This is what really bugs me. I hate lying to your mom and keeping secrets. Just tell her so we can all hang out together."

"I hate keeping secrets from your mom, too," Faith added. "If the relationship has to be secret to be special, then the relationship isn't special."

How she wished she could go back in time

and tell her teenage self the same thing. She knew what it was like to be caught up in the excitement of having something that was forbidden. Unfortunately when the veil was lifted, it turned out to be nothing.

"She hates him for some reason," Lily complained. "I don't even know why."

"Maybe she wouldn't if you didn't sneak around with him. Maybe she'd like him if he came to the door and said hello when she answered it. Invite him to dinner. Give your mom a chance," Faith pleaded.

"My mom is not cool like you. She doesn't understand."

"Your mom is way cooler than me and she has been in love before, so she understands completely. Give her a break."

"Fine, but you have to be there when I tell her so she doesn't kill me."

Faith would do anything for this to be over. She hoped Josie would be as cool as she'd hyped her to be. "Deal."

Dean showed up at the Sundown fifteen minutes before Sawyer was scheduled to sing. Faith and the girls had talked to Josie. Jonah and Lily were outed as a couple and Josie took it better than Lily thought she would and a little worse than Faith had hoped. With

Josie's blessing, the girls had called Jonah and told him to find a friend and meet them at the movie theater. Lily had admitted to being excited for their first date out in the open.

Faith's ex-secret boyfriend took the seat next to her at the bar. It was the same spot he had occupied one week ago when he had walked back into her life. Had it really only been one week? It seemed like a lot longer.

"What's the cookie and drink special?" he asked, resting his elbows on the old mahogany bar.

"Margaritas." Sawyer tossed a drink napkin down in front of him.

"I'll take the cookies but pass on the drink. Beer for me instead."

Josie slipped behind the bar and snatched some pretzels from the bowl near Faith. "So, Mr. Presley, how much would it cost to bribe you to go down to the movie theater and spy on my daughter and a boy she's been lying about seeing for the last month?"

"You are not sending him to spy on her," Faith said, stealing a pretzel from her. "She came clean, now you have to trust her."

"I wouldn't trust Dean anyway, Josie." Sawyer placed an opened beer bottle in front of Dean. "He probably empathizes with the kids given his history of lying about the same thing."

Dean grimaced at Sawyer before taking a swig.

"Don't hate the liar, hate the lie," Faith said.

"Thank you." Dean tipped his drink in her direction. His eyes were emerald in the dim light of the bar.

The fluttering in Faith's stomach was back. She grabbed some more pretzels to try to settle it.

"You ready to play tonight?" Dean asked Sawyer. The two of them talked about his set and what he was going to sing first. Josie added her two cents. The four of them laughed and it felt so…normal.

It was strange how easily Dean fit. He was the piece of the puzzle that had been missing for so long that people forgot about it until they found it and realized it made the whole picture complete.

Faith had to remind herself that he wasn't sticking around and to not get attached. He was the missing piece that didn't want to be a part of this particular puzzle.

Sawyer went to go set up and Dean excused himself to sit closer to the stage. His interest in Sawyer's performance created more unease. The two of them had struck a deal. Faith still didn't know what it was; she'd been too afraid to ask.

"I think you should give me your blessing to play Sugar Mama to that man," Josie said, staring in Dean's direction.

"You don't want to be someone's sugar mama."

"That's true. I want to be the younger one in the relationship. Not to mention, he's too pretty. I need to be the prettiest one in a relationship, too. But he's so dreamy. I've been in love with him for a whole week."

Faith had been in love with him for practically her whole life. He had been her ideal for as long as she could remember. It wasn't surprising that other people felt the same way.

Dean had his phone pointed at Sawyer. When he started to sing, Dean recorded the whole thing. Faith watched him take video after video. The pit in her stomach grew bigger.

Why did it seem like every time she fixed one problem, a new one would pop up?

CHAPTER SEVENTEEN

SAWYER WANTED DEAN at the farm at the crack of dawn. On a *Saturday*. Dean didn't do anything this early in the morning on the weekends. It was unnatural.

"Pep up, look alive!" Sawyer snapped his fingers in front of Dean's face. He hadn't gotten enough sleep last night. Not because of wild dreams or not enough blankets but because he had spent the late-night hours uploading videos and photos to Sawyer's social media accounts.

They had a couple hours before the NETA evaluator might arrive. Faith had called and clarified after the disaster with the first woman. Like the cable company, they were given a window of time to expect someone to show up on their doorstep.

"Let's walk the facilities one more time to make sure we know everything is working and meets the requirements," Sawyer said, holding Faith's clipboard.

"Where is your sister this morning?"

"In the arena with the horses." Besides checking all the records on the animals, they needed to prove that all the therapy horses could follow a list of commands.

They started in the parking lot and moved to the horse barn. From there they went to the arena. Faith was riding Sassy, who was being stubborn about getting close to the new and improved mounting ramp.

"I don't know what's spooking her, but she won't get close," Faith said, backing the horse up to try again.

Sawyer checked the ramp and couldn't find anything that would cause the horse to disobey. He called Sassy over and she lined up fine. Faith didn't look relieved. The stress took all the color from her cheeks. Her lips fell in a straight line, refusing to curl up even when Dean tried his best to be funny.

"The horse can probably sense your stress. You need to relax," Dean suggested.

"Easy for you to say. This isn't your life's work on the line. Today doesn't decide if your company will continue to thrive or be shut down."

In some ways, it did. Sawyer wouldn't pursue music until he knew that Helping Hooves had the advantage of being a NETA facility. Grace Note Records had a very real stake in what happened here today.

Dean and Sawyer were on their way to check on the fencing they had put in yesterday when a white SUV with Alabama plates pulled in. This time, a man stepped out of the car and apologized for being early, offering to wait in his car until it was time for their appointment.

Sawyer didn't have the patience to wait any longer. He gave the NETA evaluator the green light to get started. Dean waited on the front porch for what felt like hours. It was no wonder that many of the farms and ranches that applied for this accreditation didn't receive it. There were just so many hoops to jump through.

Both Faith and Sawyer walked the man back to his car when he was finished. They shook hands and exchanged goodbyes. Dean could see the weight had lifted off Sawyer but a new one had planted itself on Faith.

"So, what did he have to say? Did you pass?"

Sawyer's expression went from apathetic to ecstatic. "We passed!"

Dean stood up and high-fived him. "Why aren't you two jumping for joy right now?"

"He said based on what he saw today, we most likely passed. They have to go over some of the staffing information and he had to score the horse assessments," Faith clarified. "Sassy was still stubborn during her evaluation."

"It's going to be fine," Sawyer said. "We had everything we were supposed to have and in the condition it needed to be in. We did good. Sassy was having an off day. Her mom died yesterday. I think she deserves an off day."

Faith wouldn't hear it and went inside to fret.

"I would have thought she'd be relieved," Dean said to Sawyer when they were alone.

"I thought so, too. Maybe she's worried about what passing means." It could mean a possible career change for Sawyer. "I am going to go put the horses out to pasture. Can you check on her for me before you go?"

Dean went inside and found Faith in the kitchen. She had that hot-pink apron on again.

"Whatcha making?"

Faith screamed and dropped the bag of

flour she had just taken out of the cabinet. Flour exploded into a dusty cloud.

"Why do you have to be so quiet when you're in my house?"

He apologized profusely while helping her clean it up. "At least flour is better than mud, right?" He wiped some flour onto her nose.

"I'm making a rule that you have to whistle when you walk into a room. I need some sort of warning system."

They both laughed. Hearing her do something other than worry was nice. He felt good about that even when she purposely left a floury handprint on the back of his shirt.

She was so beautiful when she smiled. Her eyes lit up and her cheeks pinked. He wanted to do something to keep that look on her face.

"There's the smile I was expecting to see when you found out you passed. Helping Hooves is going to be accredited and things are going to be easier, you'll see."

Her gaze fell to the floor. "I sure hope so. I need things to be easier so badly."

Dean grabbed her hand and was surprised by how much he wanted to pull her close. "Is that little place in Collinsville still open? You know, the one we went to because we thought no one would recognize us?"

"The Filmont?" Faith's brow furrowed and he fought the urge to reach up and smooth it out. "I think so. I can't remember the last time I ate there."

"We should go. Tonight. Do something to celebrate this all being over. You passed, Faith. Be happy."

She leaned back against the counter, creating some space between them. It made Dean want to move closer even though he knew he shouldn't.

"I don't know," she said. "Sawyer's going bowling with some friends tonight. Maybe tomorrow?"

He hadn't realized the invitation had come out like he wanted to have a family dinner. "I didn't mean all of us. I meant me and you."

"Oh." Faith blinked a few times like she needed to let it sink in. "Me and you on a date at the Filmont?"

"Not a date. A celebration dinner. As friends."

She frowned. "We're friends?"

"Aren't we?" There wasn't any other title that would work. Thanks to the mistakes made in the past, they couldn't be more than that. But friends was better than the strangers they had allowed themselves to become.

"We are," she replied softly. The frown remained. "What time are you picking me up?"

"THE FILMONT IS where people go on their anniversary or to get engaged," Faith said to Sawyer as she pinned her hair back so it was out of her face.

Sawyer sat on her bed, eating a bowl of cereal, his third and, supposedly, his dinner. The man would live off of cereal and ramen noodles if he ever moved out and lived alone. Like the dog on the floor, he looked completely disinterested in what she was saying, but had come upstairs when she'd called because he was a good brother.

"I'm overthinking this, aren't I?"

"You're absolutely overthinking it," he replied. "Do you have a problem with me and some of the guys coming back here after we bowl to have a bonfire? We might be up late. I'm celebrating."

Faith wanted to be more excited about what Mr. Camden had said at the end of their walkthrough. There was no reason they shouldn't get NETA's seal of approval after everything was checked and double-checked. But instead of being relieved, she felt this terrible sense of foreboding. Like with the good could only come bad.

"I don't care what you guys do as long as you don't make so much noise I can't sleep."

"Cool. I'll try to keep them under control, but you know Daryl. I swear that man has two volumes—loud and loud enough to wake the dead."

Faith was glad to hear Sawyer had plans to hang out with friends. Sometimes he worked so much he didn't make time for himself. And if Sawyer could go out with friends, so could Faith. Dean could be her friend.

"Am I too dressed up?" Faith checked herself in the full-length mirror that hung on the back of the door. She had chosen a dress but was rethinking that decision. Maybe dress said "date" and pants said "dinner with a friend."

"You look fine." He drank the milk from his cereal bowl and set it on her nightstand. Sprawling out on her bed, he folded his hands behind his head.

"Don't get comfortable in my bed," she warned. "And please do not leave that dirty bowl in here. I am not your maid."

"Well, I am not your girlfriend. I suggest you call Josie if you want real fashion advice.

I'm not really good at picking out outfits and trying to figure out why guys choose one restaurant over another. Although, as a guy, I can tell you we usually pick places to eat based on the food. We aren't thinking about anniversaries and engagements. We're thinking about filling the hole in our bellies."

"Good to know." Faith laughed and realized she wasn't as tense as she had been a few minutes ago. Sawyer was right—the things that women thought about were not the same as what men thought about. Men focused on their basic needs while women made a big deal out of everything.

Dean wanted to go out to dinner. He'd invited a friend who deserved a good meal. The Filmont had amazing food. It was as simple as that. She ignored the butterflies in her stomach and the way her blood was rushing through her veins when she thought about being alone with Dean all night.

It was going to be an interesting dinner.

COLLINSVILLE WAS TEN MILES south of Grass Lake. It was the next town over and had a rival high school. When Faith was young and her dad got bored of eating at the same old restaurants in Grass Lake, they would make the drive to Collinsville.

When Dean and Faith had been dating, Dean had made reservations at the Filmont for a romantic getaway that didn't go exactly as planned.

"I'll never forget pulling up and having no clue how to use the valet. I turned the car off and took the keys—I didn't know any better. Not sure how I thought the guy was going to park it without the keys," Dean said as they drove in his rental car, which, they'd speculated, might have belonged to Kim Hanson, a girl they went to high school with, when she was actually in high school.

"That was a little embarrassing. But you played it cool. I remember watching you drop the keys in the guy's hand like you meant to do that. Of course, you could do no wrong in my eyes back then."

"But now it's a different story, huh?" he asked, glancing at her before returning his eyes to the road.

"Only because I'm not a naïve little girl anymore." The rose-colored glasses Faith had viewed the world in had broken when Addison died.

Collinsville and the Filmont were on the

other side of the lake from the town that shared its name. By boat, someone could get there in a matter of minutes, but by car it took a good twenty. From the outside the Filmont looked more like a cottage in the woods than a restaurant. It had a fairy-tale appeal to it, which was why it was so popular with couples.

Dean pulled up to the valet and left the keys in the ignition this time. He offered his arm as they followed the flagstone path to the entrance. Inside, the hostess greeted them.

"Celebrating anything special tonight?" she asked as she guided them to their table.

"We are, actually."

"Oh, good. Birthday? Anniversary?"

Faith quickly let go of Dean's arm. She didn't want anyone to get the wrong idea.

Dean took it all in stride. "My friend here owns a horse farm that passed a big test today."

His friend. That was going to take some getting used to.

Dean pulled Faith's chair out and his chivalry was unnerving. He stirred up all these old feelings, and it wasn't very fair. This wasn't the same as before. She had to remind herself of that throughout dinner.

They ate. They chatted. Dean made her laugh and was his charming self, which made putting her feelings for him to rest more difficult. When the waiter came to clear the dinner plates, he asked about dessert.

"I hear you're celebrating a big accomplishment. Can I bring you or your lovely wife… girlfriend…" He was fishing.

"Friend," Faith said before Dean had to.

Properly chagrined, the waiter apologized. "Would you like to see the dessert menu?"

Dean took him up on the offer and ordered chocolate cake with two forks. When the waiter left, Dean leaned forward. "Why do you say 'friend' like it's a disease?"

"I didn't mean to. I just didn't want you to have to explain again. You already had to do it once. It's sad that more men and women can't be friends. That everyone assumes that if a man and a woman are together they must be together in every sense of the word."

"Right? Maybe it's because we're so good-looking. No one would believe we could resist each other. I mean, look at me, I'm pretty much as good as it gets."

Try as she might, Faith couldn't keep from laughing. Tears leaked from the corners of her eyes.

"Are you trying to tell me I'm not devilishly handsome? I'll have you know I'm wearing my dad's shirt right now, and Ted Presley wears clothes that lead to women throwing money at him. Never mind that he works at the bank. He swears it's the shirt."

Faith dabbed her eyes with her napkin as other patrons began to stare. "Stop, please," she begged.

"I'm just saying." He threw his hand up. "You're beyond beautiful. Always have been."

His compliment quickly put an end to her laughter. Faith didn't want to hear that he thought that way about her. The chocolate cake came, followed by the bill. Faith excused herself to go to the ladies' room after fighting to pay for her half of dinner and losing. Behind the closed door, she checked her reflection in the gold-framed mirror above the sink.

Her cheeks were flushed. Maybe it was from the laughing fit, but most of it was probably due to his words. Beautiful wasn't how she saw herself. She had a narrow face like her mom. Her eyes were boring brown, not at all like Sawyer's. His had soul, hers looked like mud. Hard work and physical labor on the farm meant she'd never had a manicure and there was always hay hiding somewhere.

"He was being nice. Trying to lighten the mood. Stop overthinking everything," she told herself. She washed her hands even though she hadn't used the restroom for anything other than a temporary hiding spot.

Dean was waiting for her by the front door. His dress shirt was a pale green. It worked with his eye color. His dad did have an impressive wardrobe.

"Want to take a walk down by the lake?" he asked as they stepped outside. The sun was setting and the clouds took on a pinkish-purple tint.

"Sure." Being outside, breathing in some fresh air, sounded like a great idea. Maybe it would clear her head.

They made their way down the gravel path that ran alongside the Filmont to the water's edge. They had a white gazebo in the back with paper lanterns hanging from the roof.

"I thought you'd be more excited about how things went today, but you still seem tense," Dean said, leading her down to the dock where the bugs were chirping and the frogs were beginning their nighttime lullabies.

"I'm happy. I just know there's still a lot to do. If we get more business, I might need to hire another therapist. I read that people have been using horses to help veterans with PTSD. It would be a great service to add. I'd need a social worker on staff, though."

Dean laughed through his nose. "You and I are so much alike it's scary."

"What's that supposed to mean?"

"We're always thinking about the company. What do we need to do next to stay relevant, to pay the bills, to survive?"

"Your record business seems to be doing pretty well. You've got Boone Williams on your label."

"Who hasn't been able to write one song since his last album three years ago and needs to go back to rehab."

Faith cringed. "I was hoping that was all tabloid nonsense."

"They unfortunately get it right sometimes," Dean said with a sigh.

"I'm lucky the only drama I have to deal with is between two teenage girls."

Dean rested his arms on the dock railing and gazed out over the water. The warm spring breeze created small waves that reflected the setting sun's fading light. The water looked like diamonds were floating on top of it.

"I heard you played social worker to Lily

and Kylie. Maybe you won't need to hire anyone else, after all."

"Ha!" Faith had no time to get another degree. One was enough. "Talking to them was like getting to redo what happened with us. I could relate with both of them—all three of them, really."

"Is that why you said 'hate the lie, not the liar' yesterday?" Dean asked, staring straight ahead.

Faith wrapped her arms around herself. "The lie is always the bad guy in the story. My brother would be proud of me for giving up a little of the blame. I might encourage him to look into getting his degree in social work. I think he'd do really great with injured vets."

"Sawyer?" Dean's head turned in her direction.

"Yes, Sawyer." Faith didn't think he should be so surprised. "He's honest, straightforward. What you see is what you get. It would save me the trouble of finding someone else. No Boones coming to work for me. I don't need that headache."

Dean got quiet, contemplative. Faith hadn't meant to remind him of his worries at work. "I'm sure the next big thing is just waiting to be discovered. When you go back to Nashville, they'll be waiting at your door."

He dipped his head and rested it on his hands for a second before righting himself. "I'm sure they will. We should go, huh?"

The walk to the car was silent, as was the drive home. Dean seemed stuck in his head. He had said they were alike, always thinking about work; maybe that was all it was. When he parked outside her house, it felt like they were about to share a much bigger goodbye than "see you tomorrow."

Faith played with the hem of her dress. "Thanks for taking me out and for everything you did to help us get this place ready. We couldn't have done it without you."

"Don't thank me, Faith," he said with a bite while staring a hole through his steering wheel.

She took that to mean it was time to go and pushed open her door. The sound seemed to snap him out of his stupor. He jumped out of the car and came around to her side, holding the door open for her.

He even walked her to the porch. She needed to fill the silence. "I forgot to ask when you're heading back to Nashville."

Shoulders slumped, Dean didn't make eye contact. "Soon," was all he said.

"Well, don't be a stranger. We're friends now, right?"

His green eyes lifted and she saw the sadness and regret in there. He didn't need to feel bad about going. They weren't meant to be, and they were on their way to mending their broken hearts for real this time.

"Friends," he whispered.

Faith didn't think, she just did what her heart told her to do. She reached up and ran her hand down the side of his face. The hair of his beard was softer than she'd expected it to feel. Stepping toward him, she lifted up on her toes and kissed him.

It was supposed to be a friendly good-bye kiss. A no-big-deal, if-I-don't-see-you-again-at-least-I'll-have-no-regrets kiss. It started that way, but she didn't pull back and he didn't step away. Instead her whole body tingled as her heart thumped wildly in her chest. She wrapped her arms around his neck and he pulled her closer by holding her around her waist.

Her fingers slid through the hair at the nape of his neck. It wasn't like the hungry, sloppy kisses they'd shared when she was eighteen.

Back then, they were driven by desire and puppy-dog love. This kiss was grown up, full of things they couldn't say.

When it finally came to an end on Faith's darkened doorstep, her breaths came fast, like she had been under water for the last twelve years and Dean had finally arrived to resuscitate her. He rested his forehead on hers and kept his eyes closed.

"I'm sorry," she said before slipping into the house, regretting nothing.

CHAPTER EIGHTEEN

ANGER. IT WAS THE only thing besides numb that Dean had felt since they'd heard the news five painfully long days ago. Addison was dead. Faith had told her the truth and it had sent his sister into a tailspin.

Why? Why did she tell? There was a reason they were hiding. Of course, Dean had assumed the worst that could happen was that Addison would make Faith break it off. She'd dig her little heels in and be a brat about it until Faith couldn't handle it anymore. Faith would surely choose Addison over him.

But that wasn't what happened. What happened was much worse.

He sat outside her house for thirty minutes before he rang the doorbell. The house was dark apart from the one flicker of light coming from Faith's bedroom window. She probably had candles lit.

She answered the door, wearing her pajamas. Pajamas that looked like she'd been in them all day long. Her hair was in a messy ponytail and her eyes were rimmed red.

"Are you alone?" They were the most words he had spoken to her since they'd heard about the accident.

"Yeah, come on in." She opened the door wider. He knew she was. Her brother had a baseball game and he'd seen her dad's truck parked in the lot near the diamond on his way over. "I was getting some water. Do you want something to drink?"

"I'm good."

"Good" was a relative term these days. "Good" basically meant he wasn't curled in a ball sobbing.

He followed her to the kitchen and purposely kept his distance. There was a tiny part of him that still wanted to take her in his arms and kiss her until this pain went away. But this pain would never go away because it was their fault Addison was dead.

Faith didn't bother to turn on the light. The two of them dwelled in the shadows. There was no light that could pull them out of their personal darkness, anyway. She opened the refrigerator and pulled out a can of soda but didn't bother to open it.

"I came to tell you I'm leaving."

"Where are you going?"

"Back to school. I can't stay here. I can't live in that house."

She nodded in understanding. Addison's ghost probably lingered around this house, as well. It was her home away from home.

"I'm not coming back, either."

Her gaze lifted. "Not for Thanksgiving? Christmas?"

Dean shook his head. "I'm never coming back."

"Oh," she whispered, staring back down at the can in her hands.

No tears. That was good. No pleading for him to stay. That was even better.

"Well, that was all I wanted to say." He started for the door.

"I'm going to miss you," she said, her voice thick with emotion. "I'm sorry."

There they were. The two words he was waiting for her to say. He felt every muscle in his body tense. He was a tightly wound wire and her apology caused him to finally snap.

"I don't want your sorry. I don't forgive you. I'll never forgive you." It only felt good to say it out loud for a moment, then he saw the look of complete devastation on her face. But he couldn't feel bad for her. He couldn't *care about her anymore. Not after what happened.*

Tears rolled down her cheeks. She set the can on the counter, unopened. "I never wanted any of this."

Addison was too possessive, too dependent on Faith. Dean had known that all along and still pursued her. He was so stupid. "I told you she would see this as you choosing me over her. She's such a…"

Addison wouldn't be anything ever again. Except for dead.

Was. *His sister was a brat. If she hadn't been the kid who had to have all the attention all the time, this never would have happened. Everything between them had always been some sort of competition in her mind. Heaven forbid their dad asked Dean how his day was before he asked her; that would mean he loved Dean more.*

Running off, hanging out with the wrong crowd, drinking—all of it was for attention. Plain and simple. Attention she wouldn't have thought she needed if Faith hadn't told her the truth.

"I tried to tell her it didn't have to change anything. I love her and I'm in love with you." Faith reached for him.

"Don't touch me," he spat.

Faith recoiled like his words were a flame capable of burning her. "I wish you wouldn't push me away. I need you. I love you and I know you love me, too."

"I don't want you," he said plainly. "You're stupid for loving me and even more stupid for thinking I could care about you after everything that's happened."

Faith covered her face with both hands as she dropped to her knees. The sounds coming out of her were enough to make Dean want to crawl out of his skin. Her shoulders shook as she unloaded all her pain at his feet.

Part of him wanted to make her stop. He wanted to hold her in his arms and tell her he was sorry. They'd both messed up. He loved her. He did love her. But his compassion was so deeply buried under all his anger, she would never know it even existed.

Without another word, Dean left the Stratton farm and Faith for good.

DEAN WOKE UP in his childhood bedroom with a thin sheen of sweat covering his body. The room was still dark and a quick glance at the clock told him it was still the middle of the night.

He felt like a thousand-pound weight sat on his chest. He was a horrible person. He wished that had only been a nightmare, but he knew it had been more than that. It was a memory like the others.

The way he had acted toward Faith, the things he had said, were uncalled for. He could blame the anger, but that was no excuse. He could say he was young and hot-headed. But all that mattered was that what he'd said was inexcusable.

Faith was an easy scapegoat. It had been better to blame her than to admit all of it really rested on his shoulders. He had initiated the relationship. He had asked that she keep it a secret. He had put off telling Addison. He had forced Faith into the uncomfortable position of lying every day while he got off scot-free because Addison didn't care what he was doing. She didn't quiz him about why he wasn't able to be somewhere or why he was acting different. Faith had carried the burden alone.

And when she'd needed him the most, he had abandoned her and left her thinking he didn't love her at all. The truth was he had hated himself, not her. Never her.

Worse yet, if things went as planned, he'd

be devastating her once again. This time, he'd be taking her brother with him. When she'd shared all her ideas and plans for Helping Hooves, Dean knew his ideas and plans for Grace Note were in direct opposition. Only one of them could have what they wanted.

Just like that night in his dream, she had apologized when it really should have been him sharing his regrets.

He sat up in bed. It was too late to call her, although he wanted to. But there was someone else he could apologize to who didn't sleep. *Or who's always asleep*, he thought. Getting out of bed, Dean knew what he had to do.

He was more than surprised to see a light under Addison's closed door. A shiver ran down his spine. It was like she knew he was coming. Pushing the door open, his heart raced. There were no ghosts behind the door, but Dean's mother sat on the bed.

"Are you okay?" He could see she had been crying and sat down next to her.

"I woke up from a dream and needed to come in here," she answered, wiping under her eyes. "I'm not usually this weepy. I think having you home has stirred up some old feelings."

"Dad said we were alike, and he's right. I've been having weird dreams since I got here, too."

Dean's mom put her arm around him. "I'm sorry, honey. It probably doesn't help that I haven't cleared out this room. I know it's time. I just…" She let out a sad sigh.

She found comfort in here. Dean didn't understand it, but he knew that was what it was. Like Faith had to go to the gravesite every week. They needed to be close to Addison somehow.

"Maybe we can work on it together, you and me. Seems like I need to open this door and you need to close it."

Marilee leaned against her son. Her hair looked more brown than gold in the dim light coming from the lamp on Addison's nightstand. "I'm so glad you're home. I miss not having any of my kids in this house."

"I've been hiding from this—this room, these memories," Dean said, waving his hand around the room. "But they're still here, waiting for me to deal with them. What do you say we start by taking all these pictures off the wall?"

He stood and offered a hand to his mom.

She took a deep breath and then his hand. "Sounds like a good place to begin."

Addison had taped hundreds of photos to her wall. Some were trimmed into smaller squares or rectangles. Others were cut into hearts and diamonds. Dean and his mom peeled each one off the wall and removed the tape, setting the photos on Addison's bed so they could eventually be stored in a photo box.

"Oh, my gosh, this one is hilarious," his mom said, holding up a photo of Addison and Faith when they were about four years old. Both of them were dressed up for Halloween— Faith as a princess and Addison as a dragon.

Their smiling little round faces could melt a grown man's heart. "She always found a way to get attention, didn't she?"

"Never wanted to be like everyone else," his mom said, setting it on the bed. "She truly wasn't like anyone else. She was special."

"Weird, special. I guess you can say they're both the same thing." Dean pulled off a picture of her and the cast of the high school's version of *Alice in Wonderland*. Addison was the Mad Hatter, of course.

Photo after photo came down. Young Addison and Faith jumping off a dock with their arms and legs spread wide so they looked like giant X's. Faith and Addison with way too much makeup on from the time they got themselves ready for their first junior high dance. Addison and Dean one Christmas morning sporting the sweaters their grandmother had hand-knitted them. The fake smiles on their faces had been the only things in that picture that were ever worn again.

Each picture carried with it a memory. Sometimes Dean shared that memory, sometimes not. Every one of them filled him with both sadness and joy. She'd had a beautiful life. It had been happy a life, full of both momentous and insignificant events, lots of firsts and lasts.

"I stopped staring at these when I'd come in here a few years ago," Marilee said, taking a minute to sift through the ones Dean had removed from his side of the room. "My goodness, Faith is in ninety percent of these."

"They were inseparable." There was a tug at Dean's heart. The two of them had known one another their entire lives. Looking at how many of Addison's memories included Faith, Dean realized how much Faith had lost that day. Addison may have been his sister, but she was more than that to Faith. What they'd had couldn't be labeled.

He peeled off one of the last pictures taken of the two of them. Graduation. Faith had bent down a bit so they were the same height. They were hugging cheek to cheek with the most picture-perfect smiles gracing their pretty faces.

The tightness in Dean's chest made it hard to breathe as the tears welled in his eyes and spilled over. He dropped to his knees, the emotion overwhelming him. He cried like he'd never cried before. All the feelings he had buried and covered up with anger and guilt came flowing out. None of it could be held back.

His mother held him and whispered words of comfort, but it felt like there would never be any relief from this hurt. He had loved both girls and lost them both that day. He still loved them. His heart ached and the tears didn't stop.

Until they did.

"She loved you so much," his mom assured him. "You were such a good big brother. She knew no matter what, you'd always be there for her."

"I wasn't, though. I wasn't there that night. I didn't protect her because I was selfish."

"Oh, honey. That's not true."

"She found out about me and Faith. She was mad. That's why she went to the lake and hung out with those people. She wouldn't have done that if I hadn't taken Faith away from her."

"Dean Francis Presley." His mother let him go and lifted his chin so he could see her. "Are you kidding me?"

He wasn't. That was what happened. He'd wanted Faith. He hadn't cared if it would cause trouble or if Addison would get jealous. He'd lied about it because he didn't want Faith to choose Addison over him. They were everything to one another; she would have picked his sister.

"Your sister and Aaron had been dating for months. She would have gone to that party at the lake whether Faith had been around that night or not."

Dean blinked and blinked again. "What? Addison wasn't dating Aaron Evans."

"Well, they were writing some pretty provocative notes back and forth for two people who weren't dating. I found them when I was cleaning her room and confronted her about what was going on."

"Addison and Aaron were dating? All summer?"

"She claimed they fell in love when she tutored him in math. I don't even think she told Faith. I've never talked to her about it."

"She didn't." There was no way Faith knew that and hadn't told Dean.

"We argued that she was too young to be so serious. Can you believe they were talking about getting married?" Her tone verged on hysterical. "Leave it to your sister to fall for the bad boy of Grass Lake."

Dean had a hard time accepting this new information. If what she was saying was true, it changed everything Dean believed about that night. It changed everything he believed about who was responsible for what happened.

"You know me, I try to give everyone the benefit of the doubt," his mother continued. "But that boy's father had been in and out of jail how many times? Too many to count. And his mother had problems with alcohol. I know I shouldn't have judged him based on his parents' wrongs. I just didn't want Addison to get herself mixed up with someone like that and give up everything she was working toward. And I was right. Look at what happened."

"When did you two fight about this and where was I?"

"That night. We fought that night. She stormed out. The last thing she said to me was that she hated me." His mother's face twisted and it was her turn to weep.

Dean hugged her. "She didn't hate you, Mom. She didn't."

"I know," she said, wiping her face. "Oh, why am I even crying? I've made peace with what happened. It took a long time, but I do know she loved me. Moms and daughters fight. I just wish fighting wasn't the last thing we did together."

"How did I not know this?" Dean felt like history had rewritten itself in a matter of minutes. Everything about that night had a different slant to it.

"You left." When he cringed, she added, "And I understand why you felt like you needed to do that. But you weren't here to process it all with us."

Dean definitely needed time to process

this. He also needed to talk to Faith. If anyone needed the burden of guilt lifted, it was her.

He knew exactly where to find her once morning arrived.

CHAPTER NINETEEN

FAITH CHANGED OUT the flowers in Addison's vase. The periwinkle hydrangeas were Faith's favorite. Addison used to draw pictures of them and tape them inside Faith's locker at school.

"So this week has been…interesting. I think more happened in the last seven days than in the last seven years."

It really was unbelievable how much had occurred in such a short time. Dean had shown up and Faith's whole world had started spinning off its axis. She had lost Duchess, passed the NETA inspection, repaired the relationship between Lily and Kylie, and kissed Dean.

That last one was the real mindblower.

"I don't know what I was thinking except that he's probably never coming back and that was the last time I was going to see him. I know what *you're* thinking."

Addison would be rolling her eyes so hard

they'd probably roll right out of her head. Faith was still in love with Dean after all this time.

"It doesn't matter how I feel. He doesn't feel that way about me. I'm not sure if he ever did. When I look back, I wonder if he was hiding our relationship for more reasons than because you wouldn't have liked it. I remember the way his friends used to treat us like we were nothing more than annoying little girls."

It had felt real back then, though. His "I love you" always had seemed sincere. But loving someone and being in love with someone were two different things. Maybe they were always better off friends, given their long history of being practically brother and sister.

"He's going back to Nashville and Sawyer and I will spend all our time and energy on Helping Hooves. None of this will matter. We live in two different worlds and I don't think he'll ever really get over the fact that I told you the truth when he asked me not to. It's a hurdle I'll never be able to jump over."

The squeaky cemetery gate announced the arrival of another visitor. Faith glanced over her shoulder and did a double take when she saw Dean walking toward her.

Dressed in khaki pants and perhaps another one of his father's dress shirts, Dean looked like a model for J. Crew. He held a bouquet of flowers from Harriet's in his arms. The ends of the pink ribbon fluttered in the Sunday-morning breeze.

"I thought I'd find you here," he said as he approached her.

Faith rose and brushed off the grass clippings that stuck to the skirt of her floral-print dress. "I was just finishing up. If you want a few minutes by yourself, I can go."

"I don't want you to go. I didn't come here to talk to Addison. I came to talk to you."

Faith swallowed hard. She wasn't sure how to read the easy smile he was wearing or the way he didn't seem anxious being near Addison's grave. "What did you want to talk to me about?"

Dean pulled one flower out of the bunch and placed it on Addison's headstone. "She'd be jealous as all get-out if I didn't give her at least one, right?"

He held the rest of them out for Faith, whose stomach was doing a few backflips.

She took the flowers as her eyebrows pinched together. "What are these for?"

"I have this mountain of regret that I don't know what to do with. The way I treated you before I left here, the way I've acted since I've been back... There's a million things I wish I'd done differently."

Faith shook her head. "You have a right to your feelings. I don't blame you for being mad at me for what I did, for setting Addison off even all these years later."

"I'm not angry with you. I have never really been angry with you. I can see now that it was my way of coping with my own feelings of guilt. Blaming you was a lot easier than taking responsibility."

"It wasn't your fault." He didn't force Faith to fall in love with him. He had told her not to say anything to Addison.

"It wasn't your fault, either."

"It wasn't all my fault, but I got the ball rolling." She'd still give just about anything to go back.

"It wasn't your fault *or* my fault. Addison would have gone to that party and gotten in that car no matter what."

Faith let out a weary breath. Couldn't he say he forgave her and let them both move on? Why did she have to work so hard to convince him that he was justified in being mad in the first place?

"If I hadn't told her about me and you, she would have chilled out at home. We didn't go to parties alone. And if there hadn't been a me and you, Addison and I would have been together. I would have talked her out of going to the lake or I would have gone with her. Had we gone together, we would've had a ride or called you. Either way you look at it, I was the reason she was there."

"If you hadn't been with me, Addison would have snuck off to the party without you."

He was making no sense. "How do you know that?"

"Because we weren't the only ones having a secret love affair."

"Did you have something to drink so you could make it through mass?" Faith's furrowed brow and arms folded across her chest made it clear she was not ready to accept what he was telling her.

Dean let out a laugh. She was so stubborn. A week ago the woman was letting the whole town take advantage of her. She would have done or accepted anything anyone said because she didn't want to upset a single person's apple cart. Now she wanted to argue until she was blue in the face.

"My mom and I had a long talk last night… well, more like this morning."

The wind picked up and blew Faith's hair in her face. Dean took the opportunity to touch her. He swept the unruly strands out of the way and pressed his palm to her cheek.

"Addison was in love with Aaron. She tutored him at school…they started writing love notes to each other. My mom said they had been throwing around the word 'marriage.' It was way more serious than any of us knew."

"Marriage?" Faith's arms fell to her sides. She shook her head back and forth. "No way. I don't believe it."

"My mom found the notes. She probably still has them. She kept everything."

Faith clearly couldn't reconcile what he was saying with what she knew. He watched her face while she battled it out inside her head. "When did your mom…?"

"She confronted Addison that night and they fought about how serious the relationship was," he told her. "Addison snuck out to that party because my mom forbade her from going. She got in the car with Aaron because she was in love with him, not because she was mad at you or me."

Dean watched as all the pieces fell into place for her. He expected her to laugh or cry, then laugh. But the look in her eyes wasn't anything close to humored. She was seething.

Faith turned toward the grave and bent over to pick up the flowers in the vase. She marched over to the wrought-iron fence that surrounded the tiny cemetery and tossed the flowers over it. Blue petals were caught by the wind and floated in the air, scattering across the grass. She stormed back to the grave.

Instead of talking to Dean, she knelt down in front of the headstone and spoke to Addison. "Are you kidding me? You were in love with Aaron Evans? You made me feel like the worst friend in the world for hiding my relationship and the whole time you were doing the same thing to me?"

Dean wasn't sure what to do. He had planned on this being good news, not bad. He'd thought she'd jump right into his arms and celebrate the weight of their guilt being lifted. He'd never seen Faith so angry, so hurt.

"I've spent the past twelve years of my life trying to figure out what possessed you to get in that car and hating myself because the only reasonable excuse was that you were so mad at me, you weren't in your right mind! When the truth was you were nothing but a…a…a stupid, love-struck girl?'"

"Faith," Dean said, placing a hand on her shoulder. It didn't snap her out of her fit.

"You wanted me to choose between you and him, and when I said I couldn't, you told me I was ridiculous for thinking he could really be in love with me. That was so unfair! You had someone. You cared about someone else. You were allowed to be in love, but I wasn't? Why? Because he was your brother?"

Addison had done exactly what Dean had known she would do. But Faith had come with him to the concert that night. She hadn't given in to his sister's demands. She really had chosen him by refusing to choose. The realization made his heart swell.

"I've hated myself for twelve years because I thought I had chosen wrong. Now I know you had no right to ask me to choose in the first place. You were so selfish."

The church bells began to ring and Faith stood and fixed her dress again. She didn't say a word to Dean, who thought about wrapping his arms around her and telling her it was okay to be furious. She didn't give him the chance, though. She slipped past him, heading for the gate, and kept walking until she was inside the church.

FAITH WAS SEATED next to Sawyer in the pew in front of Dean's parents. Dean sat next to his mom, directly behind Faith, who sat ramrod-straight. Sawyer leaned in her direction and whispered something Dean couldn't hear over the sound of the choir. Faith did not respond.

The choir finished their song and Pastor Kline opened with a prayer. Dean couldn't hear a word he said because his sole focus was on the woman in front of him. He couldn't see her face, but he could imagine the grim line of her lips and the flush of her cheeks thanks to her frustration.

Sawyer glanced back at Dean, his eyes questioning what had happened before his sister came in. Of course, he blamed Dean. Lately he was the cause of all her misery. He wanted to proclaim his innocence this time. He had come bearing good news. It was Addison who had made Faith so upset. All he could do was give Sawyer a shrug.

Halfway through the next choir song, Faith got to her feet and headed for the back of the church and the exit. Sawyer started to go after her, but Dean stood and stopped him.

"I got her."

Sawyer didn't look too pleased with that idea but let him go. Dean was much more aware of the stares and disapproving shakes of the head from the congregation as he left the building. When it had been his anxiety that had sent them out, he had been oblivious to what anyone else thought.

Outside, he scanned the parking lot for her and Sawyer's pickup. She wasn't near the truck and nowhere out front. Dean walked around the side toward the path that led to the cemetery.

Faith wasn't easy to catch. She strode with such purpose around the fence to where she had thrown the flowers. She gathered them up and returned to the gate. The wrought iron screeched as she opened it. Dean waited for her on the outside while she placed the flowers back in the vase connected to Addison's headstone.

NEVER IN A MILLION YEARS would Faith have believed Dean had a story to tell her like the one he had told her today. Addison had been a giant hypocrite.

Sitting in church, Faith had remembered how her best friend had complained about having to tutor Aaron Evans the final couple months of school. He needed to pass math in order to graduate, and a tutor was the last resort. Given his bad attitude, Addison had believed the teachers were desperate to get him out of the school and off their list of problems, which was why they had recruited her to do it.

Leave it to Addison to have been the better liar. Faith couldn't think of one time Addison had shown any interest in him. She probably hadn't felt half as guilty about doing it as Faith had about Dean, either. The whole thing made Faith want to scream. When had her friendship dissolved into lies?

The longer she thought about it, the madder she got. All that time she had spent blaming herself was a waste. How could Addison have made her feel so bad about sneaking around with Dean when she was doing the same thing? Granted, Aaron wasn't Faith's brother, but the lies were the same.

Then it hit her. Addison had been in love with Aaron. Addison had been in love enough to talk about *marrying* Aaron. Why hadn't she told Faith? Because Faith would have tried to talk her out of it. She would have tried to convince her that Aaron Evans was nothing but bad news. Faith would have done the same things Dean was afraid Addison would have done to them. And she would have been right.

"I wish we could have talked about it. I wish we could have been there for one another instead of worrying about being judged." Faith had returned to the cemetery to make peace. The tears she'd held back in church rolled freely down her face. "I've hated him for so long. I don't even know what happened to him after he got out of jail. I need some time to wrap my head around the fact that there has to be something worthwhile about him if you loved him. You didn't love just anyone."

This was the biggest revelation of all. Addison had been so wild and carefree. She had never taken boys very seriously. She'd had some dates here and there. She'd been to some school dances. But there was never that one big love of her life. It was one of the things that Faith had felt the worst about when Addison died—knowing she'd never experienced true love. But she had. At least that was what Dean had told Faith.

She wiped her cheeks and took a cleansing breath. "I'm so glad you know what it felt like. I'm sorry you didn't get more time.

And sorry about the flowers. I hope I didn't ruin them."

Dean was standing behind the gate when she made her way back to the church. He was exactly the person she needed at this moment. Her heart needed him to be close.

"You two make up?" he asked with a wary half smile on his face.

"I think so. I never could stay mad at her for very long."

Dean's smile widened. "She hated it when people were angry with her. Especially you. Remember that time she made me drive her over to your house so she could do the 'I'm sorry' cheer she made up on your front lawn?"

"At ten o'clock at night when my dad had already gone to bed? Oh, I remember. He was *not* pleased with her...until she did it for him, too. She really didn't want people to be mad for long." Faith opened the squeaky gate and closed it behind her with a clang.

Dean took her hand. "I thought you'd be relieved to hear that your fight with her wasn't the last fight she'd been in that night. My mom has been walking around with the same kind of regret and I had no idea."

"It is a relief and a new heartache. I wish

we could have been there for each other. I want to know how they got together and what sweet things he said that melted her heart. I want to know when they had their first kiss and what she loved about him. I'll never get to hear about that."

"I'm sorry." Dean pulled her closer. He smelled like soap and sunshine. Warm and safe. "I'm sorry for so many things. Especially not realizing how hard all this was for you. I'm not sure I can ever forgive myself for making you lie."

Taking that as an okay to let go of her anxiety when it came to Dean, she leaned into him, resting her head on his chest. His heartbeat was steady and strong. The sound of it helped her calm her own.

"Hate the lie, not the liar. How different things might have been if we had all been honest."

"I can't imagine my sister wanting to hear about what a good kisser I was," Dean said. A chuckle shook his chest.

Faith looked up at him. "She would have probably asked me to skip the details."

"I would have been fine with keeping some things between you and me. I wish I could have told the world how much I loved you, but kept *how* I loved you for myself."

Hearing him say he loved her, even in the past tense, sent a tingle through her whole body. Her heart began to race again. The love they had shared had been gentle and innocent. It was everything she had wanted it to be and something that could never be recreated. It was once in a lifetime. But that didn't mean they could find something new.

Dean pulled back and his eyes almost seemed to twinkle. "I think I've loved you for longer than you realize. Even when I told myself I couldn't or shouldn't."

"I've been in love with you my whole life. When your sister asked me to choose, I couldn't imagine turning it off. It's like your name is written on my heart. I can't erase it, no matter how hard I try. No matter how hard *you* try."

Faith once again gave in to the emotion she could no longer hold back. She threw her arms around his neck and planted a kiss on his lips. From now on, no one was ever going to tell her to hide her feelings. Dean didn't object until the kiss was over.

"Do you think I'll ever get a chance to kiss

you first?" he asked, holding her face in his hands.

Faith planned to live and love without fear. Not only did she deserve to be happy, she owed it to Addison to enjoy every minute. Life was too short and too much time had already been wasted.

"I don't know. When are you planning on kissing me ag—"

Dean didn't wait for her to finish. He covered her mouth with his and made her forget that she had kissed him first. Hope bloomed inside her for the first time in forever.

CHAPTER TWENTY

"I REMEMBER THE football game when your dad got the whole crowd to chant your name," Dean's dad said to Sawyer as they all sat around the Presleys' kitchen table.

Marilee had invited the Strattons and Harriet over for brunch once church services had ended. Everyone was laughing as they ate and reminisced.

"Dad thought I'd get more playing time if he got the crowd behind me. Little did he know that coach played the kids who could actually throw, run or catch the ball. I tended not to be great at any of those."

Dean couldn't stop staring at Faith as she plucked a grape from the bunch in the bowl that sat in front of her. Her eyes met his as she popped it in her mouth. Her smile was enchanting.

"Your dad had a wonderful spirit." Marilee set some warm muffins on the table, fresh from the oven.

"He did," Sawyer agreed.

Faith took another grape and tossed it at Dean to stop his ogling. But he couldn't be distracted. She was too adorable to not look at.

"Dean and I were cleaning up Addison's room this morning and were cracking up at some of the pictures." Dean's mom didn't notice they were fooling around. "There was the one of you guys decorating that cake in the shape of a horseshoe for your dad's birthday."

"It was the ugliest cake I have ever seen," Dean chimed in, reaching for his own grape. "Your dad must have loved you if he ate that thing. It was this weird shade of gray and the frosting looked like it had melted or something."

Faith covered her mouth with her hand and laughed. When she caught her breath she explained. "We didn't wait long enough for the cake to cool. Addison is the one who said we had to make it look realistic, which is why it was gray. That wasn't my choice. I wanted it to be purple."

"Purple?" Sawyer questioned. "What kind of horseshoe is purple?"

Faith's smile finally reached her eyes. Dean

had been waiting to see that smile. "I don't know. I was twelve. I loved purple."

Dean's phone rang, somewhat pulling his attention away from the beautiful woman across from him. He checked to see who it was. Landon was calling and wouldn't stop until Dean answered.

"Excuse me a second," he said, getting up from the table. He answered as he stepped into the family room. "What's up, Landon? It's Sunday. Your day of rest."

"I think we should sign the kid. Piper shared his first video and it's gone viral. If we don't sign him, someone else will. I trust you—we should act and act fast."

Dean froze. The hair on the back of his neck stood on end. He'd been waiting for Landon to come around. Until this morning when he realized he was still in love with Faith and they weren't the reason his sister died. The thought of taking Sawyer away from her made him want to throw up everything he'd had for brunch.

"Are you there? Dean, did you hear me?"

"I'm here. I haven't had a chance to get on social media today. Let me give it a look and I'll get back to you."

"What?" Dean could picture Landon pacing on his back patio. "What's the matter? I thought you wanted to sign him and were waiting for me to say yes. I'm saying yes, Dean."

"Let me check it out and I'll get back to you. I'm not sure he's ready to pursue this right now. The more time I spend with him, the more I see he might have too much on his plate. I will get back to you, I promise."

"He's not ready? You said this was the one. What's changed?"

Everything had changed. He had finally made amends with Faith. That would be ruined if he offered Sawyer an out. How would she ever run Helping Hooves by herself? There was no way.

"Nothing. I'm in the middle of brunch with my family. Let me go online and see what's happened this weekend and I'll get back to you. Relax."

"Relax? This company needs more than Piper for it to survive. You are in charge of finding the talent. You told me you found talent. Sign the talent."

Dean felt sick to his stomach. Grace Note needed Sawyer just as much as Helping Hooves. If what Landon was saying was true and Piper's fans were taking a liking to him, he absolutely was the answer to their troubles.

"I'll call you back." Dean hung up, but needed a minute before returning to the kitchen where they were still laughing and sharing memories.

Once Sawyer began making music, there wouldn't be time to work on the farm. He'd be traveling and touring. He'd be up late, and mornings on the farm were much too early for a music star. There wouldn't be a compromise. They couldn't share him.

Dean sat down on the couch and rubbed his face. All the weight that had been lifted off his shoulders this morning was quickly replaced by this burden.

"Everything okay?" Faith took a cautious step into the room.

Just the sight of her made him feel better. And worse.

"I'm fine. Work," he deflected. "You know how that is."

She sat beside him and ran a hand up and down his back. Her touch was so familiar. It felt more like home than this house did.

"It never ends, right? I wish I could help the way you helped us."

She could help. *Give me Sawyer*, he wanted

to say. It would make things so much easier if she let him go than if Dean had to take him away.

"You're sweet to offer, though." He put his hand on her knee. "I don't want to think about work right now. I'm having too much fun laughing at you."

She playfully pinched the back of his neck. "Nice."

"How does someone who's now an amazing baker make the ugliest cake-fail ever?"

Faith shrugged. "I blame Addison, one hundred percent."

"That I do believe. She was a menace in the kitchen. Somehow that girl could create a sink full of dishes and dirty every surface by pouring a bowl of cereal. She was so messy."

"It's nice to see you talk about her without getting that look on your face."

"What look?"

Faith traced the line of his jaw with her finger. "This would get really tight and kind of pulse. And your eyes would narrow into angry slits. And this spot—" she ran her finger between his eyes "—would wrinkle up."

"That doesn't sound very attractive."

"I'll admit, it made you look mean. And it made me sad," Faith said, running her finger down his nose and onto his lips. He gave it a kiss.

"I don't want to make you sad anymore."

Her finger was quickly replaced by her lips. "Good, because you make my heart happy when you smile. You smile more when you talk about her. It's my favorite."

"You were right about needing to tough it out and get through the sad stuff. It wasn't easy, but it wasn't as impossible as I thought it would be." Dean had been so afraid of unleashing the sorrow. The anger had been safer somehow. It made him feel in control even though he was far from it. "It almost felt good to cry about it. I held all that in for so long, I wasn't sure what would happen if I loosened my grip. But this morning I let it go and it was exactly what I needed."

She took hold of his hand and kissed it. Dean quickly realized how much he had missed kissing her. He felt twenty years old again, when everything was right with the world...when he held her in his arms and kissed her until their lips were sore. If only kissing her now would solve all their problems.

"I'm still trying to wrap my head around how different everything is. A week ago I was sure you would never want anything to do with me. I thought we were destined to be strangers."

"A week ago, at the picnic, I wanted to kiss you after we danced. So it's not all that different for me."

Faith's cheeks turned red as she bit down on her bottom lip. She turned her head, embarrassed. "We should go finish brunch before our families wonder what we're doing out here."

That was probably for the best. Dean had used up all his self-control when it came to Faith a long time ago.

DEAN WALKED THE Strattons to their truck when brunch and the friendly socializing came to an end. He made sure Faith got in the truck and resisted making a fool of himself in front of Sawyer. No kiss goodbye, just a promise to talk soon.

He was climbing the porch steps when Sawyer called his name. He jogged up behind him. "I didn't want to say anything in front of my sister, but is this normal?"

He handed Dean his phone. Sawyer's Instagram account had thousands of followers that hadn't been there a few days ago.

"I keep getting notifications that all these people like the photos Lily made me take. I have my phone on vibrate and it's been shaking all day. Tell me that's what we wanted to happen."

It was exactly what Dean had wanted a few days ago. Piper's fans were falling in love with Sawyer just as Dean had predicted. Only, he hadn't thought it would happen so soon.

"It's good," Dean replied, trying not to make too much of it. He didn't want to get Sawyer excited about something he might no longer be able to offer him. "We'll have to see if it keeps up. You might want to turn off the notifications."

"Maybe I'm blowing up," Sawyer said with a hopeful grin.

"Maybe."

Faith waved from the passenger seat as Sawyer ran back to the truck. Dean lifted his hand and tried to keep his expression neutral. He didn't want her to worry before she needed to do so.

Once Dean got inside the house, he went straight for his dad's home office. He sat down at the computer and pulled up everything he had set up for Sawyer. Everything he had wanted to prove to Landon was right there. Piper had helped launch him into the stratosphere.

"What's going on?" his dad said, poking his head in the room.

"Checking some things for work. Do you mind if I use your computer?"

"Fine by me." His dad sat down on the small leather couch in the corner. "It was nice to spend time with old friends today."

He was baiting Dean into a conversation about Faith. Dean wasn't sure he could talk about it given the current situation. "It was very nice."

"I take it you and Faith have made amends. You two seemed…happy to be around each other."

"We didn't know about Addison and Aaron until Mom told me this morning. It made a big difference. We've been blaming ourselves this entire time."

"Goodness, you and your mother are exactly the same. Except she wouldn't do work on a Sunday. What's so important that you have to worry about work on this beautiful day?"

Impressing his father had always been a goal of Dean's. He wanted his father to be proud of him and aware only of his success. He didn't bother sharing information about his trouble.

"Just checking on a few things. Music happens 24/7. We don't take a day off."

"Something changed after that phone call you got in the middle of brunch. You sure nothing's wrong?"

His dad's probing wasn't going to end. Dean had to give him something. "We're on the lookout for some new talent. There's been some issues with Boone. Landon's worried, but I know we'll get it figured out."

"Hence why you were down in Birmingham last weekend. Looking for the next big thing, huh?"

"I'll find him."

"Him? How do you know it's going to be a him? Maybe the next big thing is a woman," his dad challenged.

Dean's gaze fell back on the computer screen and Sawyer's smiling face, which now had ten thousand likes. Where would he find another guy like this?

"I have a really good lead. And it's a guy."

"Really? You've been trapped here since you left Birmingham. Where'd you find this someone?" His dad sat up a little straighter.

"Wait...are you thinking about signing Sawyer?"

There weren't a lot of other country singers in Grass Lake. It was amazing it had taken his dad this long to figure it out.

"Sawyer is very talented, but he also has a lot of responsibilities at the farm."

"Well, what's he want?" His dad waited patiently for Dean's answer. But Dean hadn't been thinking about what Sawyer wanted. His focus had been on what Faith needed.

"I think I have to talk to him some more. Make sure he's ready to make a commitment to something that could really change his life."

Dean's dad rose and hitched up his pants. "His life and Faith's." He blew out a breath. "That will be interesting."

It would.

"What are you smiling about over there?" Sawyer asked as Faith stared out the passenger window, admiring the wildflowers that were blooming along the roadside.

"It's been a really good day, that's all."

"You seemed ready to kill someone when you first came into church. Then you left and came back like life was beautiful. And I think you and Dean ran off to make out in the middle of brunch, but I guess I should be glad he didn't jump across the table and kiss you in front of all of us because he sure looked like he wanted to."

Faith pressed a hand to her warming cheek. She closed her eyes and took a breath. It had been so long since she'd felt so free. No guilt, no worry, no heartbreak. It didn't seem possible and she didn't want this freedom to be taken away.

"Remember when you told me Addison's death wasn't my fault?"

"Yeah," Sawyer said, glancing over at her.

"I believe it now."

Sawyer grinned and nodded. "It's about time."

"And I think maybe I want to be more than friends with Dean." She waited for a smart or teasing remark but none came. His smile had faded. She nudged him with her elbow. "What? No comment on that one?"

Sawyer inhaled and exhaled loudly. "I feel like we should talk about something."

Faith turned back to the window. "No way, little brother. Do not try to pretend to be Dad having The Talk with me. That was excruciating enough the first time. I do not want to relive that even as a joke."

Sawyer turned into the drive that led to the farm. "I wasn't talking about that. It's about me and Dean."

Faith gave him a good smack on the arm. "That is not funny."

"I didn't mean it like that. I'm trying to be serious here. I've been meaning to talk to you for a couple days, but there was never a good time, and I almost hate to do it now because you're in a good mood."

"What are you talking about?" Faith asked as he pulled the truck up by the house.

Sawyer ran a hand through his hair and scratched the back of his neck. "Dean and I made a deal."

The deal. Faith knew there was a deal. She'd let it go because, deep down, she was worried it was going to take away the little bit of happiness she had going on. Now it threatened to ruin the big happy she'd been given today.

"What kind of deal?"

Sawyer kept his eyes forward. "I asked him to help us get the farm ready for our inspection in exchange for letting him experiment with my stuff online."

Faith had thought for sure he was going to say he planned to go to Nashville even though he had promised her he would stay here. This seemed much less worrisome, except it didn't make a whole lot of sense. "What does that mean?"

"We set up some profiles on some social media sites and Dean stirred up some interest. I guess his partner wasn't as gung ho about signing a complete unknown as Dean was, so this was supposed to help Dean prove to his partner that I was worth the risk."

"But you aren't going to Nashville, so it doesn't really matter, right?" She waited for Sawyer to agree, but he didn't. He didn't say anything at all. "We passed inspection. We're going to be listed as a NETA-accredited facility. We're probably going to have to hire some staff. There's a lot of work to do."

Sawyer's grip on the steering wheel turned his knuckles white. "You're right. We're going to need some more staff. We can hire someone or get volunteers to help you in the mornings with the horses. You can hire a maintenance person. The things I do around here don't have to be done by me."

Faith's whole body was trembling. This could not be happening. "Yes, they do."

Sawyer parked and faced his sister. His eyes locked on hers in a way that silenced her completely. "No, they don't."

"What happens when this music thing doesn't pan out and you have to come home and I have to fire some poor guy because you decided to play country star for a couple months?"

"Wow. Thanks for the vote of confidence there, sis." Sawyer pushed open his door and jumped out of the truck.

Faith scrambled to catch up with him as he stormed toward the house. "I didn't mean it like that. I'm trying to be realistic. How many talented people end up singing in dive bars their whole lives? A lot. Becoming a famous singer is like becoming an NFL star. Very few people make it to that level. It's just a fact, not a put-down."

Sawyer stopped and spun around. His face was as red as the tie around his neck that he'd loosened on the ride home. "Dean thinks I have what it takes and he's in the business. His opinion matters a whole lot more than yours."

He headed into the house without another word, leaving Faith at the bottom of the porch steps. She tried to come up with another argument for keeping him in Grass Lake. She considered bribery and guilt trips that included using their father's wishes for both kids to run the farm when he was gone. She did her best to think of a way to change Sawyer's mind. That was when it came to her. Maybe it wasn't Sawyer's mind that needed to be changed.

CHAPTER TWENTY-ONE

DEAN'S MOTHER HAD had enough. "How long you gonna stare at your phone like that? Doesn't it make you go cross-eyed after a while?"

Dean had watched Sawyer's popularity increase by the hundreds every hour today. By ten o'clock in the evening, he had more followers on Instagram and Twitter than some of Dean's currently signed acts.

Sawyer had been feeding his fans new pictures and videos all day. Shots of him and his dog. A picture of his guitar. A video of him singing on his bed—shirtless. The boy suddenly had it all figured out and he was working it all over the internet.

Landon had been right about it being possible that he could attract the wrong kind of attention, aka the competition. Even if Dean backed off, he'd already got the ball rolling for Sawyer in a big way. Other record labels could come a-knocking.

"Sorry, Mom, but some of us have to work no matter what time or day it is. Plus, I think I've seen this one. The husband killed her."

The family was all gathered around the television to watch some police drama. It was Dean's mother's guilty pleasure.

His dad turned the volume up a click. "It's always the husband. And if he's the victim, it's always the wife. What does that say about our society, huh?"

"Marriage makes you homicidal?" his mother guessed.

Dean laughed. His parents were more entertaining than the show. "I hope that's not true. I don't want to have to visit one of you in jail."

"It would be your mother doing to the killing. I am much more tolerant of her quirks than she is of mine."

"What? That's not true." Marilee perked up from her spot on the couch. "I don't have any quirks."

Dean turned his attention back to his phone. At the rate he was going, Sawyer was going to have an agent within a few days and then his price would go up.

Faith sent a text. Can I come over?

Dean smiled. When he wasn't thinking

about what he was supposed to do about her brother, he was thinking about her.

Always, he replied and got up to wait for her outside.

"Where are you going?" his mom asked.

"Gotta talk to a girl and make sure she's not the kind that'll kill me if we get married someday."

"Good luck with that. The odds are apparently not in your favor, son," his dad said without looking away from the television.

Dean sat on the old porch swing his dad had installed but rarely used. He hoped Faith was coming over to spend time with him, but something told him she needed to talk, most likely about Sawyer.

Faith pulled in a few minutes later. Her little blue sedan wasn't much newer than Dean's rental car.

He got up and moved to the railing. "You must have known I was thinking about you all day," he said as she got out of the car.

Faith didn't smile like the way he had hoped. Her hair was pulled back in a ponytail and she was dressed in what appeared to be makeshift pajamas.

"I'm sorry about coming over so late. I had to wait until Sawyer went to bed."

"I thought we were done with having to sneak out of the house to see one another," he said, hoping for that smile but not getting it. "What's the matter?"

Faith joined him on the porch. "I need to talk to you."

"Okay…" He took her hand and led her to the swing, but Faith didn't sit with him. He had a bad feeling about where this conversation was headed.

"Helping Hooves is my dad's legacy. I always imagined myself carrying on his work after he was gone. I just didn't expect it to be as soon as it was."

"I know how important it is to you." Dean could relate better than anyone. His business was like his child. He loved it and would do anything to protect it.

"My dad left the farm to me and Sawyer. Not just me. Not just Sawyer. Both of us. He knew neither one of us could do it alone."

"I get it. I do."

Faith took the seat next to him. "Do you really think Sawyer has what it takes to become a country music star?"

"I wouldn't have told him so if I didn't believe it."

That was clearly not the answer she was

looking for. "But it's not an easy business. There are no guarantees, right?"

"No, there aren't. You have to have talent, but a whole lot of luck is involved. It's not easy to predict what or who is going to hit."

The worry lines around her eyes made Dean feel even guiltier. "Could he live on the farm and travel to Nashville to record songs or play shows at night?"

"For periods of time, yes," Dean said, hating to get her hopes up. "But to be successful he'd have to hit the road. He'd be gone more than he was home."

Faith sat back and dropped her head in her hands. Dean put his arm around her. Why was it that their siblings were always driving a wedge between the two of them?

"Sawyer said your business partner isn't sure you guys should sign someone who's a complete unknown. Do you still want him to come to Nashville with you?"

"I do," Dean answered honestly because there weren't going to be any more lies in this relationship. "Landon, my partner, is on board. We put some things online and Sawyer has gotten an amazing response. But I understand he has responsibilities here. I don't want to take him from you."

Faith jumped on that. She lifted her head and begged, "Then don't. Don't take him. I know that sounds so selfish, but I'm begging you to un-invite him."

Dean took a deep breath and shook his head. "Your brother has real talent. I'm not the only one who sees it. If I don't invite him to Nashville, someone else will. And what if the next guy doesn't have his best interest at heart like I do?"

"He won't go with anyone else." Faith's desperation grew. "He trusts you and if you told him he should stay here, he would believe you."

"You want me to lie? You want me to tell him he's not good enough when he is? I don't know if I can do that."

The lies they had told other people in their lives had ruined their relationship the first time. Dean didn't want to go down that road again.

Faith got up and walked over to the railing. Leaning on her elbows, she stared down at Dean's mother's rhododendrons. "This isn't easy for me. The last thing I want you to do is lie. I hate the lies."

"Then don't ask me to, Faith. I think we should let Sawyer decide."

She spun around and the tears in her eyes made that pain in his chest reappear. "There are talented people everywhere. You're more than capable of finding another singer. I only have one brother. I can't replace him. Sure, I can hire someone to do the work he does, but that's not all I need him for. Everyone I love leaves, Dean. Everyone. My mom. Addison. My dad. You. The thought of Sawyer joining that list…" She began to tremble. "Please."

Dean went to her and held her close while she cried. Grace Note Records had been the most important thing in Dean's life until he'd returned to Grass Lake. Now everything had changed.

WEAK.

Pathetic.

Insecure.

Cowardly.

Those weren't the words Faith would usually use to describe herself. Until tonight.

Standing on the Presleys' front porch, begging Dean to lie to Sawyer so he wouldn't desert her was pretty much the lowest Faith had ever been. If the world used this as her defining moment, it would be a shameful one at that.

Knowing this didn't stop her from asking, though. Her fear of being left alone was bigger than her need for self-respect at the moment.

"I'll do it," Dean said in nearly a whisper. Faith almost thought she'd imagined it until he said it again. "I'll do it, but I hope you understand what this means."

She did. That was one of the reasons the tears were falling. Asking Dean to do this meant there could be no hope for the two of them to be together. There was no way she could ask him to break her brother's heart and then be a part of their lives.

"It means this is really goodbye," she managed to choke out.

Dean squeezed her a little tighter. She could feel his reluctance to let her go. Her fingers dug into the soft cotton of his shirt. She didn't want this to end before it even had a chance to really begin, either. But the choice had been made.

THE NEXT MORNING Faith went out to the barn before Sawyer even woke up. She wasn't even sure she'd be able to face him today. Her head throbbed from a mixture of crying and lack of sleep. She had spent the early morning hours reconsidering her decision. What was done was done, though. There was no going back.

Sassy greeted her with a whinny. Winston made himself known, as well. The youngster of the bunch was Renegade. Sawyer had named the jet-black quarter horse. They were still training him to do therapy, but he was proving to be a little more stubborn than the others. Greta rounded out the bunch. She was a beautiful palomino quarter horse who had been put into the therapy rotation about a year ago.

Faith knew them all like they were her family. She could name all their likes and dislikes. She knew which ones preferred to stand around eating and which ones loved to play games and be active. They were all quick learners and inquisitive. Each one held a special place in Faith's heart.

She had refilled their water and hay before Sawyer made it out to help. He had on his favorite cowboy hat and Tim McGraw T-shirt.

"You're up earlier than usual. Did you even sleep last night?"

Faith avoided making eye contact. "Thought I'd take them all for a ride this morning. They need to run today. I feel like we haven't been exercising them enough since Duchess died."

"That's probably a good idea. I was going to work with Renegade today so he's ready to take the spot that's open when camp starts."

"Thanks," Faith said with her heart heavy in her chest. He was always looking ahead and thinking about what they needed for whatever was next. How could she ever find someone who knew this place well enough to do that?

She couldn't, which was why she had done what she'd done.

They worked in silence, mucking the stalls and laying fresh bedding. Faith didn't have the guts to make small talk. Nothing she could say would ease the tension between them. Tension that would inevitably grow once Dean and Sawyer spoke.

Faith saddled up Sassy and went for a ride. When she got back, Sawyer was on the phone. Her stomach dropped. Would Dean tell him the bad news so impersonally? Maybe that would make it easier on him. She couldn't fault him for going that route.

"Dean wants me to stop by this afternoon. I'll only be gone for a little bit, and I'll pick up the supplies we need when I pass through town."

"Okay." Faith's emotions were all twisted as she dismounted Sassy.

"I'm going to tell him I want to go to Nashville with him when he heads back."

An enormous lump formed in her throat. Faith didn't know how to reply. She prayed Dean would stay true to his word.

"You've got nothing to say to that?" Sawyer asked as Faith led Sassy into the barn.

"What do you want me to say? That you're breaking my heart? That I can't believe you'd leave me to run this place by myself? Is there really anything I can say that's going to change your mind?"

Sawyer hurled a hay bale into the stall next to the tack room. "That's great, Faith. Perfect. I really appreciate your support."

Faith bit her tongue. She didn't want to fight with him. She wanted him to go to Dean's and get the bad news. Once Dean left for Nashville, everything would go back to normal. At least, that was what Faith wanted to believe.

CHAPTER TWENTY-TWO

"I WISH YOU didn't have to go." Marilee stood in the doorway of what used to be Dean's bedroom.

He shoved all his new clothes into a bag his mom had let him borrow. "It was never going to be forever." He could say that about a lot of things.

"I know, but everything's been better with you here. I hope with all the secrets out in the open, you'll come home again soon. Maybe to see a lovely young lady you seemed very cozy with yesterday."

If she only knew. New secrets would make Grass Lake off-limits once again. Maybe he could come down for a day visit. But sticking around too long would certainly spell disaster.

"Faith and I are just friends, Mom. Don't start planning a wedding."

His mom smiled like she was trying not to

laugh. "I never said anything about a wedding, but it's interesting that you did."

Dean sighed. "Mom, I'm serious. Faith and I will never be more than friends." If he could even call what they had that. This new lie ruined their chances of having any kind of relationship. In a few years they'd be strangers once again.

"Fine," she said, throwing her hands up. "I don't care why you come home. Whatever the reason, it would be nice to have you, that's all I'm saying."

He lifted his mom into a bear hug. "*Is* that all you're saying?"

She wiggled in his arms. "Put me down. Goodness, you're just like your father."

He set her on her feet. "I love you, Mama. I promise to come home again if that will make you happy."

"It will." She touched his face. "It really will."

Dean didn't need much time to pack the small bag of things he had accumulated over the past ten days. Ten days. It was hard to believe how much had happened in such a short time.

"Sawyer just pulled up. Is he coming to see you?" his mom shouted from the hall.

Dean went to the window and pulled back the curtain. Sawyer was checking his hair in the side mirror of his truck, most likely worried about making a good impression.

"Yeah, he's here to talk to me." Dean sat on the bed and rubbed his throbbing temples.

"Try to look more excited once he's inside," his mom said, walking by his room to go downstairs as the doorbell rang.

There wasn't much to be excited about. He had to tell his most promising prospect that he wasn't interested in signing him even though Dean was the exact opposite of disinterested. And he still had to break the news to Landon that there was no new talent on the horizon. That wasn't going to go over well, especially since it was Dean's influence that had sparked so much interest over the past week.

Always the hospitable one, Dean's mom welcomed Sawyer with open arms. "Can I get you something to drink?"

"I'm fine, Mrs. Presley. Thank you very much, though."

Dean jogged down the stairs with his bag and greeted Sawyer with a firm handshake. He suggested they go sit in the family room. Sitting down was the only way to take bad news. But maybe that only made it easier for the bearer of the bad news. Dean quickly dismissed that theory. There was no easy way to say this.

"Did you see what I posted last night? More importantly, did you see the girl who asked me to marry her?" Sawyer waggled his brow. "I'm trying to figure out why I didn't think to use social media before."

"I'm glad you're having fun. It's a really good place to start. I hope you'll keep it up."

"You're going to want me to, right? I thought that was how I'll let people know what's happening when I start recording and playing shows."

Sawyer had been an excellent student. He listened and paid attention, which was huge. There werc lots of guys out there who were just as green but thought they knew it all.

"If you get to that. Yes, social media is the perfect way to communicate with your fans, create buzz."

"Well, I'm ready to start. I want to do this. I've talked to Faith and we're good to go. Looks like you're packed. When do we leave?" Sawyer's eagerness was evident in his cocky grin.

Dean rubbed his jaw. It had been so tense it was getting sore. "That's what I wanted to talk to you about. I don't think you should come to Nashville. Landon—" Dean cleared his throat. The lie didn't want to come out. "—and I have decided to put our efforts into another artist. Someone we've been looking at for a few months."

Deep, questioning lines appeared on Sawyer's forehead. "Are you messing with me right now?"

Dean wished he could say yes. "It's not personal, it's business." That was the biggest lie of all. This was entirely personal because he was in love with Faith and she needed her brother.

"Are you joking right now?" Sawyer stared at him in disbelief. "Is this your way of playing hardball?"

"I'm not playing games, Sawyer. That's not what this is."

"Come on. I get it. I didn't jump at your first attempt at reeling me in and now you're making me sweat a little. Is that it?"

"I think you have a great voice. Keep singing in your free time. It's a good outlet for you, I can see that."

"Is this about my sister? I told you. I would handle her. She and I will figure out what to do about Helping Hooves. If she made you reconsider, I'm asking you to re-reconsider."

Dean couldn't address the issue of Faith. "I wish you the best, man. I really do."

"She put you up to this, didn't she? Come on, Dean, a couple days' ago you were practically begging me to come to Nashville. You told me you could make me the next Boone Williams. Then, the day after I see you making out with my sister—who doesn't want me to leave, by the way—you decide to go with another artist? I'm not some little kid who doesn't see what's going on here."

"There's nothing going on between me and Faith," Dean assured him. That much was true. "I care about her, yes. We got carried away yesterday because emotions were running high, but we can't be together, so don't make this about her."

"That's it, then? You're leaving and you don't want to see what I can do in Nashville?" The pain of rejection emanated from Sawyer's eyes. Dean had to look away.

"Like I said, I wish you the best."

Sawyer rubbed his palms on his thighs before he stood. "Yeah, well, I wish you the best, too. Thanks for nothing."

Sawyer was out the door before Dean's

mom could even say goodbye. She stepped around the corner. "What was all that about?"

Dean gripped his head. A dull ache started at the base of his neck and wrapped all the way around his skull. "Nothing good."

"I'M THINKING ABOUT changing the menu. Maybe add some specials. Serve more than just pub grub." Josie had stopped over with some mock-ups of the new Sundown logo she'd been working on for the last month or so. She had provided the distraction Faith needed while Sawyer was at Dean's.

Either Sawyer was hearing Nashville was a no-go or he was talking Dean out of the deal he'd made with Faith. Neither one was the perfect solution to things. Both ended with Dean leaving Grass Lake for good and one of the Strattons miserable.

"Whatever you do, people around here will love it."

"I also thought, what if I knocked out that one wall on the west side and built a bigger stage with a little dance floor? We could bring in more entertainment, attract more of a crowd. Maybe Sawyer could still come play there after he goes big-time."

Even Josie had more faith in Sawyer than

his sister did. Faith felt that old, familiar guilt take its place on her shoulders. Before she could confess to ruining any chance Sawyer had of making it big-time, he came storming into the house.

"What did you do?" Sawyer's blood must have been boiling. He threw his truck keys across the room. They hit the picture hanging by the pantry so hard it fell off the wall with a clatter, causing Scout to bark. "Did you call him at the crack of dawn and tell him to leave me behind? Is that what you were doing in the barn so early this morning? Did you make him promise to do whatever you wanted when you were playing kissy-face yesterday?"

Faith had no comeback. Pretending she hadn't known it was coming and telling him she had nothing to do with it were two very different things.

"Hey now, cowboy." Josie stood in between the two of them. "Why don't you head back outside and find your cool before you come in here and talk to your sister?"

"Did she tell you how she meddled in my life like she had a say?" Sawyer's heavy breaths made him sound like he had run there from the Presleys'. "You don't get a say, Faith. I'm not a kid!" He knocked over one of the kitchen chairs in his rage and left out the back door, Scout hot on his heels.

"What in the world?" Josie picked up the chair and righted it. "I've never seen him throw a temper tantrum like that before."

Faith ran her hands over the goose bumps on her arms. Her whole body felt electrified, like Sawyer had come in and used a Taser gun on her. She'd thought he'd be disappointed, not full of fury.

"He's not going to Nashville with Dean."

"Why not? Is that guy crazy? Did he not hear Sawyer on Friday night? That was his best show yet!"

Dean had heard him just fine. He also believed in Sawyer more than Faith did.

"Because I asked him not to take him."

Josie sat down. The stunned expression on her round face said it all. "Why would you do that?"

"Because I can't run this place without him. What would I do if I lost this farm? How disappointed would my dad be?"

"Nobody in this town would let you lose the farm. You and Helping Hooves are part of this community. We'd help you."

"I can't rely on the kindness of others. Eventually even the kindest people have to take care of their own. Sawyer and I are responsible for this place, and he wants to walk away without a second thought."

He wanted to walk away from *Faith* without a second thought. All the insecurities that came with being left behind by their mother reared their ugly heads. Sawyer hated her for abandoning them, for thinking Grass Lake and her family weren't enough. Yet here he was, doing the exact same thing.

"He won't be gone forever."

"Dean said if he pursued that life, he'd be gone all the time. That the road would become his home."

Josie put a hand over Faith's. "This will always be home, no matter what. Home is where your heart is and Sawyer loves this place. But what if he can do something amazing somewhere else? Can you really sit here and tell me you would deny him the chance to try?"

Faith's head hurt almost as much as her heart. She wiped her face, not wanting to cry any more today.

"I have to get back to the bar, but please don't do something you're going to regret the rest of your life—or that's going to make him resent you for the rest of his."

Faith saw Josie out and noticed Sawyer and Scout by the equipment shed. She couldn't stand that he was this angry with her. He hadn't bought the lie, but maybe he'd understand the truth.

He came around the side as she made her way over. He put a hand up to stop her from saying anything as he stomped past her, headed to the field where the horses were grazing today. She followed him even though she knew he didn't want her to.

He rounded up Renegade from the pasture and brought him into the barn. Sawyer tied him up in the tack room and gave the horse some fresh hay to keep him occupied while he gathered up his hoof-trimming equipment.

"We have to talk about this."

"No, we don't, because it's obvious that you only care about yourself."

Sawyer was justified in much of his anger, but Faith didn't take too kindly to him acting like this was only about her.

"Maybe I could say the same thing about you," she shot back. "If either of us is being self-centered, it's you. I'm thinking about all the horses, all our clients, the volunteers. You only care about you."

Sawyer picked up one of Renegade's legs

and secured it between his own. He used the hook knife to clean the hoof off. Sawyer didn't get mad often, but when he did, he often channeled his frustration into physical labor. Apparently it wasn't working today. When he was done, he set Renegade's leg down and glowered at Faith.

"Maybe it's about time I thought about me. Dad didn't ask me if this was what I wanted to do, he just acted like it was expected."

"You told Dad you didn't want to be a therapist, that you preferred taking care of the horses over the people." Faith petted Renegade's head to calm him. The horse was picking up on their discord.

"So college was only an option if I wanted to be a therapist? Some people go to be engineers and accountants, you know. Shoot, some go just to party and be young and wild."

"Is that what this is about? You feel like you missed out on being young and wild?" Faith had to step away from the horse. "Welcome to the club, little brother. Do you think I dreamed of being in charge of running this household since I was ten? We both had to grow up fast because Mom bailed."

"Well, you got to go off to college and only worry about yourself for four years. You know where I was during that time? Here, doing this. You know where I was during the four years my friends were in college? Here, doing this. The next four? Here, doing this. Next four? Here—" he raise his arms up and motioned around the room "—doing this. This is all I've ever been allowed to do, so excuse me for thinking maybe I could try to do something new for the next four years."

Sawyer had never complained. In all their years of living on the farm, he'd never been the one who balked at having to get up early or at all the work that had to be done. This was literally the first time Faith had ever heard him question if this life was what he wanted for himself.

He went back to clipping Renegade's hoof. The horse kicked, agitated by their argument. Brother and sister set aside their differences momentarily to calm him back down.

"I didn't know you felt like that," Faith said as she distracted the horse with hay.

"I didn't know I felt like this, either, until Dean came along," Sawyer admitted. "He inspired me to dream, but I guess that was stupid because I'm stuck here."

Faith never wanted him to feel stuck. This was the kind of work people should do because they loved it, not because it was their only choice.

"You aren't stupid." There was only one stupid Stratton in the barn right now, and it wasn't Sawyer.

Sawyer went back to work, using the rasp to file down Renegade's hoof. Checking and double-checking that he had the entire surface level. He was always so careful and never cut corners. His love for the horses showed in the way he took care of them.

Faith was at a loss for words. She'd never thought of her brother as unhappy. She didn't fully believe he was. Wanting more didn't mean he had a terrible life to begin with.

"You're not stuck, either," she finally added.

"I know," Sawyer said, setting the hoof down. "That's why I'm still leaving. I don't care if Dean doesn't want me, I'm going to knock on some doors, find someone who thinks I'm worthy of a shot."

Faith took the blow pretty well considering it felt like he'd knocked the wind out of her. Sawyer had made up his mind and nothing she said was going to stop him. She had forced Dean to lie and Sawyer was still leaving. She had lost the two men she loved most in the world in the same day.

"I called my buddies and got you some backup. Logan said he'll come by in the mornings and help you muck the stalls. You can call Caleb whenever you need something fixed. He's pretty handy. They'll buy you enough time to hire someone or set up a new volunteer schedule."

He wasn't going to be deterred. He'd made plans, set up replacements. Sawyer already had one foot out the door.

CHAPTER TWENTY-THREE

DEAN GOT BACK to Nashville around dinnertime on Monday. His condo felt emptier than usual. The sparse furnishings were nothing like his mother's overly accessorized, *Southern Living*–inspired home. The refrigerator was empty, which was completely normal since Dean rarely cooked for himself. It was easier to order in or to go out.

He indulged in a hot shower in his recently updated bathroom. There were jets and sprayers everywhere, making it more like a massage than a simple washing. It was supposed to help him relax. It wasn't doing its job.

He towel-dried his hair as he made his way into his bedroom. His phone alerted him to a text. Landon had been trying to get hold of him all day. Dean had avoided him so far, still not sure how he was going to move Landon off of Sawyer and on to someone else—that mysterious someone else who was yet to be discovered. Dean tapped Ignore on his phone.

Explaining the issue with Sawyer was a conversation they needed to have in person in the morning.

When he finally slipped into bed, he relished in being able to stretch his legs all the way out. The bed he had slept on at his parents' house wasn't much better than the couch he'd had to curl up on at Faith's, but it was still small.

Faith.

He shouldn't have thought her name. Her name alone conjured up all these other images and feelings. He could almost smell the soft, flowery scent of her perfume, and when he closed his eyes, her smile was somehow plastered on the inside of his eyelids.

It was so unfair that as soon as one obstacle was removed, another fell right in its place. The lies ruined everything. It didn't feel right, but the alternative would have been worse. Dean wouldn't have been able to focus on Sawyer's career, knowing Faith was miserable back in Grass Lake.

If Faith was happy, Dean would be happy. *Eventually.*

As he struggled to slip into a deep sleep, Dean wished they could have been happy together. Maybe Addison really didn't want them to be together and was still messing with him from the other side.

"Don't you want me to be happy?" he asked the ceiling.

No one answered. Thank goodness. But he hoped Addison still heard him.

GETTING TO THE OFFICE in the morning felt like a complete rat race. Traffic was bad, the line at Starbucks was endless, people scurried along the sidewalks without acknowledging one another with a hello or good morning. Nashville was the complete opposite of Grass Lake.

Dean arrived at Grace Note Records' home base a full hour later than he'd intended. The overpriced office space they currently rented was in the perfect location in the heart of the city. Grace Note occupied the upstairs loft of a narrow brownstone. Landon and Dean each had their own office, and there was an open space that housed the front desk and a lounge for musicians to hang out in.

Dean pushed open the door and was greeted by his assistant. "Good morning! It's so good to have you back! How was your visit with your family?" Peggy put the *P* in pep. With her blond curls and cherubic face, she always reminded Dean of a grown-up version of Shirley Temple.

"It was good, Peggy. My mother says hello."

Peggy rested her chin on her hand. "I love your mom."

The two of them had met a total of two times when his parents had driven up to the city for visits. Peggy had a way of making friends instantly, without having to put any effort into it.

"I'll let her know." Dean pointed at Landon's closed door. He still hadn't decided what he was going to say about giving up Sawyer. "Is he not in yet?"

"No, he's here. He's in there with someone. I'm supposed to tell you to join them once you get settled."

"Who's here?" Dean asked, praying it wasn't Boone or anyone who worked for Boone. That was a headache Dean did not want to deal with his first day back.

Landon's door opened. "I thought I heard your voice. We've been waiting for you."

Dean's business partner stepped out of the way so Dean could enter. Seated in front of Landon's desk was Sawyer. His easy smile might fool someone else, but Dean knew the truth behind it. He was there to make Dean suffer.

"Sawyer and I were killing time getting to know one another while we waited for you. We didn't get into any specifics just yet. We wanted you to be here for that." Landon took his spot behind his desk. Piper's platinum and gold records hung on the wall to the left.

"Traffic was a killer this morning. Good to see you, Sawyer," Dean said through clenched teeth. He set his stuff on the ground.

Landon was oblivious. "Sawyer tells me you used to work on his family's horse farm. I've been trying to picture you on a horse. It's been making me laugh all morning."

"He's a decent rider. Of course, the summer he worked there, he spent more time in the hay stall than with the animals," Sawyer said, getting his dig in.

"What was he doing—?" Landon started to ask.

"I'm a little confused," Dean cut in as he turned toward Sawyer. "I don't remember telling you we should meet today."

Sawyer's expression changed to one of false surprise. "Did I get the meeting time wrong? I must have misunderstood you. I could have sworn you said come on by first thing tomorrow morning. Landon said he couldn't reach you yesterday, but he had told you he wanted to get together to talk about our next move. Wasn't that what you said, Landon?"

"We didn't have a meeting time. I didn't even know Dean was back in town. But I think we're all on the same page here about getting Sawyer signed to this label as soon as possible."

Dean was mad at himself for not getting to Landon first and a tiny bit impressed with Sawyer's shameless audacity.

"I apologize for being off the radar yesterday. There are some personal things going on. In fact, do you mind if Sawyer and I step out for a minute? There's something I need to get off my chest that has nothing to do with this."

Landon eyeballed his friend. There would come a day when Dean would have to confess what had really gone down here. "Why don't I give you two a minute? Sawyer, you want something to drink? Coffee? A Coke?"

"I'm good, thanks."

Landon left the room and Dean shut the door behind him. "What are you doing here?"

Gone was Sawyer's pleasant expression. His eyes were narrowed into angry slits. "I was coming to beg you guys to reconsider, and imagine my surprise when your partner, who you said wanted to go in another direction, was happier than a pig in mud that I was here!"

Being caught in a lie was even worse than having to tell it. "He and I got some wires crossed. Did you tell your sister you were coming here?"

"My sister," Sawyer said knowingly. "I am very aware of what my sister did, Dean, and you're lucky I haven't lost all respect for you and how you do business. I'll chalk this up to being head-over-heels for Faith, but this is your one and only free pass."

Dean sat down and scrubbed his face with his hands. "I don't want to hurt her anymore, Sawyer. She needs you, and I don't want to be the reason you're not there for her."

"You aren't the reason I left Grass Lake. *I* am the reason. This is *my* life. You and Faith don't get to manipulate what direction it takes. I want this and it doesn't matter if you sign me or someone else in this town does. I am not going to spend my life on that farm unless I've done everything I can to make this work."

Dean admired the young man's tenacity,

as well. "So you told her you were leaving? How did that go over?"

"Not well. But she's stronger than she thinks she is, and she's going to be fine. I believe in her even if she doesn't believe in me." There was a lot of hurt underneath all that rebellion.

"Your sister loves you. She did what she did because she's afraid. And she's tired of losing people she loves. I was trying to spare her one more loss."

"Yeah, well, I think lying was wrong, for the record. You told me you don't make promises, but I hope you'll make me one here today. What goes on between you and my sister is separate from what goes on between you and me. That means if I fail at this thing, you can let me go like anyone else. You don't have to treat me differently because you're in love with my sister."

Dean stiffened at the word love. How could Sawyer know how he felt about Faith? Dean barely understood his feelings. "I can do that. In fact, let's not talk about your sister at all."

"Deal," Sawyer said, reaching over to shake on it. "For what it's worth, though, I thought you and Faith could have had something good."

"What kind of deal are we making when you break the deal in the very next sentence?"

Sawyer laughed at himself. "That was it. I had to get that out there and now I'm done. I just want to make music, Music Man."

"I can help you with that."

"THANKS FOR YOUR HELP, Logan. I really appreciate it," Faith said as she walked her new volunteer to his car. Logan and Sawyer had been friends since kindergarten. Short and stocky, he had always had a cowlick sticking up on the top of his head. It was cute when he was five. As an adult, it made Faith want to take scissors and cut it off.

"No problem. I'll see you tomorrow. Tell Sawyer I better get front-row tickets to all his shows for this."

"You deserve that at the very least."

With the morning chores done, it was time to start going over the financials and figure out how she could possibly afford to hire someone to do the work Sawyer usually did. Logan wasn't going to work for imaginary concert tickets forever.

There had been months Faith and Sawyer weren't able to pay themselves. She couldn't have that happen if she was going to bring on a stranger. It would be great if she could hire a speech pathologist and perhaps a social worker like she had mentioned to Dean. Unfortunately there wasn't nearly enough money for that if she had to replace Sawyer. The daily upkeep of this place was a full-time job.

The day flew by. Faith made some phone calls and placed a couple Help Wanted ads. The saddle pads needed washing and she cleaned the water troughs. The farm seemed a lot less lively without Sawyer around and the work a bit more tedious. When she finished her afternoon chores, it was so quiet Faith ended up falling asleep in the rocking chair in the front room with Scout at her feet. The poor dog was as lost as Faith without her brother around.

"Knock, knock." Josie let herself in. "Do you know what time it is?"

Faith checked the old clock on the mantel. Freddy was due any minute for his therapy session and the horses were still out to pasture. Faith had never taken a nap in the middle of the day before. Not having Sawyer here was making her lazy.

"I had Lily grab Winston and bring him in to get ready," Josie said, easing one worry. "She said he's the one Freddy likes to ride."

"Thanks," Faith said, nudging Scout out of the way and pulling on her shoes. "I don't know what happened to me."

"You've been working too hard, apparently. Kylie went to clean up the turnout paddock. I don't know if that was what you wanted her to do."

"Perfect. You guys are lifesavers. Sawyer's been gone less than a week and I'm already sleeping on the job. We'll be out of business in no time!"

"Don't say that," Josie said with a stern look. "It's a transition. You're doing fine. I have a present for you."

Faith watched her with a furrowed brow as she pulled out a wrapped package from her purse. She couldn't imagine what Josie had up her sleeve.

"Why are you buying me presents? I'm trying really hard not to throw myself a pity party and gifts are never required at those, anyway."

"This is from your community, which wants to step up to help you keep this place running." Josie handed her the gift.

Carefully, Faith unwrapped the package, wondering what the community could do for her that would fit inside a...notebook. Faith opened it up to find a list of names, phone numbers and days of the week they were available.

"That is your complete list of everyone who wants to volunteer at Helping Hooves," Josie explained. "Some of them are kids from the high school who need the service hours, but most are the people in this community who have relied on you for a variety of things and want to repay you the kindness."

Given the amount of people willing to help, there would be no need to hire someone to do Sawyer's work. Faith could save her money to pay more therapists. She could update some of the facilities.

A bunch of Lily's friends had offered a few hours a week this summer to help at the camp. A couple of the retired guys who loved to hang out at the Sundown were ready and willing to take care of mowing and running the heavy equipment. A few ladies from town promised two or three hours a week to pitch in with the clerical work that Faith often felt burdened with doing. Mrs. Ortiz, who worked at the hospital in Claims Processing, was willing to assist with all of Helping Hooves's insurance woes.

Josie was all too pleased with herself.

"You've got people committed and signed up through the summer. If you look, we started a calendar on the next couple pages."

Faith wanted to cry. No one had ever done something this huge for her before. She hugged her friend, finding words hard to come by at the moment. Maybe Helping Hooves would make it, after all. Even without Sawyer.

CHAPTER TWENTY-FOUR

"MR. PRESLEY, IT'S DWIGHT. I've got some good news. Your car is all done and ready to roll." Dean hit Save Message on his phone. Thank goodness his car was fixed. One less thing to worry about. And a legitimate reason to go back to Grass Lake.

"Sawyer, let's do it again. This time, relax and let the words come a little slower." Jimmy Young was one of the record producers Dean admired most. He had the best ear and the patience of a saint. Jimmy had produced both of Piper's albums. "You're rushing for some reason. You can do this, buddy."

Dean watched Sawyer nod from inside the sound booth. They'd been working on this song for a couple hours and Sawyer wasn't feeling it.

"Actually, can we take five instead?" Sawyer asked.

Jimmy looked to Dean, who was footing the bill for the studio time. It wasn't cheap, especially on the weekend. Lately, Grace Note barely had enough money to book any studio time. They had to be so cautious, and hopefully Sawyer was worth it. In a perfect world Dean would have his own recording studio that would help pay the bills, not create more. But in Nashville, quality space was at a premium.

"If he can't do it without a break, let's take a break."

Jimmy let Sawyer know he had ten minutes to get himself together. Sawyer stepped out of the booth and Dean followed him down the hall, where there was a small break room set up.

"Everything okay?" Dean asked as Sawyer scrolled through his phone. He couldn't figure out where this particular mental block was coming from. Up until now, Sawyer had been nothing but professional.

"I'm fine," Sawyer said distractedly.

"Is there something you'd rather be doing right now than recording this song?"

They had a clear plan with a tight timeline. Record the single, get a video out, record the album, get on a tour, single, tour, single. None of it could happen without the first track getting laid.

Sawyer shoved his phone back in his pocket. "I'm not allowed to talk to you about it."

"You can talk to me about anything," he assured him.

"Not this particular person," Sawyer replied, shaking his head.

Dean's chest constricted. He'd been worrying about Faith for three weeks now. He'd thought about texting her but had decided against it. His sole source of information was his mother, who could only report she'd seen Faith looking lovely at church on Sunday. He needed a new spy.

"What's wrong with Faith?"

Sawyer sighed. "I don't know. Nothing. She never answers any of my calls. I text her and she texts back a word or two. I know she's busy, but is she really so busy that she can't check in with me?"

Dean also worried about her overdoing it. She was much better at saying no now, but old habits died hard. She could still be overextending herself and not maintaining a good balance. The difference between Dean and Sawyer was that Dean wasn't letting his concern interfere with his work.

"You're homesick, is that it?"

Sawyer shrugged. "I can't even remember the last time I went this long without talking to my sister. I don't like it."

Dean had no solution to this problem. He understood; there were plenty of times he wished he could talk to his sister, as well. Faith was alive and hopefully well. Sawyer might have to be happy simply knowing that.

"This isn't going to be an easy transition. The busier you get, the less time you're going to have to connect with the people back home. Lots of musicians get homesick, but you have to do your job or else you won't have to miss home—you'll be back there permanently."

Sawyer frowned. There wasn't a way to sugarcoat it for him, and Dean didn't have the time or the money to waste if there was.

"I'll do better," he promised.

"My car's fixed. Got a call from Dwight just a little bit ago. If you get this done, maybe I'll take you with me when I go to pick it up."

Twenty minutes later the vocals were finished and the mixing could begin. Dean and Sawyer celebrated with some tacos back at Dean's condo. Sawyer's stuff was scattered around and never seemed to stay confined to the bedroom Dean was letting him use. The boy had no money to get an apartment or to pay for a hotel. The only person he really knew in Nashville was Dean. It seemed only fair to put a roof over his head...temporarily.

Dean set the box of tacos on the coffee table and went to grab some napkins. Sawyer turned on the television and found the hockey game. The Predators were playing well and had a good shot at making the play-offs. Sawyer made himself comfortable on Dean's leather couch and started unwrapping his first taco. "Do you have any hot sauce?"

Dean was a man living in Nashville. Of course he had hot sauce. He didn't have bread or anything close to a fruit or a vegetable, but he had four bottles of hot sauce in the cabinet.

"Do you think you could keep your dirty clothes in your room?" Dean picked up a T-shirt he was certain he'd seen Sawyer wearing two days ago.

Sawyer snatched it from his hand. "Sorry. Faith used to complain I was a slob. But I'd leave dirty clothes lying around and they'd magically appear in my drawer clean and folded a few days later. Don't blame me. She didn't train me very well."

Laundry fairy. Man, Dean missed her.

"Yeah, well, that isn't going to happen here. So you're going to have to learn to pick this stuff up. The only place I'm going to put it is in the garbage."

Sawyer grunted as he shoved half a taco into his mouth. Dean took that as a "yes, sir."

"Why don't you try to call your sister?" Dean sort of hoped she'd want to talk to him if she heard he was watching over her brother.

Sawyer checked his phone. "She's probably in the barn doing the evening chores. This is what happens—when I have downtime, she's busy or asleep, and when she's free, I'm not."

"Well, you have nothing going on tonight. Set a timer or something so you remember to call her before she goes to bed."

Sawyer put his taco down. "Why are you so eager for me to call her? You hoping she's going to ask about you?"

"No," Dean said in a huff.

Sawyer grinned annoyingly. "Yes, you are. You want me to put in a good word for you?" His smile slipped. "If she'll even answer my call."

"I thought we agreed we weren't going to talk about her. You promised."

"You're the one who keeps bringing her up," Sawyer accused.

"Well, I'm done."

"Oh, so we can talk about her when you

want to, but I'm not allowed to acknowledge her existence otherwise. Real fair."

Dean ignored him and focused on the hockey game instead. Nothing about Faith was fair. It wasn't fair that she had to run the farm alone. It wasn't fair that she'd asked him to lie. It wasn't fair that she couldn't see it wasn't Dean's fault that Sawyer had chosen to come to Nashville. Dean hadn't asked him to come, but he had allowed him to stay. Not that Dean had any idea how she felt about the whole situation.

Dean's phone rang and Kevin's name appeared. Boone's agent had better have a really good reason to call on a Saturday. He tried not to get his hopes up, but he really wanted this to be the news he'd been waiting for.

"Kev, what's up?"

Dean said a silent prayer that he was about to say Boone would go to California and work with Piper.

That wasn't exactly why Kevin was on the phone. "He isn't going to go. I've tried everything. I even threatened to quit and he said he'd save me the trouble and fired me."

The headache Dean had been fighting off all day quickly returned. "He fired you?"

"He'll hire me back by tomorrow. This is

how he handles things lately. I'm not sure I'll accept his offer, though. Part of me is as done as he is."

Boone needed an agent and the publicist who, as rumor had it, had been fired twice already.

"I've been patient," Dean reminded him. "I've been more patient than most labels would be."

"I'm fairly certain if he was with anyone else, he'd be out. I'm sure under all his nastiness is someone who's grateful for that patience."

"What's his excuse this time? And it better be good because I am about to make going to this place nonnegotiable."

"Too far. He doesn't want to leave Tennessee."

Dean had promised to look for a facility closer to home and hadn't done it. He wasn't even sure they existed around this part of the country. Places like that were very west coast.

"I'm going to find him something here in Tennessee and I won't listen to any excuses. He'll go or we're going to terminate the contract."

"I'll pass that on. Not sure it's going to get

me rehired, but I'm also not sure if I care at this point."

"Good luck," Dean said before hanging up.

Sawyer stood and picked up every stray piece of clothing in the room, tossing it all into the spare bedroom. He closed the door to his room before sitting back down.

"What got into you?" Dean asked.

"I forget you're my boss now. I better start behaving or else." Sawyer drew an imaginary line with his thumb across his throat.

"You're lucky I like you better than others."

The sad thing was, he had really liked Boone in the beginning. There was a time when he used to be someone Dean respected. The first time he'd met the man, Dean had been truly starstruck.

"You're not really going to drop him, are you?" Sawyer unwrapped another taco. "I mean, he's Boone Williams."

"He needs help. I need to find a facility that will take him. Somewhere they'll help him work on his issues without him realizing that's what they're doing. You know any place like that?"

"What's he supposed to think he's doing there?"

"Recharging his batteries. Getting away from the pressures of Nashville."

Sawyer didn't have any good ideas. Just as Dean suspected, places like that didn't exist around here. Dean went back to watching the hockey game.

At the beginning of the third period, Sawyer's phone rang and both men exchanged a hopeful look. Sawyer held it up and showed Dean the photo of Faith.

"Hey," he said. "I'm glad you called."

So was Dean. He didn't want to be creepy, but he considered asking Sawyer to put her on speaker phone so he could hear her voice, too.

Brother and sister caught up. Dean listened to Sawyer tell her about recording in the studio. He couldn't be sure if Sawyer was oversharing every detail or if she was asking him for it. When it was her turn to talk, Dean had to decipher what she was saying by how Sawyer replied.

"Seriously? How many people signed up to help? Wow, that's impressive."

Dean couldn't figure out what that was about. He got up and tried to make himself look busy and not like the eavesdropper he was. He threw away some garbage and flipped through the pile of mail that had arrived today.

"Sounds like you aren't missing me at all." She must have said that wasn't true because Sawyer smiled. "I feel bad saying good. But good."

They talked about the horses and Sawyer made sure Faith was keeping an eye on the bump on Sassy's hind leg. He seemed satisfied with her answer.

"I miss your cooking and your laundry talents, that's for sure." Sawyer got up and walked to his bedroom, where Dean couldn't hear him as well. "I miss Scout and the horses, but most of all I miss you, Faith. I miss talking about the day and planning for the next one. I miss hearing what you think. I miss laughing with you and at you. No, really. I miss home. This isn't as easy as I thought it was going to be."

Sawyer wasn't the only one who missed her. Dean missed her laugh and the way she bit her lip when she was embarrassed. He missed how soft her cheeks were and how it felt to kiss her there. He missed kissing her, period.

Sawyer came back out. "Well, Dean really wants to talk to you. Do you have another minute?" Dean shook his head but it did not deter Sawyer one bit. "He's right here. He's been waiting to hear from you…just talk to him for a second. Here he is."

Sawyer held out the phone but Dean couldn't bring himself to take it. What could he even say that would not make him sound like an idiot?

"Just talk to her," Sawyer whispered.

He was going to find out.

"Hello?"

"Hey, there," she replied. Her voice sounded so small, so far away. He wanted her to come closer.

"How are you?"

"Good. How are you?" she asked.

Better now that he could hear her. "Good. Your brother is keeping me busy."

Faith was quiet. Maybe she didn't want to hear about them working together. She finally said, "That's good."

The awkwardness of this conversation was making Dean's blood pressure rise. There were so many things he wanted to say but couldn't. Shouldn't.

"You hanging in there? Things aren't too busy, are they?"

"I'm doing my best, and this town is full

of some really great people." She went on to tell him about how Josie had organized a couple dozen or so volunteers to help her keep Helping Hooves up and running in Sawyer's absence.

"I'm not nearly as busy as I was a month ago. I've got people here doing most of the work. I've focused on training them and finding some new therapists. I think I found a social worker who's willing to work here part-time."

"Sounds like getting rid of your brother might have been the best thing to happen to you."

Sawyer balled up a napkin and threw it at Dean's head.

"All the volunteers make the workday much easier, but at night, it's just me and Scout. I think I need to get a roommate."

"Trust me. Roommates are definitely overrated." He threw the napkin back at Sawyer, who batted it away.

"Take care of him, okay? He might be a pain in the butt, but he's important to me."

She was as protective of him as ever. She had accepted his choice to leave her behind and still wanted the best for him. That was a good step.

"I know he is. I will do my best."

He handed the phone back to Sawyer and let them say their goodbyes. Grass Lake was an impressive community. It was amazing that the whole town had rallied around Faith. That kind of cooperation didn't exist in a lot of places.

The two men went back to watching the hockey game and finished off all twelve tacos. Dean's mind kept wandering back to Faith. He hated thinking about her in that big farmhouse all by herself. If she got lonely enough, there was no telling what she might do. He imagined her on a date with Charles Hackney and almost threw up his entire dinner.

"You know, if Boone Williams spent a couple weeks on the farm, Faith could whip him into shape in no time. Can you believe she's overseeing all those volunteers? She gets to be bossy for hours on end—I can't imagine."

Dean sat up a little straighter. "What did you say?"

"My sister is probably loving every minute of bossing those volunteers around. Remember how she was with you?"

"No, no. The part about Boone."

Sawyer kicked his feet up on the coffee

table. "I just said a couple weeks on the farm would be plenty of time for Faith to help that guy get his act together. Have him take care of the horses, think about someone other than himself for once. All that fresh air and hard work would definitely get him out of his head."

It was a brilliant idea. It was quite possibly the best idea anyone had ever had. The more he thought about it, the more he wanted to make it happen.

"Go pack."

"For what?" Sawyer asked.

"We're going home."

FAITH FINISHED SWEEPING the aisle and was hanging the broom up in the tack room when she heard the slamming of a car door. Scout barked and ran out ahead. Her morning helper had already come and gone and she wasn't expecting anyone else this Sunday.

When she stepped outside, there was no one there, not even the dog. She shielded her eyes from the bright morning sun. Maybe she had been hearing things.

"Scout! Come here, boy!" she shouted, figuring the dog had run around the house, chasing who knew what.

The dog didn't reappear. Faith didn't have time to chase him down. She needed to shower and get ready for church. Scout would show his face eventually.

She crossed the yard and climbed the porch steps. Just as she went to the push the front door open, it moved on its own. Sawyer and one happy chocolate Lab were on the other side.

"What are you doing here?" Faith threw her arms around her brother. He had been gone less than three weeks, but it felt like years.

"I came to take you to church. You better go get ready—you smell like the barn," he teased but didn't let her go.

"Why didn't you tell me you were coming when I talked to you last night?"

Sawyer released his grip. "I didn't know I was."

"I'M GLAD YOU'RE HERE." She'd been missing him so much during the down times of the day. Evenings alone in the house were the worst. She also hated going to church by herself. He'd arrived at the perfect time.

Faith went up to shower and change. She smiled when she saw Sawyer on the floor, playing with the dog. "I don't know who's happier to see you—me or Scout."

"I'm happy you're happy," Sawyer said, giving Scout's belly a rub. "I thought maybe you were still mad and that's why you haven't been calling or texting as often."

Faith plopped down on the couch. "It's been really crazy around here and I sort of wanted you to get acclimated to your new life. I didn't want to be the bothersome sister, calling you all the time, telling you how much I missed having you around."

"Well, that's good to know. I don't want things to be bad between us."

"I'm sorry for how I handled everything," Faith confessed. She was ashamed to admit it. "I shouldn't have asked Dean to turn you away. I should have been more supportive of you."

Sawyer stopped messing with the dog and glanced back at his sister. "I accept your apology."

"I felt abandoned. Like you were treating me the way Mom treated Dad."

Sawyer scowled at the mention of their mother. "Don't ever compare this to that. Mom left us to fend for ourselves before we were old enough to do so. She truly abandoned us. I left totally certain you could do this because you are one of the smartest, strongest women I know."

Faith appreciated his belief in her. "I know it's different. It's just always been us. You and me, we take care of each other. That's what we do."

"And that's what we'll continue to do. It's not like I'm never going to be here. And when you need me, when you really need me, I'll be here. You can believe that."

Faith put a hand on her brother's cheek. It was hard not to picture the little boy he had once been. The one who'd asked to sleep in her room for months after their mother left. The one who'd asked her to come to school with him for show and tell because she was his lucky charm when he was six. The one with dirty knees and a backward baseball cap who once told her she would make a great mom someday because she was the best big sister.

He wasn't that little boy anymore. He was all grown up and it was time for him to live his own life. It was wrong of her to try to clip his wings when Sawyer was always meant to fly.

FAITH CARRIED THE bouquets of daisies she'd picked up from Harriet's and unlatched the gate to the cemetery. She'd gone simple today for both Addison and her dad. The summer sun would not be kind to any of the flowers she left out for them.

A robin fluttered by, landing on one of the headstones and chirping away. Its song was quickly replaced by the sound of someone's voice. A familiar voice.

"… And that's what I'm thinking. Not sure it's going to work, but I should try, right? I have to try because I'm in love with her. I've always been in love with her."

Faith dropped the flowers and let out a gasp loud enough to get his attention. Dean stood in front of Addison's grave in dark pants and a crisp white dress shirt that fit him like it was custom-made.

He turned slowly and a smile spread across his face. His green tie was the same color as his eyes when they weren't hidden behind sunglasses. "Good morning."

Faith was too flustered to reply. She crouched to pick up the flowers at the same time as he bent over to help.

"Sawyer didn't tell me you came with

him," Faith said, unable to acknowledge what she had just overheard.

"I had to come get my car, which is finally fixed. Sawyer was feeling homesick, so I brought him with me."

"That was nice of you. I'm sorry I interrupted your time with Addison. I can go switch out the flowers by my dad's grave and give you some privacy."

He grabbed her arm and stopped her from going. "I don't need privacy. I was waiting for you."

The butterflies in her stomach soared. No one had ever made her feel this way. He had done it when she was a teenager and he did it to her now It was always his voice, his touch, that sent her heart into overdrive.

"Were you talking about me? About being in love with me?" she asked even though the answer could send her over the edge.

Dean covered his heart with his hand. "I thought I knew what it meant to be in love with you, but had no idea until I fell in love with you again."

"Even though I asked you to lie? I was pathetic." It was embarrassing to even talk about. She was lucky Sawyer had forgiven her, but to think Dean hadn't lost all respect for her seemed impossible.

He pulled her to him. His hand brushed her cheek as he dipped his head close to hers. "You were scared. You're still getting over losing your dad. We've all done things we regret because of grief. I can forgive you if you'll forgive me for the way I acted after Addison died."

"Don't be sorry. The past is the past. We didn't know the truth." She touched his tie, needing to focus on something other than how close he was standing and how badly she wanted to kiss him.

"I don't want to spend my life running from the past. I want to embrace it and move forward. And I want to move forward with you by my side."

Her heart dropped. Why was there always a choice to be made when it came to Dean? Dean or Addison. Dean or Sawyer. Dean or home. Why did it always come down to tearing herself in two?

"I can't leave Grass Lake. This is my home."

He lifted her chin and kissed her so softly. "I want it to be my home, too," he said against her lips.

"But—"

He stopped her with another kiss. It was dizzying. His declaration seemed too good to be true. Maybe she hadn't heard him right.

He rested his forehead on hers. "When I came home, all I wanted to do was leave. But you reminded me what home has to offer. When I got back to Nashville, it wasn't the same. I'm not the same. I want to be here. With you."

Faith fought to control her breathing. She rubbed her nose against his as her eyes fluttered. "Then stay."

The church bells rang, reminding them of the other reason they were there. Dean waited for her while she placed her flowers by her loved ones' resting places and then took her hand.

He smirked as he opened the church doors. "Maybe we'll make it through the entire service this week."

"Stranger things have happened," Faith said, giving his hand a squeeze. Stranger things, indeed.

CHAPTER TWENTY-FIVE

"TALK ABOUT STATE of the art. This place is amazing." Sawyer pressed one of the buttons on the sound board.

"Look, don't touch, please," Dean said, resisting the urge to smack his hand away. The recording equipment had been the investment of a lifetime and he needed it to be fully functional if he was going to pay it off someday.

"This is so cool. I wish I would have thought to build one of these. I could have been famous a lot sooner."

"You aren't famous…yet," Faith reminded her brother.

Dean slipped his arm around her waist. It felt so good to be able to do that without any worry. There would never again be a need to hide how they felt for one another—from themselves or anyone else.

"Is this going to be enough for him?" she asked Dean, turning so they were face to face. She smelled like her fruity shampoo and

Irish Spring soap. She'd been working in the barn all morning and had to clean up before finally coming to see the final product of a month's worth of hard work.

Gone was the unused storage shed and in its place was Dean's new recording studio. Grace Note Records had moved to Grass Lake, where artists could come and get away from the madness of Nashville and focus on the music.

It surprisingly hadn't taken much to convince Landon that this was the best solution to all of their problems. Cheaper rent, no studio fees, close enough to Nashville to keep their connections but far enough away to give them some breathing room had made it the right choice.

"Who? Boone? He's going to balk at it at first, but then he's going to realize this is where his soul is going to reunite with his music." Dean had no worries. He'd put a lot of thought into how he was going to help his fallen star. Boone deserved a second chance... just like some other people Dean knew.

"I want this to be a good experience for him. And I also don't want my horses or my staff traumatized."

Grace Note and Helping Hooves were joining forces. Artists could come ride the horses, reconnect, recharge. Faith had hired a part-time social worker, who had experience with children and adults. Boone was going to get therapy without even realizing it.

"They won't be."

"What about me?" Sawyer opened the door to the sound booth. "This is where I'm recording my album, isn't it? Don't you want to know if I like it?"

Dean gave his beautiful fiancée a kiss instead of answering her brother's ridiculous question. Life was so good, he had to remind himself it wasn't a dream.

"He works best when he gets some positive reinforcement," Faith said, giving Dean's side a tickle.

"So do I," he replied with a sly smile. He slipped his hand under her shirt and rested it against the small of her back. Another kiss was the perfect motivator.

"Can you two stop? I miss the days when you used to hide in the hay stalls. I don't need to be constantly subjected to all this lovey-dovey nonsense," Sawyer complained.

"You're lucky I still need you," Dean grumbled. Sawyer's single had been released and was getting a better-than-expected response.

He was one of the hottest newcomers since Piper. His video had been on the internet for three days and had already been viewed half a million times.

Landon thought Dean was a genius once again. Life wasn't good. It was great.

"We need to get going. The parade starts soon," Faith reminded them.

Letting her go was a little easier, knowing he'd get the chance to hold her the rest of his life. He'd asked her to marry him the day he'd moved back to Grass Lake for good. In the gazebo behind the Filmont was the ideal setting. Harriet had helped him surround it with practically every flower in her shop. Faith had cried while she'd nodded yes.

It had been one of the best days of his life. And it was only the beginning.

The three of them headed downtown for the annual Fourth of July parade. The streets were lined with people dressed in red, white and blue. The same American flags that had hung limp from the light posts back in May were fluttering in the wind.

The little kids on their fathers' shoulders waved tiny flags or held signs that proudly read "We love USA!" All the businesses along Main Street had their windows deco-

rated for the festivities. Hand-painted fireworks covered Harriet's store window.

Dean's mother had saved a spot for them in
front of the flower shop. Dressed in her red-
and-white-striped T-shirt and her blue shorts
that were covered in little white stars, she
looked like the flag personified.

"You made it just in time. Here they come!"
She hugged Dean and Faith, handing them
little flags to wave. The only person more
excited about their impending nuptials than
Dean was his mother.

The parade was led by two of the Grass
Lake police officers on motorcycles and the
pace car ridden by the mayor and his wife.
People walked beside the various floats with
bags of candy to hand out to the eager children along the route. Grass Lake Community
Bank had a nice banner and Dean's dad was
riding in the car behind it.

After the Grass Lake High School band
passed by, a cherry-red Mustang convertible
drove Sawyer and his guitar down the street.
His new single blared from some speakers inside the car. The crowd went wild, cheering
on their homegrown rising star.

Faith leaned against Dean and smiled up.
She was so beautiful. If they weren't stand-

ing in the middle of a crowd, he would have kissed her until it was time to meet up at Mockingbird Park.

"My dad would have been so proud," she said with watery eyes.

"Of both of you," Dean murmured in her ear.

NEARLY EVERYONE IN TOWN came to Mockingbird Park after the parade to continue the celebration before the fireworks. Food booths were lined up along one end of the park while the kids enjoyed jumping in one of the two bounce houses that had been set up on the other.

While Dean and Sawyer were off chatting it up with the mayor and Dean's dad, Faith was helping Josie in the Sundown's booth. Josie was testing out some of her new menu items while Faith supplied the dessert.

Faith had made twenty dozen cookies for this event with Dean's help. There would have been more had her helper been able to demonstrate some self-control. Dean had one very big sweet tooth.

Having both her brother and Dean back in Grass Lake was a dream come true. This was the life she'd never imagined was possible. Harriet swore it was thanks to those angels she had up in heaven, helping her out. Whatever the reason for her good fortune, Faith was more than grateful.

Helping Hooves had everything it needed to be successful. Its potential for growth was enormous, and with Dean's ideas and ingenuity, they were sure to thrive.

"You got any of those mudslide brownies?" Mr. Middleton asked. He squinted up at Josie's price list.

"Not today, Hank. We went with Fourth-of-July inspired goodies this time. Want a Firecracker Sugar Cookie instead?"

He tried to peek behind the counter. "You sure you aren't hiding something else back there?"

Josie set a sugar cookie in front of him. "You do know that all the alcohol is cooked out of those cookies she makes, right?"

Hank scowled and waved her off, taking his nonalcoholic cookie with him. The two women laughed and shook their heads.

"Mind if I steal my fiancée away for a little bit?" Dean asked, sneaking around the side of the booth.

"Are you sending someone to replace her?"

"Oh, come on now. You know she's irreplaceable. But I'll make Sawyer do it. Hang on." He ran back through the crowd and pulled Sawyer away from a group of admiring female fans.

"That boy is a keeper," Josie said, pouring herself another glass of lemonade. She'd been drinking more than she was selling. "I'm happy you two worked things out and found some happiness."

"I didn't think it was possible. In fact, if you had told me three months ago that I'd be engaged to Dean Presley, I would have checked you into a mental hospital."

"The look on your face when he showed up at the Sundown that first night, soaking wet and looking so fine—it was like you'd seen a ghost. Funny how things turn out."

Maybe it was divine intervention that had brought Dean back to town. Maybe it was just dumb luck. Either way, Faith was grateful.

"Okay, here you go." Dean pushed Sawyer next to Josie and grabbed Faith. "He's ready to serve up some delicious treats."

"Wait a minute! You said they needed someone to taste test the chicken wings!" Sawyer protested.

"Did I say that? Whoops." He pulled Faith along. "I want to show you something," he said, leading her away from the throngs of townsfolk and toward the line of trees that provided some nice shade on the east side of the park.

"Where are we going?"

"I want to see if it's still there."

"See if what's still where?" Faith nearly tripped over her own feet as he dragged her in front of one of the larger oak trees.

"I swear it was one of these ones," he mumbled. "Aha! It is here."

Dean came to a stop. He put his hand on the trunk of the giant oak and traced the letters that had been carved in it long ago: DP + FS.

Faith started to laugh. "We were the cheesiest couple on the planet."

"Remember sneaking down here that one night? I thought it would be a romantic gesture and you were mad that I had defaced the tree?"

"I was not," Faith argued. "I was worried that Addison would see it and figure everything out. She loved to come to this park and hang out."

"She also loved to take pictures." He spun her around and threw an arm over her shoulders. With the other hand, he held out his phone. "Say cheesy gesture!"

Faith smiled for the selfie. What was she going to do with him? Kissing him seemed right.

The sounds of the laughing children filled the air, competing with the music booming from speakers set up in the back of someone's pickup truck. But it didn't matter that hundreds of people were celebrating the holiday a few feet away. Hiding was no longer required in this relationship.

Dean held her face while he pressed her back against the tree with their initials. He tasted like popcorn and smelled like fresh-cut grass. He was everything she loved rolled into one person.

"Thank you," he whispered when they finished.

"For what?"

"For bringing me home. For being my home."

Faith's heart swelled in her chest, pushing on her rib cage. She hadn't realized what was truly missing from her life until he came back into it.

"Thank *you*," she replied.

"For what?"

"For making my home complete."

"We are the lucky ones," Dean said. His

silly little grin made her ridiculously happy. Faith kissed that smile and thanked her lucky stars.

Luck was a funny thing. People might be cursed with the bad kind and then blessed with a string of the good. The bad kind popped tires in the middle of rainstorms and flooded all the roads home. But sometimes that bad luck wasn't bad at all. Sometimes that bad luck was nothing more than the good kind in disguise. That was Faith's and Dean's kind of luck—the kind that brought two lost loves back together and healed old wounds. It mended their broken hearts and gave them a shot at something they both held dear—a family.

How very lucky, indeed.

* * * * *

LARGER-PRINT BOOKS!

GET 2 FREE
LARGER-PRINT NOVELS
PLUS 2 FREE
MYSTERY GIFTS

Love Inspired®

Larger-print novels are now available...

LILP15

LARGER-PRINT BOOKS!

GET 2 FREE LARGER-PRINT NOVELS PLUS 2 FREE MYSTERY GIFTS

Love Inspired®
SUSPENSE
RIVETING INSPIRATIONAL ROMANCE

Larger-print novels are now available...

WESTERN WP PROMISES

YES! Please send me **The Western Promises Collection** in Larger Print. This collection begins with 3 FREE books and 2 FREE gifts (gifts valued at approx. $14.00 retail) in the first shipment, along with the other first 4 books from the collection! If I do not cancel, I will receive 8 monthly shipments until I have the entire 51-book Western Promises collection. I will receive 2 or 3 FREE books in each shipment and I will pay just $4.99 US/ $5.89 CDN for each of the other four books in each shipment, plus $2.99 for shipping and handling per shipment. *If I decide to keep the entire collection, I'll have paid for only 32 books, because 19 books are FREE! I understand that accepting the 3 free books and gifts places me under no obligation to buy anything. I can always return a shipment and cancel at any time. My free books and gifts are mine to keep no matter what I decide.

272 HCN 3070 472 HCN 3070

Name _____ (PLEASE PRINT) _____

Address _____ Apt. # _____

City _____ State/Prov. _____ Zip/Postal Code _____

Signature (if under 18, a parent or guardian must sign)

Mail to the **Reader Service:**

IN U.S.A.: P.O. Box 1867, Buffalo, NY 14240-1867
IN CANADA: P.O. Box 609, Fort Erie, Ontario L2A 5X3

* Terms and prices subject to change without notice. Prices do not include applicable taxes. Sales tax applicable in N.Y. Canadian residents will be charged applicable taxes. This offer is limited to one order per household. All orders subject to approval. Credit or debit balances in a customer's account(s) may be offset by any other outstanding balance owed by or to the customer. Please allow 4 to 6 weeks for delivery. Offer available while quantities last. Offer not available to Quebec residents.

WPBPA16R

LARGER-PRINT BOOKS!
GET 2 FREE LARGER-PRINT NOVELS PLUS
2 FREE GIFTS!

⊕ HARLEQUIN®

super romance®

More Story...More Romance